REPARATION

REPARATION

Entwined Victorian Lives and Cotswold Gypsies.

Gail Fulton

YOUCAXTON
PUBLICATIONS

ISBN 978-1-914424-50-2
Published by YouCaxton Publications 2022
YCBN: 01

YouCaxton Publications
www.youcaxton.co.uk

Dedication

I have never had to look far for inspiration, when I consider my darling sister. Those who know her would agree, that as frail and incapacitated as she might be, she has never given up. With fortitude and determination she has fought against the odds throughout life and has proved to me that if you want to achieve something, keep going and never give up. She will never understand the concept - but this book is dedicated to Karina, with my deepest love always.

Acknowledgements

With love and grateful thanks to my dear husband Rob, for his positive encouragement whilst I tap away at the keyboard writing my stories. His advice and input is much valued, especially in the finishing stages of my work and I am very grateful for him taking the time and patience to read and comment, scrupulously picking up on typographical errors or acting as my personal fact checker! Thank you darling!!

And, of course, I can never forget the constant love and support I am so lucky to have from our two gorgeous daughters Nikki and Becky and our fantastic (nearly) son-in-law, Chris. I want you to know how much I love you all, always and forever.

§

Contents

CHAPTER 1

1846

Two gunshots blasted out across the peaceful dawn country air and echoed across the valley. A spooked flock of mallards batted their wings on the lake's surface in shock, some flying away low, across the rippling water. A blooded body slumped to the ground, certified dead, then unceremoniously lifted and carried away. The successful duelist was reluctantly congratulated.

Nine year old Nancy May, lay belly down in the long damp grass, perched atop the embankment, watching the scene unfold below her from the secret vantage point. It was early morning dewy cold. She did not fully understand that which she had seen unfold before her eyes, nor did she realize the full impact that this event would have on the rest of her life.

She scurried back home before anyone would discover her disappearance. Luckily she knew which pathway to take to avoid the likelihood of being seen. Sneaking in through the back of the unassuming cottage, she creaked open her bedroom door, grimacing at its noise in the hope she had not been heard. Unfortunately, she had! Hearing her brother coming, she quickly dived into bed, covering herself completely and lying instantly still, feigning sleep.

Not falling for her trick, Giles crept up to the bed and shook her shoulder hard. "Where have you been?" he whispered, knowingly.

Her eyes shut tight, she flinched with the unexpected brusque contact. "Shut up and go away before you waken mother" she snapped, infuriated that she had been caught out.

"I will find out, you know!" he warned.

"Go back to bed or you'll get us both into trouble!" Nancy May chided. Hearing the door click as Giles returned to his room, Nancy May gave into the tears and wept until her pillow was soaked.

Breakfast was as usual: A meagre meal upon the table, eaten in silence. Giles held his twin sister's stare knowingly. She returned it with an exaggerated mocking face, cleverly avoiding the line of vision of either parent. Unusually however, once the shared bread was eaten, their father demanded attention whilst he delivered some news. It was simple. They were to move house, to Stapley Manor. Questions were as always, unwelcome and explanations were unnecessary.

Albert Turner liked to think he ruled the household with an iron rod and believed everyone was fearful of him. Most people were. Nancy May was not. She thought she was indifferent to him but on reflection, she decided she disliked him. She knew she shouldn't, since after all he was her father but as she grew older, she realized she had neither respect nor love for the man. In fact she loathed and despised him. Worryingly, he set no example for his son. Nancy May hoped with all her heart that Giles would not take after him in either temper or character.

CHAPTER 2

What Nancy May had seen in those early hours of the morning, was truly unforgivable. She could read her father like a book. The night before that fateful morning, she had known that her father was about to do something catastrophic and secretive. Call it a sixth sense. It was as though his body language was bursting to say 'I am about to do something brave. I am fearsome. I will kill a man.' She observed the nuances of his behaviour and watched with intrigue the nervous tick, which would betray his inner excitement.

That previous night, Albert had been to one of the several village inns in Broadway, as he often did after work on the estate. There were a few local inns in the vicinity which he could have chosen to frequent but the Bell and Donkey had greater allure for him, as it sat conveniently between his place of work and his home. He justified his regular patronage to this particular inn, by reckoning his job was thirsty work, although on occasions the quantity he imbibed could have saturated a pond, let alone his kidneys. Deep in his psyche though, the Bell and Donkey was a place where he felt he could throw his weight around and inflate the importance of his work role to the locals, making out his job was above its actual station and how he was an irreplaceable cog in the running of the estate. He always had a tall story ready and the locals would roll their eyes at the often, preposterous tales he told. Sometimes, with lapsing memory, the same stories were retold with greater elaboration and he would embroider detail for effect. He loved the sound of his own voice and the Bell and Donkey gave a captive audience. Nobody believed him but neither did they challenge him. It was simply not worth their while. They just went along with it and laughed on cue at his boring jokes and shook their heads in disbelief behind his back. Some, after a little too much ale, would be brazen enough to goad him into telling stories: "Go on Albert, tell us the one about..." and off he would go on a half hour over-dramatized fictitious tale, to make them laugh. Their laughter however, was at him not with him but he was too obtuse to realize and misinterpreted the joviality for esteem or even friendship.

It was one of those nights when he had drunk beyond the limits of rationality and sitting at the bar, loudly boasting about resolving an exaggerated critical issue on the land, hours before and relating to nobody in particular how against the odds, he single-handedly corralled the herd of cows into the yard for breeding.

"That lucky bull is going to be having some fun tonight, eh lads!!" He began. "Aww he'll be giving it some, he will! Those girls are going to get lucky alright..." and the gestures were as graphic as his insinuations. "They'll be up to some 'nanty narking' all night I reckon, that they will hey boys?!" He guffawed laughing again. Most of the men just dropped their eyes to avoid having to laugh along with him, others did what was expected of them and laughed heartily, encouraging him to continue. Persisting with the euphemisms as though nobody had quite got the image yet... "Aye he's a big lad he is! I expect he'll be doing a bit of 'bread and butter' like you know, one on top of the other!" He swigged at his ale then spluttered laughing again. "Oh yes, reckon he'll give it to 'em proper. Those girls'll all be well satisfied come the morning."

Finding himself hilarious, he gave another riotous laugh, when he heard a muttered comment from another equally inebriated fellow drinker behind him. Not quite sure he had heard correctly, he turned to the man and with a stern expression, asking him to repeat himself.

"What was that you just said then?" The room fell silent with dread. The man was sick of hearing Albert's inflated stories of self-importance and had reached his own level of tolerance. Albert had this coming and so without qualm, the man began to repeat himself. His good friends tried to hush him. One even spoke up, pretending his drunken friend had said something quite different. Albert knew instinctively this was a cover up. He stood up from his chair and faced the man seated in front of him. "Did I just hear you right then?" Not waiting for a reply, he stepped closer to the drunk, he himself swaying with effects of the ale.

The man looked up to him as Albert towered over him. "Aye" he replied bravely. "I expect you did!" Albert grabbed his collar with both fists and dragged him up off his chair and lifted him to his feet. Nose to nose, through gritted teeth he insisted, "Say it again!!"

"No point, 'cos you heard me the first time." He replied provocatively, inflaming the moment. Raised eyebrows around the room suggested they thought he had lost his mind. Others looked on admiring this man's courage. Oh that they could be so brave. A tense stillness fell about the room as though time itself had stopped.

Spitting out the words slowly and deliberately, "I said .... say it again!" He insisted. Albert's eyes were virtually bursting out of their sockets with anger. The air was solid with anticipation and dread for what was about to happen.

The man gloated, tantalizingly and began, "I said..." He paused and nobody dared breathe. "Your missus had to go there to get satisfied too."

Albert picked him up like a sack of coal and flung him against the wall with an almighty thud. Some of the men stood ready to intervene. Albert continued. "What the hell does that mean?"

The man smirked in his face, bravely eyeballing him. "Seems you obviously couldn't give her what she needed at home, so she went looking for it! Yea ... didn't you know? Your boss had to satisfy her for you!"

Albert's face turned puce with rage. It was as though he had taken on the power of an incensed beast and set about battering the man with an intensity of strength he did not know he had. The man made a fair fist of returning his blows, knowing he had delivered what he had coming to him for years. Blood spattered across the room, tables and benches were upturned, tankards smashed to the floor. Chaos reigned into a right 'collie-shangles'. The innkeeper was helpless to intercept the unruly brawling locals as they all joined in battering each other, having made a bad job of stopping the first fight but continued to yell at them and kick those he could, outside.

Albert had never felt anger like it. In the first instance, to realize that perhaps the whole village had known and kept the secret about Peggy's infidelity behind his back, for who knows how long, was beyond him! He had been made a laughing stock of! He knew nothing. Suspected nothing! How could this possibly be so? Was this affair still going on? How long had they had been mocking him - for years and years? Imagine, holding this story without a word. Could it be possible that each time he spoke to villagers, they knew! Why? Why has this been kept from him? Surely he was well liked? Surely he was looked up to, respected?

Considering this, he wondered if people were frightened to tell the truth for fear of the bruising they would get? Maybe they were right, for that is exactly what happened tonight. God his jaw ached! The split above his eye and cut lip were all evidence that he was disrespected – or worse, a laughing stock! It was a just return for his aggression. He heard one say it was his 'comeuppance'... Really? Surely he had a right to be angry to find out that his wife had been unfaithful and this had seemingly been a village secret? But to find out this way, so publically! It was mortifying. It had stripped him of dignity and questioned his masculinity. It had made him look a fool and a weak one at that. He could not see himself returning to the Bell and Donkey anytime soon, for he felt belittled, stupid, embarrassed and scorned.

Enraged, he wanted to beat up both his wife and the man who paid his wages at the same time. In fact, he truly felt he could kill them both. Leaving behind him the disastrous scene of an angry brawl and without any logic, he staggered out of the Bell and Donkey and turned left, heading towards Stapley Manor.

The man, who had dealt the heaviest blow of humiliation, became the focus of attention as the continuing scuffle eventually calmed down. His drinking companions curious to know why he had chosen that moment to tell what he knew and how did he know it anyway? He confessed to holding a secret, which he had not shared with anyone until that night and only did so now, because he was pushed to his limits with Albert's irritating arrogance. It had been years ago, that early one wintry morning, he had taken the opportunity under the obscurity of early morning darkness, to poach for food on the estate, when he chanced upon a shocking sight. Henry came out from the Mill House with a young woman, whom he recognized as Albert's wife. Their parting embrace could lead him to only one conclusion.

It was dark but Albert knew the track as well as anyone, since he had walked it daily for some years. The walk did nothing to cool his frenzy and he ran the last distance to hammer hard on the front door of the man he had called boss for all these years. He wanted to rip him apart there and then. The door was opened and without preamble, he pushed aside the butler and barged in shouting for his employer.

The butler chased after him with no chance of halting this bizarre intrusion and they both found themselves abruptly in the dining room in front of the family. A clatter of cutlery dropping on china vessels heralded a shocked silence. Before anyone could speak any words of sense, Albert had pounced upon Henry and attacked him venomously, in front of his shocked wife, Elizabeth. With frightened shock, the maid, standing ready to serve dinner, dropped a large bowl of fine stew to the floor but quickly gathering her senses, she instinctively grabbed Elise from her chair and ran out of the room to protect the little girl from this madman.

"What is the meaning of this?" Henry shouted between bouts of fist slamming. "Get this man out of here!" he instructed the staff. The butler and footman managed to grab the apoplectic intruder and yanked him backwards away from Henry. Elizabeth was wailing crying, her heart palpitating with unexpected shock and fear.

Freed of this onslaught, Henry stood to address his employee. "What in God's name is all this about? You stink of ale. You're totally blootered man!"

Trying to fight off the servant's restraint, Albert wrestled against their grip. "Believe me Sir I am of sound mind!! A slight sway in his stature belied his statement. Know what I found out tonight??? Go on, guess!! Ha!! Thought you were a gentleman

I did... Ha! No... the man I work for is nothing more than a dark cully...." Sharply thrusting his index finger and stabbing the air towards Elizabeth, "Does she know??" A split second lapsed before he asked again he asked again, "Does she?? Does she know you cannot keep your whore pipe buttoned up? Eh?? You disgust me!" He spat at Henry's feet. Turning to Elizabeth he added, "Made a dolly mop of my wife he has... did you know? Did you?" He insisted threateningly. Elizabeth just hung her head and wept. After all this time, when they thought it was too far behind them to come back to bite them, here it was staring her in the face. This would destroy them.

Henry ordered the servants to get this belligerent employee out of his house and addressing Albert directly, added firmly, "You will leave this house now and not come back. Do you hear me? You are no longer welcome in this house nor on my land. You no longer work for me. Now get out!!" He shouted his command.

Albert fiercely resisted the two puny servants' struggles to remove him. Henry could feel his heart banging and that familiar pain in his chest was returning acutely. His left arm felt strangely painful but he did not wish Albert to see his discomfort and bravely stood his ground. In his fury, Albert was able to free himself from the struggle and stood firm, casting his eyes around the room in which he had never before stood. He was filled with sudden and acute jealousy. This man had everything, which Albert did not: Wealth, servants, money, social standing, respect. He wanted all of this. In fact, that's exactly what he wanted! The idea struck him like a bolt of lightning. He wanted Henry dead and to claim his home – Stapley Manor and its extensive estate. Without a second thought and with complete clarity of mind, he turned to Henry and threw him the challenge. A duel at dawn! The temerity! An employee, bursting in like this and throwing about such challenges. Henry looked at Albert, square on, eye to eye. It was of course preposterous. Incredulous. The man was clearly mad!! The servants froze to the spot, looking from Albert to Henry, aghast.

Elizabeth looked up from her tear-wet hands, towards the intruder, her mouth wide open with disbelief. "What? ... What did you say?" Glancing then at her beloved husband as though in search of reassurance for her own sanity, she saw a look of what appeared to be consideration, across his face. Believing she must be living out some kind of nightmare, she screamed to him "Noooo!" Not knowing if the sound had actually come forth from her lips, she raised herself from her chair and threw herself into his arms, pleading for him to reject this outlandish notion. Henry remained statue like, firmly rooted to the floor, silent, wincing against his increasing chest pain.

Elizabeth had been aware for some time of Henry's occasional but sudden moments of severe discomfort but had accepted his reassurances, claiming recurring dyspepsia. In fact, Henry had been quite ill of late and often in great pain, such as he was suffering at the moment. His distress had also been aggravated by another secret he was withholding from his dear wife and that was his encounter with the gypsy.

He simply no longer had the desire to go on. In fact, he realised, that in accepting this bizarre challenge, it would not only rid the man from his house, before he felt he might collapse and at least keep his own dignity... but, with clarity of mind, as though he had been considering this temptation for hours, he almost welcomed the idea. This would give him the chance to exit life, as he had so craved of late. It was the decision of a man who no longer had fight. In that moment he had not considered his dear wife and child. It was an uncharacteristic, unprecedented, selfish moment of lapse that comes with exhaustion and perhaps even melancholy.

This unwelcome intrusion therefore, suddenly made absolute sense and so, without further preamble or dialogue and much to the horror of Elizabeth, Henry, picked up the gauntlet and agreed to this hare-brained challenge.

The two men hastily set an agreement, witnessed by household staff as they stood observing this bizarre episode unfold in front of them, as the opponents stood across the dining table from each other. Elizabeth could barely credit what she was hearing. Screaming her pleas to stop this nonsensical pantomime, it was as though they were deaf to her desperate attempts to cease the agreement. She was all but invisible. It was as though they were arranging how to escort sheep from one field to the next as she had heard them do many times before. The verbal contract hastily concluded, Albert left the house with as much fury as he entered. As the door slammed behind him, Henry collapsed to the floor, clutching his chest in pain whilst the staff rushed to his side in concern. The interlude had severely taken its toll on all present. Henry allowed himself to be assisted to his bedchamber where he whispered his instructions for the next morning to his butler and life long trusted friend, who had also agreed to be his dueling second.

Somewhat later his wife came weeping to his bedside. Little did she realize their shared words of love would be their last. He offered her calming words of reassurance and she countered these with continued pleas to retract from the contract, whilst knowing this was never likely to happen, given her husband's acute sense of stubborn pride.

Albert, slamming the door behind him and feeling only a little more satisfied that he might reap some revenge on this recent revelation, began his bad tempered walk home. The fiasco at Henry 's home, with its drastic outcome of an agreed duelling challenge, his fury was far from quelled as he set off to take out his still incensed, filthy mood on his unsuspecting wife.

His vile temper pervading his every sinew, he finally arrived home and wildly swung open the cottage door, blaspheming. The sharp pull of draught all but extinguished the last dying embers of the fire in the stone grate and all those inside flinched with the shock of the abrupt entrance. Roaring furiously, he propelled his body across the room swinging his grubby flat hand towards his wife, slapping her across the cheek, the impact jettisoned her to the floor. His face was already bloodied and bruised, clearly having already been in a fight. He continued to spit insults and curse the terrified woman, without respite. The twins flinched at his every movement and quickly left the room without being instructed, more in fear than obedience.

Shouting matches were commonplace in the Turner household but that night, these angry voices and harsh words were like no other the twins had heard before. Their parents never really argued as such, since her mother did not generally respond to his taunting. What was the point when he always insisted on winning and having the last word because he was always deemed right. It was usually the case that his tirade was more of a continuous monologue of his angry booming voice, followed by a slap or a smashed plate, then it would end hours later with a rhythmic banging of their bed headboard against their bedroom wall and her mother's screaming plea to stop.

This night, however, was different. His fury was specific. He had heard someone say something about their mother. He was incandescent beyond words. His roaring voice permeated the cottage walls. The twins could hear almost every furious sentence and he thrashed about the place threatening her. Beating her. Their mother's crying was pitiful. She was screeching her words pleading with him, trying to reason with him, begging for forgiveness or understanding. Beseeching him to listen to her. Her efforts to contest his accusations just seemed to provoke him more.

The twins stood, shaking behind the fragile door, desperately wanting to help their mother but equally terrified to intervene and find themselves as the brunt of his anger. As long moments passed and for the first time, Nancy May found herself wishing her brother was old enough to challenge their father's power and overcome him to protect their mother. As it was, she eventually turned to see her sibling, curled up against the wall, sobbing.

At a very young age, with great maturity of insight, Nancy May realized her father was nothing more than a bully. His narcissistic ways showed in every aspect of his life. He assumed he had the right over everyone else and was entitled to the best of what was on offer without consideration of others. He loved attention, as though he was the most important person in the room, or the village. He craved admiration and most people gave it, rather than get the sharp end of his tongue or worse still the back of his hand. He liked to do that – use the back of his hand. It made him feel powerful. Important. He liked the feeling of people fearing him; shrinking away from him. The irony was however, that he was neither the most important person in the village nor at home. He was nothing. Nobody liked him. Nobody admired him. They just did his bidding to avoid pain or upset or a scene. Nancy May saw him for the nasty, selfish domineering man that he was.

The venomous tirade seemed endless and although Nancy May did not understand some of the words her father used. Unable to shut her ears against the explosion of his bad language, she remembered he called her a 'whore', whatever that was.... She knew that her mother must have done something very wrong to make him this angry. More curiously, he told her he had 'thrown down the gauntlet' and would be leaving before the sun came up the next morning. Her mother begged him over and again through her frenzied tears, not to do this but the banging of his fist on the table, indicated his firm resolve. In that moment, Nancy May decided to follow him.

Staying awake for most of the night so that she would not miss his departure, she finally heard his preparation to leave and waiting some moments longer, silently crept out behind him.

It was barely light and the moon was still apparent. The cold air took her breath away and caused her to shiver. She thought how insane she was for undertaking this expedition. In the first place, she risked the already mighty wrath of her father should he discover her but also how preferable her comfortable bed seemed, to this hare-brained idea. In addition, she was not sure if her father was going to take his horse, in which case, how was she going to follow him? How could she be so stupid?

Fortunately he had set off on foot. She followed at a distance trying to marry her steps with his so as not to create excess noise. After perhaps twenty minutes or so, creeping carefully, she heard voices and held back behind a tree to assess the situation. Thinking wisely, she climbed upwards to an elevated position upon the craggy rocks, which enabled her to see her father and three other men standing in a clearing below. The sun was just beginning to rise, sparkling on the mist, which hung in the valley. She could see the ducks on the lake beyond with their heads tucked under their wings, sleeping to the sweet sporadic tunes of the dawn chorus.

Her father acknowledged the men as though he were the leader. There was then a brief discussion, with an apparent agreement. Two of the men seemed to stand back to back then counted aloud one to ten, as they strode their paces away from each other and marked the ground. As one of them turned he caught a glimpse of Nancy May's movement and for a brief moment, she felt their eyes clash. She quickly ducked. He looked again but the face on the hillside had disappeared and so he dismissed the movement as an apparition.

Nancy May braved another peek at the event unfolding below her. Her father had taken up one of the two positions, facing towards the other man. They each held a pistol and loaded them. A third man asked them in turn, if they were ready and they each responded, "Present". After a silent few moments, the caller shouted, "Fire!"

Shockingly, Nancy May saw her father's opponent bring his pistol to his own head and fire. The sound slightly mismatched that of her father's bullet, which he had aimed directly through his opponent's chest. She saw the man's body buckle and fall to the earth, as though in slow motion.

CHAPTER 3

Peggy and Albert Turner were married in January 1837. It was not a marriage made of love but of convenience. She had not disliked him but it was far from the wonderful love that she had always believed in since a little girl. He was not a totally bad man but neither was he the kindest. She had grown up in a very poor part of town and was born second of nine children. As each child was born to her mother, the older children helped to rear the younger babes. They almost became young mothers themselves before they even left school. When her mother fell pregnant for the last time, she took ill. The pregnancy was difficult and labour came too soon. Sadly, both she and the baby boy died, leaving her father unable to cope. Incredulous to Peggy, he very quickly found someone else to marry, but the new wife was not one to tolerate such a brood of children and so it was agreed that the older children should be married off as quickly as possible, to reduce the family responsibility.

At the other end of the street lived the Turner family. Families all knew each other and had done for generations. Some were inevitably interrelated. They all knew the plight of Peggy's family and Albert saw his opportunity. A few years older than Peggy and full of youthful hormones, he was desperate to leave home himself and get away from his own tyrant father and set up on his own. Taking a wife would be his best way out and so it was contrived, that he would marry Peggy and she half willingly, accepted a very unromantic proposal. They were married before the parson and settled to live in a home, which was nothing more than a shack.

Less than five months later, Peggy found she was undeniably pregnant. Life was impoverished and she was unhappy. Albert, it transpired, was bad tempered and beat her. Knowing no better and without a mother to confide in, she assumed that this was part of what she ought to expect from a husband and was hugely disappointed that this side of marriage was not what she had dreamt it would be. At first he would apologise for his behaviour but as time went by, he began to blame her for his cantankerous ways and vicious attacks. She would cover up her bruises and began to believe she was a bad person or incapable wife or otherwise deserving of the beatings. She tried harder to please him but never succeeded. Always irascible, he managed to pick a fight with ease and mocked her every effort to improve and to please and so, being without reward, she spiralled downwards into depression.

Peggy's pregnancy progressed and she continued to work in the fields, just as she had done since getting married. Towards the end of what she believed was her eighth month during a cold November day, she was as usual, working out in the fields. The afternoon sky had become dark with heavy rainclouds and before the workers could get to cover, it suddenly poured down. She had grown so round, that it was difficult enough to bend over to pick the turnips, let alone run for cover. Soaked to the skin and weary, she returned home, foregoing pay for that lost time. Of course, for that, she deserved a beating from her husband and as a result went into labour. Her friend from next door heard her screams and sent for Peggy's sister. Albert had already left her alone to go to the inn for some well-deserved ale. Hours later, she was delivered of a baby girl but her pains continued. Terrified, she endured further labour, until an hour or so later, a baby boy was also born. Nancy May and Giles Turner were announced.

Albert was incandescent with rage, that she had been so stupid as to bear TWO children, when they could barely afford one.

Life had never been happy for Peggy but now her misery had become almost unbearable and she found herself living in a state of permanent fear and walking on eggshells for fear of upsetting her husband and in consequence receiving a bad tempered fist. Her newfound motherly instinct was strong and her priority was at all times to protect her children. As weeks passed by, she had on a number of occasions placed herself possessively in front of one or the other child to take a sharp slap from Albert, rather than have her babies get a bruising for crying too much.

The winter of 1837 was one of the worst. Bitter cold swept the whole country with intolerably low temperatures. The Thames froze over and pockets of the country had to survive severe conditions and exceedingly low temperatures with hoar frost and snow. In the Midlands, Blackheath, recorded an unprecedented -20°F. Albert's job as manual labourer on an agricultural farm came to a halt, with land frozen hard and what little money he had, he managed to squander much of it on ale. Peggy continued to breast feed the babies and survived on little for herself. Even that, was largely provided for by her good and kind sister, who would rather starve herself than see this young mother go hungry. Income had been sparse for everyone throughout these tough months and the spring which followed, saw a surge of people clambering for jobs as the country tried to resurrect itself. Work was consequently thin on the ground and Albert now had a wife and twin children to reluctantly provide for.

News had come through on the grapevine that the laying of the London to Birmingham railway line was slowly creeping forward, towards the Midlands. There were plans to complete the Kilsby Tunnel by 1838 but more navvies were needed before the 112 mile line could be opened. It meant living away from home for the duration but it would pay well. Albert, along with other men from the village, grabbed the opportunity and by peak summer, he left home without a backward glance.

Peggy was to be left at home for the duration, however long that might be, with two young babies to look after. Life was hard. The promise of money being sent home from Albert did not come to fruition and times had become desperate. Some days, she could barely scrape a meal together and even that was by dint of the kindness of her sister sharing her own frugal food. It was true that other women in the village shared a similar predicament in not knowing for how long their husbands would be away. Some pined for their loved ones, thinking their absence could be twelve months or more. The difference was however, that their men were true to their word and forwarded money to their families but mostly, that there was no love in Peggy's relationship for her to miss.

It quickly became clear to her, that she needed to do something to earn some money to feed herself and enable her to continue breastfeeding her growing twins. It appeared to Peggy that the only solution, was to ask of her dear sister to look after her sweet babies for a few hours a week while she went out to work, if she could find any that was! It was the best arrangement she could make.

With that decision, she took it upon herself to ask about for job vacancies but for days, walking from place to place, she did not succeed. It was exhausting, disheartening, depressing, worrying. Each night, she cried herself to sleep. She would wake the next day and feed her offspring, then set out to search again on foot, often times in the rain. Her sister worried about her.

She was willing to do just about anything. She even fleetingly, in desperation, considered wet nursing but she was already struggling to feed her own two demanding babies.

Almost defeated, she then thought of one last possibility. This last resort was to try for work at the manor house, a little way out of the village. The weather was most unpleasant that particular day with a heavily overcast sky and fine drizzling rain. She wrapped another shawl around her shoulders over her cloak and tucked her curls inside her bonnet, bracing herself for the walk.

Making her way from Broadway, upwards through the steep hillside village of Snowshill until the magnificent, honey coloured stone edifice of Stapley Manor, finally rose up in front of her. It was set against the backdrop of a lush green hillside, rising up to give protection against its northern edge. The front facade however, took in extensive panoramic vistas across as far as Evesham, as it opened out onto endless countryside.

The rain had steadily become heavier along the course of her walk until it was now pouring down. Gratefully, she found that the road finally met a heavy wooden gate, marking the periphery of Stapley Manor's estate, wide enough for carriages to pass through. Lifting its latch, Peggy pushed hard against the resisting wood as it scraped the wet gritty ground, struggling to create a wide enough gap to squeeze through, then replaced it with a clatter. Woodland skirted the pathway to her left and to her right she glanced what looked like a partly obscured building beneath considerable undergrowth.

Having trudged the quarter mile or so along the muddy, puddled pathway, Peggy, now saturated, walked nervously towards the back of the house and knocked at what she guessed to be the kitchen door of the grand house. A young maid opened the door and took one pitying look at this soaking wet woman and suggested she step inside for a moment while she fetched the housekeeper. Mud covered Peggy's flimsy shoes and her bonnet was dripping wet. She shivered.

At the beckoning of the maid, the busy housekeeper bustled into the back hallway to see this saturated, forlorn vision in front of her and her heart bled to hear her plea for work. As much as she would have loved to give this young, desperate woman a job, the household did not require any further staff at that time and she had to advise her that she could not help. Standing to go, and thanking the housekeeper for her time, Peggy reached out to open the back door to leave, when suddenly the door was snatched from her grip from the outside and flung open to reveal a handsomely dressed, elegant man about to rush in from the downpour. Immediately assuming him to be the master of the house, Peggy stood back apologizing for being in the way and dipped her eyes humbly from his gaze, thinking how frightfully bedraggled she must look. Henry walked in and realizing her imminent exit, challenged her, "Goodness me! You are surely not going to leave here in this atrocious downpour are you?" He questioned, looking completely befuddled. Glancing back up at him, astonished that he should even notice, let alone care, she gave a half smile and whispered, "Well, yes Sir. I have to!"

"Well that is simply a nonsense! You are already soaked to the skin! You may wait here a while until the storm has passed. There's a chair just there. Please be seated." Shrugging off his coat, he began to walk away but after what seemed to be an afterthought, he turned back towards Peggy and whilst shaking the rain off his coat, enquired, "Tell me! What was your business here?"

Peggy was about to sit down, when she was stalled by his unexpected question. Remaining standing, she replied politely, "Sir, I came looking for work, Sir." He looked blankly at her for a brief moment and said, "Do we have any available? I was not aware we are looking for any more staff?" Realising he thought she had come in response to an advertisement, she quickly corrected, "Oh, no Sir... that is, I need a job Sir and I came to see if you needed any extra help Sir – I am willing to try to do anything ...but no, you do not need anyone Sir."

Henry caught sight of a narrow gold band around her finger and asked if her husband could not provide for her. Embarrassed, she briefly explained her situation and felt both ashamed and flustered at having to explain her plight.

Peggy visibly flinched at a loud clap of thunder, immediately followed by a flash of lightning and brought a natural momentary pause. Then without saying any more and furrowing his brow into a frown, Henry turned on his heels and walked away, leaving Peggy to watch the rain hammering down outside and wishing it would stop, so she could leave and take her embarrassment with her.

Peggy was subsequently aware of the low voices in the room next door, the words of which were indistinguishable but she recognised them to be between the gentleman and whom she presumed to be the housekeeper. She was intrigued to know what they were talking about but it felt ridiculously rude to even try to eavesdrop. The sky eventually brightened and the rain ceased sufficiently for Peggy to leave. She stood and reached to twist the door handle to exit but jumped at the sound of the housekeeper's voice, behind her. "What is your name again?" Peggy turned to be sure the housekeeper was in fact really addressing her. "Oh, erm, my name is Margaret, ma'am but everybody calls me Peggy, ma'am."

"You said you were prepared to do anything..." began the housekeeper and Peggy responded with a nod. "I have given this further thought and believe that we would be able to offer you some hours assisting the scullery maid... she has a poorly mother and could do with some time at home, so we could use help when she is not here but it would be only be for part of each day until her mother gets better or...." She stopped short of finishing her sentence but Peggy got the drift of her intended thought. Peggy was both relieved and overjoyed to have at least something. It was true that becoming a scullery maid was far below her capabilities but only working for part of each day was a godsend, so that she could still have time to be with her beloved children. She accepted graciously and began work the next day.

On the fourth day of her employment, she chanced to encounter Mr. Carter again. She would never have dared to speak to him, had he not initiated the conversation and was rather flustered when he stopped by to see how she was settling in. It astonished her that he even remembered her, let alone concerned himself that she was satisfied with her employment. He seemed such a kind and thoughtful man. Such a gentleman in the true sense of the word and quite unlike what she had expected of the master of a stately manor. She responded timidly to his simple questions and felt herself blush under his gaze. He had a certain presence, a strength of character, an allure she could not quite put her finger on. He smiled with generosity as he bid her good day and she carried on her work in something of a dream.

On several occasions throughout the next few weeks, Mr. Carter passed through the kitchen on one pretence or another. Some of the staff commented behind his back on the unusualness of this but thought no more of it. On each occasion, he caught Peggy's eye and smiled, or even spoke to ask some inane question. Each time, Peggy found herself blush bright red and her heart thought it might burst from her chest.

As the days went by, into weeks, she found herself feeling more and more excited to go to work. She felt reassured and even proud to have found herself employment and it spurred her on with confidence and self worth. There was something invigorating about the long walk to work, through the colourful autumnal countryside with its collage of riotous fiery shades and smell of wood burning fires that warmed her soul. Scuffing her feet in the crispy fallen leaves took her mind back to happy childhood days and for a short while she found respite from her daily worries and responsibilities. The mornings often brought a low mist, which hung in the valley waiting for the mellow sun to slowly emerge and disperse the opaqueness. By the end of the day, a chill in the air made her pull her cloak tighter and hurry her steps to get back to her two babies and a welcoming fire in the hearth and a dear sister she would not trade for the world. She was so grateful to her, for taking care of the babes while she was earning some money and could never repay her for her understanding and kindness.

Walking home one late afternoon, Peggy reflected on her day and could not stop herself from thinking about the master of the house. How lucky his wife was, to have such a wonderful man for a husband and simply by dint of birth that they commanded respect, wealth and status. She could barely imagine what life would be like upstairs but she found herself imagining herself as his wife and how life would be for them. It was only when her mind inevitably drifted to the bedroom that she stopped short, ashamed of herself for her wayward thoughts. She suddenly felt embarrassed for allowing her mind to wander into the privacy of another man's marriage (how could she ever look at him in the face again?!) but also very guilty for her momentary forgetfulness of her sacred wedding vows to her own husband. Yet, despite her self-chiding, she could not shake off the thought of how different her marriage was in comparison to that of Mr. and Mrs. Carter. She imagined theirs to be a marriage made in heaven.

It was, however, rare that Peggy ever saw, let alone spoke to the lady of the house. She seemed to keep herself privately tucked away but Peggy had heard the staff speak fondly of their mistress and from one short conversation of greeting, she thought Mrs. Carter, to be beautiful. Elizabeth, had been made aware of the new member of staff by the housekeeper and she had only spoken a few cursory words with the young woman to be sure she was being appreciated but there had been no other reason for her to speak to Peggy at length. Her husband had taken pity on the new employee and insisted a simple but worthwhile position be created for the desperate woman, in order that she may feed her children.

Elizabeth was touched by her husband's kindness and generosity but not surprised. He had always demonstrated a deeply compassionate soul and it was just one reason she loved him so very much. She loved Henry's thoughtfulness for the woman's plight and her need to protect her children. How envious she was that the new maid should have two children: Oh how she would willingly exchange all her material world, for the privilege of becoming a mother. She hated to admit to herself that she was peaked with such jealousy.

Henry, her darling handsome husband, had always been attentive and loving since they first met and following a whirlwind love affair, he gained the approval of her father and they were married only months later. There had never been a moment's regret on either side that they had rushed into their union. They were mutually besotted and inseparable. Theirs was a passionate love, the enviable sort. It was the deep, spiritual connection that comes from true love. The rare sort of love, that needs no dialogue to know what the other is thinking: the sort of love that transmits silent words between two people across a crowded room, just by eye contact. A glance that speaks a thousand words, untranslatable by onlookers but completely understood by the recipients.

They needed no fashionable aphrodisiac. The lust of youth stayed with them across the two decades of their marriage and they were happy – yet not complete. Elizabeth began to sink into gloomy disappointment as each month brought the realization that she was yet again not carrying her husband's baby. They both so very much wanted a child and yet this blessing seemed to avoid them. Months ticked by into years and Elizabeth's disappointment developed into distress and ultimately, depression. Henry did not give up hope and soothed his wife's concerns, patiently hoping for the next month and then the next. Ten years passed and it seemed unlikely that a child would be born to them. Henry had resigned himself to God's will, though he still prayed for a miracle.

Elizabeth, however, had dipped steadily into a deeper depression. It seemed that she wept constantly. She barely ate. She secreted herself away in her room and grew lethargic, pale and disinterested in life. She refused her husband's advances and could barely look at him for her own sense of shame. Henry's reassurances fell on deaf ears. She did not wish to hear his platitudes. His sense of rejection slowly permeated every part of his being and an overwhelming sense of grief settled about his daily life.

In a moment of deep contemplation, his heart pained a little, to see this young woman having to plead for employment just to keep her babies alive. To give her employment was the very least he could do. He had so much in life, yet in that moment of first meeting Peggy, he was shocked to realise that he almost envied her plight, for she had what he did not. Children.

CHAPTER 4

One Monday, Peggy had popped into a shop to buy some eggs for supper later on that day, when behind her she had overheard two other women gossiping unaware of Peggy's presence. She froze to the spot with four eggs balanced in her hand listening with sickening intrigue.

"Oh it was a lovely surprise wasn't it to have them home!" one said to the other gleefully. "He just came right in and swept me of my feet he did, oh and I hugged him that tight! He looked a bit tired but he said they were all doing alright, except the food wasn't like mine!" She giggled to recall the compliment and continued as though all in one breath." He'd got quite muscly mind, quite the strongman he is now! Oh I can tell you, it wasn't long before we were up them stairs having a cuddle!!"

She gave a burst of coarse laughter and her friend joined in, "Oh I know and my George too. It was so good to have him back but I do miss him even more now he's gone again!"

The first woman continued, "Yes, I know luv but at least we had them home for a short time and with all that money too! It's been worth them going away, hasn't it?! Some of 'em didn't bother eh? My Tom, he said that that Albert's a funny one! He's been spending all his cash on ale and the rest..." She paused to give her friend an elbow nudge along with a suggestive wink before continuing, "Apparently he 'couldn't be bothered' comin' home to see his missus – and she's got two babies and all."

"Oh I know – and at Christmas too! My George said he spends his time with a certain 'lady of the night'!"

"No! Really! ..."

Peggy dropped the eggs from her hand and with her eyes prickling, hurried out of the shop, leaving the shattered shells oozing mess across the floorboards and the two women looking shamefully aghast in her wake, plus the shopkeeper shouting obscenities after her.

By the time Peggy had crossed the road, she was running. Flowing tears obscured her vision and with an unfortunate misplacement of her foot, she went over on her ankle and smacked heavily to the floor, whereupon she wept miserably. Suddenly from behind her came a strong arm and quiet, soothing voice. She flinched to look up and into the eyes of Henry. Feeling utterly wretched and embarrassed, she tried to get herself up off the floor but her injured foot could not take the strain and she flopped back to the ground with a whimper.

"Stop. Stop." he urged her. "Don't move or you'll make it worse!" His instant concern was that she may have broken something and he could not allow her to make it worse by bearing weight upon it. Wondering what best to do in the circumstance for propriety's sake, he suggested, "Can you feel if your ankle is swelling Peggy?"

Her first reaction was to note that he had remembered her name. Then pulling herself together a little, she slid her hand down towards her foot and felt, "Ow!! Yes I believe it might be, Sir. Oww!" She unintentionally repeated.

Stooping down beside her, he spoke reassuringly, "Peggy, we have to get this tended to as quickly as we can. Now... will you allow me to take you home? I can ... erm, will you allow me to assist you into my carriage?" Peggy nodded agreement but had no idea what he meant by that, or whether he intended to take her to his home or hers. Her second thought was how on earth was she to get into the carriage. Feeling utterly mortified at her predicament, she blushed bright red and hated that too!

Henry stood and took a few paces away from Peggy, waving his hand in the air to draw the attention of Bill his driver, then gestured for him to bring the carriage alongside. That done, Bill was to open the carriage door and without preamble, Henry scooped up Peggy into his arms and lifted her cautiously into the carriage. He was just lowering her onto the velvet seat when somehow she knocked her sore foot and sucking in her breath, she winced trying not to show how much it hurt.

"Oh, my dear, I am so sorry. Did I hurt you?" The endearment was out of his mouth before he realised but she seemed not to notice, which was a relief.

"No!" she blurted out sharply, "It was my fault! You are so kind!" Suddenly registering his words, she looked at him with something resembling shock but somewhat disappointingly he seemed unaware of his choice of words. He was so close, she could feel his breath on her neck and a shiver shot unexpectedly down her spine. Disconcerted by her reaction, she shuffled a little further away from his hold and simultaneously, he also moved discreetly to sit in the opposite seat.

"Now, where do you live? We need to get this ankle looked at!" Peggy hesitated hard. This was her worst embarrassment! She was so ashamed to have him see where she lived.

"Oh I'm sure I'll be fine, Sir, if you just take me to the end of Primrose Lane, that would be a great help. I shall manage after that. Thank you Sir!" He studied her face. She had dropped her pretty eyes to her skirts and even though her cheeks pinked with what he knew was bashfulness; there was something so fragile about her.

"Indeed not." He insisted. "I shall see that you get home to your door. We need to get you inside and then I can call for the doctor." Peggy shot her glance back up to him in panic.

"But Sir, I cannot afford a doctor, Sir....I..I'll be fine", she stammered.

With such benign calm, he gestured his hand toward her, "There is no need to worry about that, Peggy. I can see to that but we must have this sorted. You must not attempt to try to walk on that foot. Now, I shall have no more argument. Whereabouts on Primrose Lane do you live?" Henry knew that Primrose Lane had few houses and none of them were grand, to say the least. It was a very quaint part of Broadway but the homes he knew were quite dilapidated. Peggy had to resign herself to his generosity and thanked him graciously, explaining exactly which house she called home.

He knocked a signal loudly on the side of the carriage and shouted up the directions for Bill to pull forward. Talking to Peggy reassuringly, Henry showed her great kindness, which she had never before experienced from any other man. His voice was gentle and comforting in itself but his words were even more lulling. A stark contrast to Albert. She wondered if Elizabeth had any idea how very lucky she was? He had no idea of the whirl of thoughts spinning in her head. Perpetuating the conversation, Henry asked about her twins.

Her eyes shone, lighting up her whole face, "Oh Sir, they are my joy! They are scrambling into everything so as I can't keep up with them and I can see them as proper little people now with a mind of their own. So different to each other and I don't mind telling you, I don't get a right lot of sleep but I wouldn't change that!!" She came to an abrupt halt and dipped her head, cringing at herself for babbling.

Henry laughed. "You must be so proud of them Peggy." He said enviously. "You are very fortunate to have two healthy infants!" He too then stopped before divulging his greatest desire. There followed a slightly uncomfortable lull inside the carriage before they both went to speak at once, then laughed.

Seeing this lift in her mood, Henry risked his curiosity, "You were crying before you fell!" ... Her demeanour changed again. He persisted, "What had upset you so?" He paused. "I saw you run from the shop. Tell me what had happened, Peggy. Perhaps I can help." Naively he continued. "Were you not able to pay for something? Do you need financial help? I can help you to feed your children, Peggy!"

She shook her head. "No, nothing like that." She admitted.

"Then what is it? You can tell me!" Her eyes filled with tears again and he felt bad to have caused her to remember her upset. "Are you unwell, perhaps?" Again, she shuffled in her seat and shook her head. He gave her some moments to compose herself and eventually, she spoke.

"I overheard something." Just at this wrong moment, the carriage pulled up at her address and Bill jumped down to assist his master. Henry signalled for him to wait. He moved away discreetly.

"Whatever had you heard that would cause you such distress?" he encouraged.

Finally, she gave in to answer him, "It seems that some of the men had come home for a couple of days at Christmas." She swallowed hard to choke down the threatening tears. "But not Albert." Trying to offer reason for her disappointment, Henry sought for a possible excuse.

"Maybe he wanted to work extra hours?"

She scoffed loudly and the tears flowed hard. She wiped her nose indelicately with the back of her hand and snivelled a little. "No Sir... It seems he has been spending his time and money between the alehouse and ... and, a fallen woman!"

Henry was dumbfounded. "Surely not! Surely this is no more than gossip mongering!"

Peggy shook her head, "You do not know him like I do Sir! I believe there is truth in this!"

Fighting for some words of reassurance, he finally suggested, "Peggy, I am sure you will see, once he comes home, that this is all an exaggeration and all will be well!"

Breaking the dialogue, he gestured for Bill to come forward. Between them they manoeuvred the young woman from her seat and to the ground. Realising there was no other way to do this, Henry again scooped her up and as though she weighed nothing, carried her to the front door. Peggy's sister Mabel, opened the door aghast at the sight before her. There was quite a bit of explaining to be done!!

Over the next couple of weeks, Peggy felt the most pampered woman in the world. Never before had she had so much attention lavished upon her. Henry was as good as his word and had a doctor come to the house to examine her foot. The ankle was thankfully not broken but indeed badly damaged and would take quite some time to repair. It was duly bound up and she was to rest as much as possible. That was easier said than done, with two young children but Mabel agreed to come to stay for the duration of her recovery and so the hours passed by pleasurably together, looking after the babies. She was given a wooden crutch, which should be used as little as possible, only when she absolutely must get up from her chair. Life was going to be difficult, she thought.

Incredulously to Peggy, Henry insisted upon paying her wage, even though she was unable to go to work. In addition, he made it his business to call in on her every other day to see how she was progressing. Each visit, he would bring with him a small gift of food from Stapley Manor. Peggy was never sure if the cook realized to whom he was gifting the cakes or pies or bread, which he brought but she was extremely grateful for all his offerings. He appeared to never treat her with anything more than concern for an employee, yet he did insist on her calling him Henry. From her stance, she could not fathom his kindness.

Was this kindness how he was with everyone? He was the most exceptional man in his indulgence. He would stay for perhaps an hour or so each visit and chat with Peggy and Mabel equally and on occasion he would play with the toddlers in such a way as a father might. Peggy found this so endearing and charming and it did cross her mind to wonder why he and Elizabeth did not have a family. She found herself looking forward excitedly to his visits, yet knew that she should not. Her tummy tingled at the thought of seeing him and when she set eyes on him, she experienced an unfamiliar sensation in the pit of her stomach and it seemed to somersault when he returned his smiling gaze.

The purple swelling around her ankle was reducing and the pain was slowly lessening. During one visit, her sister had taken the children for a short walk and so his arrival found Peggy alone. He and Peggy chatted amicably over a cup of tea and their companionship felt as comfortable as good friends, without social differences. There was something warm about their friendship. For Peggy, it was something intangibly exciting. There was no awkwardness about having each other in close proximity and neither even thought about propriety in being alone together. Their relaxed chat was natural and convivial, so when Peggy happened upon a question, which seemed to open up the floodgates of his mind, she was not totally surprised at his easy honesty.

"How is Elizabeth?"

The question did however take Henry off guard for a moment and he simply responded with a deep sigh but then continued without further hesitation, "She is not herself these days and quite melancholic." It was as though the remoteness of the tiny cottage gave him the security of letting go of his thoughts.

Peggy dared to probe further, "You do not have children?" Touching the sorest of spots, he jumped to his feet in readiness to leave. Immediately realizing her faux pas, "I am sorry, Henry,

I should not have asked. Forgive me for my intrusion." She was truly sorry for her insensitivity.

Resigned to telling her the truth, as though it would purge his soul to tell someone, he returned to his seat dipping his head towards his folded hands. "It would seem that we are unable to have children. The despair has sent Elizabeth way into the doldrums and I cannot pull her back out. It deeply saddens me." It was without thought that she reached out to encompass his hand in hers, comfortingly. He did not flinch and accepted the unconventional gesture, in the genuine way it was offered. It was in this way that they sat for some time, in quiet, deep conversation, bringing a cathartic release to both.

Three weeks on and Peggy still had a limp but it was only really discernible to those who knew her well. By the time she was ready to go back to work, February had arrived with icy cold days and nights. She had begun to realise how much happier she had become of late. She had not seen Albert in some six months and without his predatory, uncouth behaviour, it seemed she had returned to her true self. She rejoiced in her newfound freedom but there still lurked a sense of dread for his unpredicted return.

At the end of her third day back at Stapley Manor, just as Peggy was about to put her coat on to walk home, Henry came through the kitchen. She was so pleased to see him and instinctively wanted to run inappropriately into his arms and let him hold her.

Unexpectedly however, in that same instant, she sensed there was something different about his demeanour. She felt a pang of disappointment and even embarrassment for her own reaction, to sense his slight aloofness. His obvious distancing was quite different to what she had become used to. Although he smiled widely and asked after her health, pointing to her foot, she could not quite read his mind. There was undoubtedly a greater formality resumed between them and her stomach plummeted with a sense of confused hurt.

Rationalising this and with a moment of further sensible thought, she began to reason why this could possibly be. After all, they were no longer in the privacy of her tiny cottage and he was once again her employer and married master of the house. He opened the door for her to leave as any gentleman would and as she exited, he followed her, walking leisurely alongside her.

Once outside, he seemed to drop his guard a little and confessed that he had missed what had become their regular chats. She was insanely relieved that by the time they were out of earshot of the house, Henry had resumed what she had come to know as his usual self and they once again fell into easy conversation, exchanging news. With greater contentment then, she gazed around her, appreciating her surroundings. Henry's rich low voice permeated her senses as they ambled at a slow pace, as though to protract their short time together until they reached the end of the pathway. Never had she wished more for time to stand still, while she absorbed the romanticism of such a cold frosty monochromatic wintry scene. They stood momentarily before the gate, surrounded by remote countryside with its mist-clad barren fields and smell of wood burning cottage fires and inexplicably, her heart soared. Was it perhaps just her imagination making more than she ought, of the person she walked alongside?

The following week, the housekeeper had asked Peggy if she might be able to increase her hours at Stapley Manor whilst the scullery maid took time away to tend to her mother in what had become her dying days. Very happy to spend more time at the house, Peggy was pleased to agree and arranged for her sister Mabel to once again help out looking after the twins. The extra money was most welcome and enabled Peggy to treat Mabel to some extras too. Peggy's primary delight however, was to enable increased opportunity to chance seeing Henry. For one reason or another, either one or the other of them, contrived to have their paths cross at some point, on most days. The rest of the household seemed oblivious to anything untoward.

The winter weather began to set in hard and by the end of February, snow was threatening. One afternoon, the weather had deteriorated suddenly. Henry had been out to the near paddocks where he had been making sure the horses had been safely brought into the stables and re-entered the house via the kitchen door, bringing an icy blast of air with him. He urged Peggy to leave her chores promptly and set off home, as a wind had whipped up and it was beginning to snow hard and it was sticking fast. He was concerned that she returned home without danger of slipping and hurting her foot again. As encouraged, she quickly finished her immediate chore and put on her coat, preparing herself as best as she could against the increasing blizzard. Henry offered politely in front of the housekeeper to escort her to the gate, on the pretext of making sure she got at least part way home safely.

The bitter blast of cold air, which hit them as soon as they were outside, snatched their breath away. They braced themselves against its strength, ready for the trudge along the long drive, heading straight into the face of the blusterous snow storm. It had come on so fiercely and increased in intensity within no time. Henry had wondered if they should simply return to the house, yet they had already fought their way this far. They could barely be heard by one another as the trees rattled noisily above their heads and Henry was very concerned for Peggy's safety beyond the gate and reaching her home. Barely able to see the gate ahead, he made an impromptu decision. Gently guiding her arm towards him he beckoned her to follow along the overgrown side pathway towards the Mill House. He managed to force the unlocked door but still struggled to open it, for it would seem it was seized up with years of unyielding ivy growth. Finally pushing hard, the door gave into his strength and they both stumbled over its threshold, into the dark space.

Standing still, adjusting their eyes to the dimness, it was clear that nobody had been in there for years. A mouse scurried across the dirt floor away into a black hiding hole, momentarily startling Peggy. Overgrown ivy at the window and such heavy greyness of the snowy clouds above, obliterated much of the late afternoon winter light within the gloomy room. Henry laughed, "I haven't seen the inside of these walls in a very long time!"

"Who used to live here?" Peggy asked with intrigue.

"When my grandparents owned Stapley, it had been home to their butler and his housekeeper wife ... but we are not so grand now!" he laughed. "My father said it originally was the site of a disused water mill running alongside that stream," he gestured outside into the bleak whiteness, "but that was demolished and so when this was built, the locals labelled it 'the Mill House'. I used to play here with my brother when we were little. It wasn't quite so overgrown with brambles and ivy then!"

Glancing about the room and seeing Peggy shiver, "... Now, I don't suppose for a moment ..." he hesitated, "We used to keep some candles in here..." Rummaging in a broken cupboard, he gave a celebratory "Whoop!" to find three tapers, one of which was broken into two. Leaving the cupboard door open, precariously hanging by one hinge, he opened his coat to better delve into his jacket pocket beneath and pulled out his pipe and matches. Placing the pipe on the fire mantelpiece, he struck a match and lit one of the precious candles. "It may take some time for the storm to pass... we must preserve what we have for later", he joked.

Peggy stood and watched in awe as he took control of the situation, caring for her safety. Not once did she concern herself about his decision to bring her in here, alone with him. Taking the lit candle from Henry's hand, she carefully placed it in a metal holder upon the mantelpiece but it wobbled unsafely. Looking about her she found a small piece of crisp dead ivy, which had found its way inside. Retrieving the candle, she touched the flaming ivy to its base to melt it a little.

Henry watched transfixed, "What are you doing?" he questioned. She then firmly secured the candle back in its holder and the soft wax instantly set cold, immediately securing it upright in its holder.

"There!" she announced, "That's better!" They both laughed.

Peggy looked around the dark room and began to focus on the bits of furniture. Henry abruptly disappeared into what she assumed was a next door room and returned with a broken chair. Stamping his foot on it a number of times, it easily smashed into pieces. Looking around the room, he spotted an old rag of sacking which at one time had been used as some sort of bag, perhaps for vegetables and setting it alight with the candle, thrust it into the fireplace, on top of which he placed a few of the pieces of chair wood. In the meantime, Peggy had found a sort of bench-bed and a wobbly table, which she pushed forward towards the fire. Slipping out of their snow-wet coats, Henry shook them and hung them over the edge of the table to dry. They both perched upon the edge of the bench, instinctively holding their hands out towards the new yellow flames which did not yet hold any heat. Peggy gave a shiver.

"I hope you are not too cold, my dear. That will not do at all! We shall soon feel the benefit of the fire!" Henry drew up closer to her and wrapped his arm around her.

"Come, take some of my warmth!" Blissfully closing her eyes momentarily, she unashamedly snugged in towards him, deliberately breathing in his masculine scent. She thought she could possibly be in heaven.

This was no short-lived blizzard. It raged on through the night. The impoverished windowpanes did little to keep the draught out and rattled constantly with each blast of wind. The room was damp with lack of use for years, maybe decades but the fire offered its constant glow and psychological warmth. Once their coats were dry, Henry lay them on the floor which offered a much more comfortable resting place from the hard bench-bed, with scarves rolled up for a make-do pillow. Peggy lay next to the fire and Henry lay protecting her side from the draughts. Without inhibition, they wrapped themselves around one another, breathing in each other's air. It was as though they had lain thus, for years. They had managed to keep the tapers going, one after the other and the fire was kept to a low ember. Conversation never ran dry. No awkward pauses. They listened intently to one another in respectful turn, learning about each other's lives, both laughing and crying in response to stories told to pass the time. There was a mutual empathy, as each spoke of their own trials and tribulations, and each showed a natural concern, one for the other. Sharing life stories and home truths, made for an understanding or closeness which was unexpected by Henry but not by Peggy. She believed she had found, in Henry, what she believed was her soul mate, no matter that he was already married. Henry however, never lost sight of his marriage and loyalty to Elizabeth, but his growing attraction to Peggy was, under these circumstances, nigh on overwhelming and temptation was brinking on the irresistible. He saw this woman, despite all that she faced daily in her abusive marriage, still finding a compassion within her, to show understanding for Henry's sorrow. She was so giving of her loving attention, that her underlying vulnerability was simply too alluring. Such seductive enticement, was just too strong for either of them to refuse and with unconditional mutual consent, they gave into their physical needs. With such gentle tenderness she never thought existed, Peggy never wanted this night to end. Henry however was left with a confused sense of remorse, for although this beautiful young woman could, in another existence, have been his everything, he was, after all, married. Conscience stricken and full of self-reproach for this foolish act, Henry knew this must not happen again.

Waking with a start as the sun rose, a noise outside jolted them back to reality. Hearts pounding for fear of being discovered, they quickly corrected their clothes and Henry peeped through the window to find deeply drifted snow outside but a clear, sunny morning with blue sky and a fox trying to forage for his breakfast. Relieved at this, they sighed away their worries, then laughed.

Their 'cover story' to everyone at Stapley Manor had been that Henry had indeed escorted Peggy home, only to be unable to get back in the storm and so he had stayed at the Lygon coaching inn for the night. Peggy simply told Mabel, that she had stayed in the servants' quarters at the manor house. Nobody thought any more of it and no more was said. Except between them, when Henry spoke with great kindness to Peggy about their wonderful night and his undeniably deep feelings for her but confessed too his guilt of such an indiscretion and begged her forgiveness and understanding that this must never be discovered. Neither would it happen again. Heartbroken, Peggy agreed.

It felt strange for Peggy to continue working at Stapley Manor yet no longer seeing Henry about the place. A huge sense of emptiness overwhelmed her and sadness took over her everyday thoughts. True to his word and with great difficulty, Henry stayed well away from the kitchens or the driveway when she would be coming to or going from the house. Her need to work was crucial for survival and without any support now from Albert, she must continue in her job.

Passing through the fields one day, approaching the Mill House, many subjects weighed heavily on Henry's mind. He reflected on his dalliance with Peggy and his concerns for his dear wife's deteriorating health intermingled with his longing for children. He then randomly recalled an encounter a month or so earlier. A colourful wagon pulled by two shabby white horses, creaked its way along the driveway leading to the house, driven by a gypsy man and his vivacious wife. Henry was always a little cautious about letting gypsies into their midst and so on this occasion he did not declare himself as the landowner of this fine estate. He stopped politely to pass the time of day, believing it was always best to keep on their good side, for their cultural reputation of dishonesty was commonly accepted. The cart had rolled to a stop aside Henry as he paused at the gate. Seeing them approach, he perched to rest on the wall alongside the gate. The man asked if there might be any work at the big house, to which Henry gave a non-committal "I doubt it!"

The young woman jumped down from her seat alongside her husband and with a seductively flirtatious, hip-swinging stroll, made her way towards Henry. "Good morning Sir" she said with a glint in her eyes. He responded with a similar greeting.

"Now Sir, I be thinking you might know more than you're a'tellin'! A handsome man like you, out here... I think you're not a worker! What would you be doin' here, I'm wondering?" She swayed her hips towards him and presumed to take his hand in hers. Feeling most uncomfortable but equally transfixed, he did not refuse her advances. She smoothed his upturned palm in her hands, sending a prickle of reaction down his spine.

"Mmm, my word", she paused, staring into his creased palm. "How interesting you are..." She circled her thumb alluringly and continued. "Would you care to cross my palm with silver

Sir and I can make things clearer for you, as I see you have much on your mind, Sir.... Something precious to you... something you crave..." She glanced up at him, as though to get a clue from his face.

He delved into his pocket and flicked out a small coin, which she caught with well practiced agility. Glancing again to his manly palm, "You have a beautiful wife, I see..." Henry was taken aback but then reasoned this was just talk and guesswork, something she might well say to every gentleman. "but I see no children..." she continued and his heart stopped. Something about her was absorbing, captivating. He spoke not a word. All too soon, she replaced his hand back on his thigh, "Soon Sir... 'Tis here in your hand, Sir. Not long now and you will be blessed with a beautiful baby girl Sir." Leaving Henry spellbound, the gypsy hopped back onto the vardo and the wagon began to roll forward, taking them away as quickly as they had come. Like a dream.

Henry gathered his senses and called after them light heartedly, "If this is true, I shall reward you!" Rosanne turned her head back towards him, beaming her smile widely, and waved an acknowledgement. The colourful caravan disappeared just as it had come, leaving Henry in a stir of emotion and not quite believing that he would make such a promise as he just had. Yet, he did not regret it either!

Months went by and Peggy saw no more of Henry, despite her daily walks to Stapley Manor. She felt a deep sadness from the moment she woke until her body and mind gave into sleep at night. She tried not to hope that their paths might cross, yet knew that if they did chance to see each other, it would only serve to painfully reignite their passion. She must accept that what had passed between them was gone and she must simply cherish the memory.

Something had been worrying her though and as weeks went by, she became more and more certain of her concern. Finally admitting to herself, she had fallen pregnant with Henry's child. A small part of her was so proud. To think that together, they had created a small life. She desperately wanted to love this child and not for a moment, despite all the repercussions she was now undoubtedly about to face, did she consider having the baby ripped from her body. Nevertheless, her future was in jeopardy. How was she to continue to keep this secret? Things would become difficult at work and she feared she would have to leave her employment but she had no idea how on earth she could explain this decision either to the housekeeper or to Mabel. Then there was the problem of how could she cope without the money? Her biggest worry of course, was Albert. She felt sick at the thought of his finding out. Without a shadow of a doubt she would be beaten to a pulp and then thrown out, never to see her children again. Mabel would not understand and would shamefully consider her a harlot. She did not know when Albert would next be home but she prayed it would be sooner rather than later. The irony! She did not want him home at all but if she was to get away with this, he must not see her swelling belly. She decided not to tell Henry for this would cause him too much heartache. It would be the child he had always wanted but it would break his wife's heart to know he had been unfaithful. In a fog of uncertainty and loneliness, Peggy could have no set plan as to her future but she prayed on a daily basis that she could hide her secret from everyone.

Two weeks later, half way through the month of May, her first prayer was answered, even though it was a bitter-sweet pill. Albert had deigned to return home for just a few days and as usual threw his weight around in his usual grotesque way. It was fortunate that Peggy was already at home and she was not needed over the weekend at Stapley Manor, for he knew nothing about her going out to work.

Peggy found herself needing to be a good actress. He had brought a small amount of money, which he threw arrogantly onto the kitchen table as though she should be graciously appreciative. Peggy tried to muster sufficient gratitude to allay any suspicion of her recent wayward behaviour. He looked dreadful. He stank of ale and his clothes and body were filthy. He paid little heed to the twins, save for the times they annoyed him with their crying or squealing and on those occasions, he would threaten a slap or the end of his foot. No sooner was he home than he disappeared out again to the alehouse.

When he eventually rolled in later that night, not only did she anticipate his expectations of her to wait up for him and have a homely welcome for her husband but she had to force herself to appear to be receptive to his rough and crude advances when she was physically sickened by them. She prayed that it would be sufficiently dark so that he would not suspect her changing shape. She found it almost impossible to accept the stark contrast between her grotesque husband, to whom she had tied herself for the rest of their lives and Henry, who had proved himself to be the most caring, gentle person she thought could possibly ever exist. Peggy knew how vital it was that she act out this wifely conduct, for fear of getting a beating of which she had not forgotten he was quite capable. She felt the days, and more so the nights were endless and she loathed every moment he was back under their roof.

For whatever reason, Albert seemed to Peggy to be even more aggressive than usual but she wondered if her perceptions had changed, now that she had known the lustful joy of being with Henry. Yet, Albert's dissatisfaction in the bedroom and the consequent bruises were proof enough that his bad tempered ways had indeed become worse, no doubt, she believed, because she did not know the seductive ways of a prostitute!

He slept off the effects of his ale drinking during the day, for which she was grateful to have him out of her way. Knowing he would repeat his routine later the second night, she lovingly rubbed her tummy and feared with dread for her safety once he returned. The mere thought of his repeat attentions made her nauseous. God forbid he was home for good. With a moment of inspiration and in an attempt to keep him from having his way with her again, she claimed to have her 'monthly unwellness', which she knew he found repulsive. Knowing what she risked, she found it preferable to take a black eye for her 'stupidity', rather than to have him maul her again. Reeling from the battering she had taken, she hoped it would be a long time before he came home again.

The weekend passed just as she had expected. He left on Monday morning to return to Kilsby, much as he had arrived and had spent much of the money he brought with him. He was filthy tempered, indifferent to her wellbeing, irritated by the children but thankfully, ignorant of her being with child. Once they had departed, she had heard say that the men would not be home again until Christmas. She had never been so thankful.

CHAPTER 5

Months had passed now, since that fateful morning in 1846, when Elizabeth had seen her husband leave in the early dawn darkness and feared for his life. Sixth sense told her that he would not be coming home again. Trying to prepare herself, she anticipated the worst news. Yet the pain was no less devastating to hear, when those inevitable words, were spoken to her. Her legs buckled from beneath her, when she heard confirmation of what she most dreaded and she collapsed to the floor. She loved him – had loved him - so very much.

Only grief can enable the sort of reflection, which Elizabeth now endured. She was deeply wounded and destroyed with shock but after some time she had ultimately come to terms with his affair, for she blamed herself for not bearing him a child. She could not help but fall in love with the tiny, helpless child, which had been laid at their doorstep and had come to accept Elise, with all her heart. At least they now had a wonderful and beautiful baby daughter and she believed it was God's way of answering her prayers.

It was now down to her, to continue bringing up this sweet little child, just as Henry would have wanted. He simply adored her and would have wanted her to be protected in life as he had done for her, these past seven years. At that moment of reflection, Elizabeth made a promise to herself, that Elise would never come to understand that, not only did her father agree to fight in a duel and allow their home to be taken from under their feet but that, in the event, she had been told by Henry's butler Noah, that in fact he believed, Henry took his own life.

This, in years gone by, would forever commit his soul to hell. The later was a tortuous thought to her and one she could not fully come to terms with, even now. She was a God fearing woman and as such, continued to pray each night for his soul. In life, Henry had been the kindest of gentlemen and did not deserve such dark finality. She hoped he had found his rightful place in heaven. Thank goodness, at least social attitudes had changed and nowadays the body of the person who had committed suicide, could be interred in consecrated ground, as was Henry. The law too, had at least come to regard all such deaths as a non-punishable offence, even if it were premeditated, so no further circumstance could consequently threaten the remaining family.

Moving to Primrose Lane had been a crushing blow for Elizabeth and she could not wait to leave there. However, until then, she had resolved to make a good fist of settling in, since they knew it was only a temporary inconvenience. She had managed to rumble along financially, by accessing sufficient funds she herself had put aside from her own parents' legacy, which she had hoped one day to pass on to Elise, upon her marriage.

Nevertheless, she waited anxiously for the reading of Henry's last will and testament. She could not believe that he would omit to ensure their security going forward. Elizabeth had been hopeful of securing a home much more suitable to them, than the basic cottage on Primrose Lane, once more substantial money had become available. Henry's solicitor, Mr. Foster, had said in his first communication by letter that there were a few complications to be ironed out, which may take some time and Elizabeth took this as normal and was ever patient. She knew, that Henry would not have omitted to make provision to protect both herself and Elise, should anything happen to him first.

At last, Elizabeth was invited to visit Henry's stalwart solicitor. Elizabeth believed that Henry's affairs had been straightforward. Walking into his office, she accepted the upright green leather chair across the dark mahogany desk from Mr. Foster, glancing around the room whilst he thumbed through some papers and shuffled them into appropriate order. The badly lit wood panelled office was intimidating and cluttered with precariously tilting paperwork. How he found whatever he needed, she could not imagine! She waited in silence while he formally scanned the top few pages, squinting through his gold-rimmed spectacles. Eventually, he began with a decisive clearing of his throat. Elizabeth sat bolt upright in anticipation.

"Mrs. Carter, there are some unusual variations in Henry's will. We need to go through this carefully." Elizabeth could not imagine what this could possibly mean and her first thought was for the mother of Elise. Had Henry placed this woman above her? Her stomach suddenly churned.

Wishing the solicitor would not prevaricate so and just get on with proceedings, Elizabeth felt relieved to finally hear Mr. Foster's serious tones resuming.

"Mrs. Carter , I am afraid that I shall not be able to conclude all our business today."

Elizabeth looked at him with a curious eye. "Why is that, Sir?" she asked politely.

Not ready to explain himself just yet, he began by reading that Henry had indeed left her the most part of his cash funds, to ensure that she and Elise could be reassured of a comfortable life ahead, if it was used wisely. Of course, Elizabeth was at least relieved to hear this. The solicitor continued. There were two other cash bequests. One of which was a small amount of money to be left to Rosanne, the gypsy. This was not entirely a surprise to Elizabeth, as she knew how charitable her husband had always been and she had no concern that he had done this. There was another separate financial provision for Elise, which took the form of a specific amount of money, which had been placed in trust for her. Again, Elizabeth was unsurprised and equally happy to hear this. It made absolute sense to her.

Next, a dramatic pause in the proceedings whilst Mr. Foster shuffled some papers and again harrumphed to clear his throat. Elizabeth could not imagine what else there might be to discuss and nothing here seemed to be in the category of 'unusual variation', which he had prepared her for. It seemed like an age later, Mr. Foster finally spoke again.

"At this point Mrs. Carter, I suggest we leave things there for the moment. I must ask you to be patient. This might take some time. There are two areas of concern, upon which I am seeking further advice, before I speak to you again."

Elizabeth found herself being ushered out of the door in a slight haze of confusion and had no choice but to agree to this unexpected hiatus. Clearly Mr. Foster was not willing to divulge any further details. Yet, exiting the building, Elizabeth's mind was not too anxious, as she was happy with what she believed to be the major concern, which was that Henry had secured them with sufficient funds to keep them comfortable going forward in life. Anything else, she decided, must be trivial.

Returning home, she sat by the fireside with a hot restorative drink and considered the events of her day. Her mind was no clearer about Henry's will but mesmerized by the flickering flames in the grate, she began to relax and her thoughts rambled through life, as one does when alone.

In deep reflection, she recalled coming downstairs that fateful afternoon in November, 1839. She had taken up her seat in the front parlour, which on a clear day overlooked the glorious Cotswold countryside, not expecting how her life was about to change forever. The fire was already burning deep red and warm and she reflected appreciatively on how very fortunate she was to have a home like this and a life in which she was loved and cared for, unconditionally by her husband. Yet still, she bore the guilt of this unshakable depression, which blackened her everyday mood. She had at least managed to come downstairs today, which was a good sign and thought she should try a little reading to distract herself. The day had begun foggy but a chink of sunshine was trying to break through and she hoped this would lift her mood, if just a little.

Her favourite place to sit, was upon the window seat where a smattering of tapestry cushions lay and she was able to lift her dainty feet to rest upon the sill and pick up her current leather bound book. She admired the reappearing near view for moments, then snuggled herself up, to recommence her reading from yesterday's marker.

Only a few moments later, her maid Alice knocked respectfully at the door, then entered with a small tray of warm milk and biscuits; her favourite treat. They exchanged but a few words, then both simultaneously stopped to listen. "What was that?" asked Alice quietly. "Shh!" said Elizabeth as she too turned her head to better hear. "A cat?" she added. Another moment and the noise came again. "Where is it coming from?" Elizabeth whispered, trying to decipher the direction of the sound. "Sounds like it's coming from outside Ma'am" Alice thought out aloud. Elizabeth got up from the window seat and stood still. The sound came louder. "It sounds like a child... a baby!" she said incredulously. With that, both women went to the front door and Alice opened it wide, to reveal a tiny, moving, bundle, wrapped in white linen. Quickly darting forward, Alice bent to pick it up, "Ohh!" she gasped, "Ma'am, it is... it IS a baby!"

she emphasized. Not being able to see anyone else through the fog, Elizabeth called out. But with no reply, she again turned her attention to the wailing bundle. "Quickly, bring it in by the fire!" she instructed her maid, closing the door against the damp air and following closely behind her maid into the parlour.

The baby was now in full voice and her tiny distressed cry could be heard across the hallway into the library, where Henry was sitting at his desk. Curious, he too came out of the room and found the two women with the baby. His first instinct was that since Alice was the one holding the child, she must have brought it for Elizabeth to see. Henry wondered if he had missed something of a staff pregnancy. "Well, well! He exclaimed innocently, so who do we have here then Alice?" Both women looked up simultaneously towards Henry and by the look on their faces, he was struck with confusion. There was an immediate silence in the room.

Elizabeth, took the baby from Alice and cradled her closely in her arms. "We have... we have just found.... She was left on the step, Henry." Looking down at the child, she continued, "She is a little cold!" Thinking quickly, she turned to Alice, "Go and fetch some clean linens and a couple of my warmest shawls, Alice, then go to the kitchens and see what the cook suggests we can give her... warm milk, I'm guessing." Alice bobbed a curtsy and speedily left the room.

"It's a girl?" Henry hesitated to ask.

Elizabeth reflected for a moment on her assumption, "I don't know! I don't know!" she repeated, confused. Carrying the baby gently towards the sofa, she sat down and placed the crying bundle beside her on the velvet surface. She began to gently unwrap the layers of pristine linen, like a precious gift. With absolute wonderment, Elizabeth half whispered to her husband, "She is but new born, Henry. So tiny and fresh. Such a fragile cry!" As she continued to carefully undo the swaddling, a small piece of paper fell from one of the folds of fabric, upon which was written a few words. Elizabeth lifted it up to read, "She is yours. Please love her, as I do."

Elizabeth looked up at Henry, directly into his eyes like she had not done in months. "What is this about Henry?" Her voice trembled with anticipation. He did not reply but stood dumb with shock, returning her stare, not knowing how to answer. Seeing his evident paralysis, she asked again, "Henry. Tell me what this is about! Do you know something about this baby girl? What does this note mean?" The questions tumbled from her mouth and her whole body began to shake, perhaps with nerves or perhaps with anger.

Surely this was some kind of misunderstanding? Silently, Henry walked slowly to the window and looked outwards into the foggy distance. The partly uncovered baby behind him, wailed louder. Elizabeth stood up and also took some steps away, distancing herself from the child. She paced up and down the room trying to make sense of what was happening. "I have to know, Henry. Tell me the truth. Why has a baby been secretly left on our doorstep, with a note saying, 'she is yours'?"

Eventually, Henry turned to face her. Very quietly, in a shocked tone, he spoke. "Elizabeth. Perhaps... yes it is possible... perhaps this child could be mine. Forgive me for I have failed you. It was never that I did not love you but yes, I have been disloyal... Once!", he emphasised, as though that mattered. He repeated, "I was disloyal but once." I do believe it is possible that this baby has my blood – but she is ours, Elizabeth. She is meant to be ours!"

Elizabeth flopped into a chair and screamed crying like Henry had never before heard but then, she had never before been hurt, as she was now. "Who is she? Tell me! Who is this hussy?"

Henry snapped back, "She is not a hu.."

Elizabeth saw the look of protection for her on his face. "You love her don't you?" "Who is she Henry??"

Henry was adamant and she knew it! "I will NOT tell you, Elizabeth, NEVER! There is no point. It's over." The room around her seemed to spin in a haze of confusion. She had never heard Henry raise his voice before. Her ears buzzed and she felt herself swoon. Henry was fast to her side, supporting her flaking body. Her head reeled uncomfortably and when she spoke it was as though it was not her own voice,

"Henry, you are naive! She would forever be in our lives for as long as we keep this child! She will blackmail you, always be here, wanting to see the child...wanting to see you! ...She might change her mind and claim her back, in years to come! Henry, I cannot bear it!"

Henry sighed and paused for her to calm herself a little, gently rubbing her clenched hands. This agitation was no good for either of them. He hated to see her thus. They were not a couple used to arguing: They never had been. He began, "You are wrong, my darling. She will not. She cannot keep the child, for her husband would kill her if he knew. Then he would come to find me - and kill me! Or worse, kill this innocent babe. I shall never tell you who she is. It serves no purpose."

His words sank in, "She is married too?" she said incredulously. She was horrified. Henry tried again to reassure her that they had no need to fear the baby's mother.

"Sweetheart! This woman... she is a kind and good person. She is the perfect person to be the birth mother of our child. This must have broken her heart to give up her child for us. If this child – our child – grows up to be as generous as her birth mother, then we shall have a wonderful, caring, loving daughter."

There was a long lull of excruciating silence and Elizabeth honed in on his word 'loving', though she said nothing. She felt she could not speak the word. It was painful and tense just to be in the room. Elizabeth wept bitterly into her pretty lace handkerchief, with her head in her hands. Henry sat by, quietly coming to terms with the shock of the day's events. His thoughts were also for Peggy and how she must be dealing with all of this. The fact that she had not told him was sad in itself, for she must have bore fear and worry in her silence and then to have given birth to their child, knowing she would not keep it. He wondered if she had been alone all this time, perhaps even during childbirth and he wished he had been there in some way at least to support her. What a stoic woman she was. She did not deserve this. His heart bruised painfully to think of this. He hoped that Albert had not had reason to beat her and found himself praying for her safety. How could he thank her for this most wonderful gift? He had no idea.

He whispered gently, "Elizabeth, please, please..." he begged, "She is meant to be ours, for there is something else I have not told you." Elizabeth looked at him again and tried to focus. Another secret!! How could this be? Did she even know her husband any more? No... this surely, could not be happening! She could take no more and shaking her head she pushed up her hand to quieten her husband, yet he persisted in his truth telling. "The gypsy I told you about, Rosanne, who comes every year to find work... she reads my palm." Elizabeth held her breath in anticipation of the next revelation. "She foretold me of this child. She saw this baby girl in our lives, Elizabeth. Destiny has brought her to us. She is ours to love, my darling."

At that point in Elizabeth's musing, she did not realise how high Henry's own emotions were as he came to terms with the joy of the baby girl's arrival but frustrated too by Elizabeth's understandable reaction as well as pained by his own guilt in admitting to his secret affair. The whole scenario reignited his feeling for Peggy and he felt the need to separate himself for a while from the shock of it all and took himself on a long walk to digest all that had happened that afternoon.

He found himself walking along the driveway towards the peripheral gate and the Mill House. His mind slowly absorbed in reliving his memories of that one blissful but secretive night and weighing up the glorious consequences of now having the little girl he had always dreamed of, against the hurt he had caused to both Elizabeth and Peggy. He stopped in his track momentarily. Could he be sure this baby was indeed Peggy's? Yet he could not see how else she could have arrived on their doorstep with such a note. Of course it was! How could he doubt it?! He thought of Peggy with concern and wondered how she was after giving birth and how on earth she had managed for the past months. He felt deeply for the predicament she had found herself in and admonished himself for all that he had brought upon her. Full of regret, for not being able to support her through what must have been a traumatic time for her, he wandered along the stony driveway, which lead him subconsciously to the Mill House. Reaching its side pathway, he was curious to notice, that the grass had been freshly trodden. Following it around the small building to the rear, he found the door to be slightly ajar. He tugged at it and entered. There was a slight warmth about the space and a meagre burnt out fire in the hearth, still smoking its dead embers. Furniture had been dragged across the dusty floor, leaving trails. His stomach lurched with realisation. Looking about the dark room for confirmation of his instinct, he saw the remnants of a candle and touched it to find that the wax around the dead flame was still malleable. Taking it out of the holder, the base had been lit to better secure it…She had been here! He knew it! His chest tingled as he pieced together the thoughts of what must have happened in recent hours. Peggy had returned to their happy secret hideaway, to give birth to their daughter, in the very place where she was conceived.

Elizabeth's devastation was all consuming. She could not look at the crying baby, let alone hold her. Once again she took to her room and languished in her despair, nursing her hurt. Henry on the other hand, chose to call the baby Elise, a French diminutive of the name Elizabeth, which was his thoughtful way of truly accepting the baby as theirs.

That decided, he informed the staff of her arrival, on the pretext that a poor relative had left the baby for them to care for it. For the next few days, Alice was instructed to take charge of caring for the baby and attending to her needs until Elizabeth was 'well enough' to do so herself.

Henry continued to plead for forgiveness and convince his wife of his genuine contrition. As time went by, she believed his sorrow and came to accept the child and indeed, to love her like their own.

It was impossible now, for Peggy to continue her employment at Stapley Manor. She recognized through her grief that it was imperative for her own psyche, that she distanced herself from both Henry and the little girl, whom she believed they had named Elise. Such a pretty name, she thought with profoundly tender emotion. The only way this heart-breaking plan would work, was for her to extract herself from the setting and pray she never saw either of them again. Perpetuating this hurt, would only serve to ultimately break her mind and soul. So, with heavy heart, she sent word to the housekeeper of the big house, excusing herself from service, due to a change of circumstance. The surprised housekeeper dutifully reported this to Henry and this confirmed his quiet belief, that without a shadow of a doubt, Peggy was the mother of this new born girl. Peggy told anyone else who needed to know, that she was no longer required to work at Stapley Manor.

CHAPTER 6

Needless to say, returning home was not the end of this story for Peggy. As a new mother, Peggy still had much to hide. She was painfully sore and still suffering light bleeding after the birth. Her breasts were uncomfortably producing milk and she grieved for the baby she no longer had. Just as much as the pain in her heart would not go away, her tears refused to stop flowing. She ached to hold her child, just one more time. She still had two other children to love and care for and she needed to conceal her deep unhappiness from them but Mabel was suspicious about Peggy's erratic behaviour and suspected she was ailing. There was no more room in Peggy's emotions to have to now also hide her desperate misery and physical discomfort from Mabel. So, it became easier to explain her loss of appetite and extreme fatigue, by suggesting that she had succumbed to a touch of winter influenza. Such convenient camouflage for her real condition, successfully arrested her sister's probing and appeased the situation, long enough for Peggy to regain her mental and physical strength.

The Broadway wives had anticipated with great excitement their husbands' arrival in time for Christmas. There was rumour that the job at Kilsby was at an end and therefore the men would not be returning there. For most women, that was mostly good news, for their loved ones would be back home permanently, although it did bring another problem of unemployment. Nevertheless, there was a tangible sense of excitement in the village. That is, except for Peggy. For her, the approaching festive season was shuddersome. She barely had enough money as it was, to put food on the table, let alone a feast. That she could afford this much, was due to the generosity of Henry's employment, which enabled her at the time to put aside a few shillings savings to see her through tough times. She had been so grateful for this after she handed in her notice but such savings were now almost expired. The children would have to go without even a small gift this year, since they were barely old enough to expect one but Albert would no doubt expect some kind of fanfare welcome. Each day her nauseous apprehension grew. Still sore after only five weeks since giving birth, she feared for herself when inevitably Albert would force himself brutally upon her. She hoped he would not notice her stretched skin across her stomach, nor the fact that she was still producing a sporadic supply of milk. She was going to have to be very careful to hide all the signs of childbirth. One thing in Peggy's favour however, was that Albert was not a man who admired his wife's body. He paid her little attention, except for his immediate needs. She prayed that after all the secrecy she had managed to hide over the past year, she could get through the next few months to secure that secret for ever.

Albert seemed to be in a permanently drunken state. He was more short tempered than ever, odorously unkempt, lazy and demanding. She bristled to hear him call her to fetch this or that and often took a slapping for no reason, just because she was within distance to do so. She asked dear Mabel to take the children as often as possible to keep them safe and that was agreed with kind understanding. Peggy counted her blessings that nobody suspected her recent history. If she hurt, she grimaced through the pain. She had become an accomplished liar, of which she was not proud but it had become a survival instinct.

Mabel was so sad to see her sister suffer at the hand of her husband. It was easy to see the cuts and bruises of Albert's aggression and she had long since seen through Peggy's excuses of 'walking into a door' or 'tripping over the cat'. Over time, she and Peggy had concocted a code between them for when the twins might be in danger of a battering and Mabel would be quick to respond and play along with Peggy's requests to take them for a walk or feed them tea, just to take them out of the situation. Mabel knew how important it was to keep secret her time employed at Stapley Manor, for she knew how desperately she needed the money whilst Albert was away but equally, he would have physically disapproved of her going out to work. Should he ever have questioned where her money had come from, the sisters had been ready to make out it was a windfall from Mabel's husband, who was also supportive of their plan.

Mabel lived but a few doors away and loved the opportunity to take care of Peggy's twins, as she and her husband Fred had no offspring of their own. She had longed to have children but although she had been lucky enough to take a husband who was kind and gentle, for which she was truly grateful, sadly he had no interest in having sex, at least not with her! Over the years, she had given up trying to lure him into bed and oftentimes she had cried herself to sleep with self-blame, disappointment and frustration. He was not a man who spent time drinking ale although he did have some good friends who gathered at the village hall to play dominoes or cards once a week. He kept good company with one good friend, Jacob, a very quiet, unassuming man, who lived with his mother on the other side of Broadway. Mabel thought this was lovely, that her husband liked to make sure, that this single man was not lonely.

CHAPTER 7

During the years to come, Peggy took pride in her growing children and learnt to deal with the controlling ways of her husband. When Albert did work, it was menial and physical and did not reward much financially. He took on labouring jobs here and there, from picking vegetables at the local farm, to hauling heavy casks in the brewery, to cleaning up at the tannery. None of these positions were for more than a few weeks until at some point, he was sacked for one reason or another. They continued to live in their tiny cottage and the children grew up grateful for what their mother provided. Nancy May, was what her mother referred to as a tomboy, who loved climbing and exploring, often coming home with ripped clothes and a smile of achievement. Giles, on the other hand was a gentle, home loving, shy, safe boy, who preferred to stay by his mother's side. He did however, demonstrate an innately courageous sense of protection for his mother, often daring to stand in front of her, as a flimsy barrier against his father's fist.

It was around the time of the twins' fourth birthday when one evening, Albert had come home from the Bell and Donkey Inn, having had his fill of ale as usual and began recounting a convoluted tale about a possible job of work. "Jacob was in the Donkey tonight and was sayin' like that the master at Stapley Manor is needing someone to look after the pigs." Peggy's heart jumped to her mouth whilst her stomach plummeted.

Thinking fast, she needed to keep him away from there. "But you don't know anything about pig breeding, Albert! Surely this Mr. Whatever-his-name-is, will be needing someone with experience?" She held her breath for he did not take kindly to contradiction.

"How hard can it be?!" he replied, swaying from the imbibed alcohol.

"Well, I don't know Albert but it's just that you don't really get on with animals do you?"

He laughed, "Well I live with three of them!" He poked a finger at the children then spat his words, "These two here, they eat like pigs anyhow!"

Peggy was deeply hurt, "Please Albert, that's so unkind. They do not! Please don't speak like that in front of them."

Knowing he was being annoying, he carried on, "Well anyhow, seems this here Mr. Carter is looking to expand the farming side of things there, so I'm going go see him tomorrow and see what he's got for me."

Peggy persisted to try to put him off this idea, "Well how would Jacob know about this anyway?"

Irritated, he raised his voice a notch, "Because he works there, stupid! He's the gamekeeper, lucky sod! That's the job I want!" Peggy could have laughed, had she not been so concerned. Seeing Albert, with his reputation of a bad temper, as gamekeeper in charge of a gun, was laughable!

Peggy hoped that by morning, Albert would have forgotten all about his idea but unfortunately, he had not. She felt physically sick as she watched him leave in the early morning. By the time he came home at night, he had called in as usual at the Bell and Donkey, this time to celebrate. Under normal circumstances, she would have been relieved to hear he had secured a job, no matter how menial but this was not good news to her ears.

As the weeks went by, it transpired that Albert's first claim that he had been hired, as a swineherd, was one of his usual exaggerations, when actually he was required to swill them out and keep the pens clean. It was a filthy, smelly task, which held no kudos. That, in itself, did not sit well with Albert, who was always inclined to crow above his station, so she was intrigued that he had accepted the job, especially since it involved quite a walk there and back. Unbeknown to her of course, his intention held a sinister motivation.

Time went by and Albert managed to bring home enough money for Peggy to offer frugal food for their bellies and keep the wolf from the door. He never said much about Stapley Manor or Mr. Carter or his job for that matter and Peggy did not want to ask for fear of showing too much interest. She was fairly sure however, that had he had any suspicions about her and Henry, she would have heard about it. So, putting it to the back of her mind, they carried on life as usual.

It was some months later that Albert came home earlier than usual and sober at that! Peggy was picking onions from the garden plot for supper and saw him, limping as he came up the lane. He was in no mood for questions but instructed Peggy to get a bowl of warm water and clean up his wound. It seems that one of the boars had bitten him on the backside, something that could be very painful and could quickly become infected, if left unattended. He had already walked the distance home, so she needed to act quickly.

The wound was ragged from where the beast had refused to leave go and it did indeed already look red and inflamed. There was part of Peggy that saw the funny side of it all and she wanted to laugh but she managed to swallow the giggles and keep a straight and sympathetic face when in front of him. Behind his back however, she could not help herself and cruelly found amusement in his comeuppance. She was shocked that

Henry or Jacob had not made arrangements to tend to his injury at Stapley Manor or even to bring him in a vehicle home but after some time, it came out in conversation that his pride would not allow him to tell them about his encounter with the beast and he made up the excuse of stomach gripes to go home to bed, rather than confess the truth. Little did he know, that Jacob had seen it happen and with such little respect for Albert that, he accepted his excuses and laughed at the arrogant fellow behind his back, as he struggled home, bleeding.

Ridiculously, upon returning to work the next day, Albert was fixated on taking his revenge on the beast. He wanted to give it a good kicking... but that wasn't enough. He wanted to kill the dratted thing. He needed to think on it but for today, it would get no food!!

It had been a hard day, especially with a sore backside, so deciding he deserved a jug of ale, Albert first stopped off at the Crown and Trumpet to quench his thirst but it was quiet in there, so he headed on to the Bell and Donkey. As he entered through its oak door, he wasn't too sure why people were turning their backs and sniggering but assumed he had missed a joke. He did ask but nobody was forthcoming, so he ordered another jug of ale and stood with it at the bar. Not long afterwards, Jacob came in and the pub erupted with laughter. He saw Albert and could barely keep his face straight. When Albert's back was turned, Jacob limped, holding his backside. The place erupted, again. He turned to Albert and offered him a seat, which Albert declined and someone shouted out, "Go on Albert. Have a seat! Anyone would think something had bitten your arse!"

Immediately, Albert put two and two together and without any warning he turned around and swung a fist at Jacob. Jacob ducked and missed Albert's knuckles but Albert had already begun his second strike with his left tightly clenched hand. Fuelled by increased anger at missing his target the first time, he gave Jacob a mighty upper cut, knocking him backwards and flattening him to the floor. He then picked up his jug of ale and poured it over Jacob and leaving him prostrate on the floor, with a hushed group of disbelieving spectators behind him, he strode out of the alehouse.

Furious, to be the laughing stock, he raged inside. He was going to get him back, that bloody Jacob! It was time to put into action his reason for taking that job at all.

Walking through the fields to work one morning soon after, he had a brilliant idea. Considering it further, it just got better! He could, as people say, 'kill two birds with the one stone'! He had been waiting long enough to get Jacob out of the way and slide ingratiatingly into his job. This could be his opportunity to finally get what he wanted!

He planned carefully ahead and bided his time for just the right opportunity and made sure that he had everything he needed, tucked away in the shed. The day came when he was to put his plan into action. He had noticed Mr. Carter walking his dog in the far paddocks. That was good because importantly, he could be certain that the dog was not with Jacob, as was often the case. Next, making sure that Jacob was nearby and within earshot, he fed the pigs as usual, but added into the swill some deadly Nightshade for the big boar. It didn't take much time for it to take effect and the pig dropped to the ground convulsing.

He quickly shouted for help, knowing Jacob would come running with his rifle, which was as always, in his hand. Exactly as he had hoped, Jacob, being an animal lover, ran to the pen and seeing the poor animal in such distress, dropped his gun to the floor and fell to his knees alongside the sick animal, with his back towards Albert, to see how he could help the sick animal. Albert promptly picked up the gun and shot Jacob, dead. He then shot the pig too. Rushing to the shed, he grabbed the rags he had left to hand for the purpose and dipped them in the pig's blood. He opened his shirt and spread blood about both Jacob and himself, doing his best to mimic having been mauled, then poked the evidence deep into the pyramid of pig manure, piled up by the sheds.

Starting now to shout as loud as he could and feigning frantic panic, Albert ran into the house yelling urgently for attention. Some of the staff had been alerted by the sound of the gun shots and not thinking too much about the sound at first, assuming Jacob had needed to use his gun on a fox at the hens perhaps, they were now horrified at the scene which Albert presented.

Deliberately stumbling in through the door, he gasped, "There's been a terrible accident!!" As though he was in utter shock, he breathlessly played out a convincing scene and confessed that Jacob had met a misfortunate end. He gave a false rendition of the boar going quite mad and attacking him. He had called for Jacob's help, whereupon the animal turned on him too. Albert claimed to have taken the gun to shoot the berserk boar and save Jacob but that Jacob had got in the way and taken the bullet instead. With a second bullet he killed the boar as it turned on him. He pretended his shock and distress very well.

Henry had heard the shots too and came running in from the fields, first finding his gamekeeper slumped beside the pig and blood everywhere. "Dear Lord!" he exclaimed out aloud. Bending over Jacob's body he rolled him over to see that a bullet had entered straight through his neck and he flopped uncontrollably forward, dead. Horrified, he ran beyond the abominable scene into the house where he was met with Albert faking his story with such drama.

"What the hell has happened here?" he interrupted sternly. Albert pretended now to be too traumatised to repeat the story again, leaving the staff to regurgitate his encounter, as he looked at the floor in theatrical distress. Henry had never known anything quite like it and was exceedingly dubious. Quickly assessing everything he had just seen and heard in the past few moments, something didn't feel right but without proof or witnesses, he had no choice but to believe the man, for the moment at least. Seeing Henry's doubtful reaction, Albert panicked and as though for further evidence, he then thought it appropriate to spin his tale further and showed the bite he had received yesterday from the same animal, suggesting it had been crazy for some time but boasting how he had dealt with it heroically.

Henry thought it was all a bit fishy. There was just something he couldn't put his finger on about Albert. More than once, it had passed through his mind, could it be possible that Albert was in fact Peggy's husband? As a casual worker, he had no reason to take formal details but perhaps this would be good reason to do so. Being very uncomfortable about the whole scenario, he decided to call in the men in blue. They returned to the scene of the incident but Henry was disappointed to witness the arrival of the police to be something of a farce and having heard Albert's story, in their buffoonery, took his statement as true and accurate. Hearing him give his full name and address, confirmed Henry's suspicions. So this was the man responsible for Peggy's heartache and bruises! His heart sank to think that she was married to him. It made him feel like punching him there and then. Such a thought had never before passed through his mind, about anyone. He was shocked at himself.

Reflecting on the scene, which first met him at the piggery, Henry was concerned about the unlikely position that he found Jacob's body lying against the pig. If Albert's account was accurate and if the beast was mauling him, why did the blood only appear on the parts of his body uppermost and not all over, without any scratches or teeth marks apparent? There was no evidence of ripped clothing either. The two police officers were young men and Henry talked them through his suspicions but doubted that they had ever seen a dead body, let alone had any idea of how to conduct such a gruesome enquiry as this. Henry took them to one side and suggested that they take Albert back to the police station in Evesham to perhaps be interviewed by a more experienced superior officer. He believed that with further probing, structured investigations and under more experienced cross-questioning, Albert would be brought to justice for whatever was his part in this hateful incident. Jacob deserved that at least. Albert was thus hauled away, remonstrating and irritated by Henry's interference.

After an overnight stay in a cell and only a further cursory interview, Albert was released to go home. Peggy had been beside herself, wondering where he had been and considering how he might have found himself a brothel to visit. He arrived home late morning to recount his fabricated tale and there was a definite insolence, even anger about his attitude towards Henry, which worried Peggy more than a little. Ultimately, the police had deemed the whole affair an accident and so poor Jacob was duly returned to his grieving mother for burial. Albert secretly laughed at how easy his innocence was confirmed. Furthermore, as planned, Albert intended to use the immediate opportunity to offer his services to become the new gamekeeper at Stapley Manor and now there was also the irritation of getting even with Henry. He knew he would find a way! He just needed to persuade the master, to give him the job!

Henry brooded over his discovery that Albert was indeed married to sweet Peggy. How on earth she coped with such a man, he would never know. He could easily see, how she could be bullied by him and even worse, be the butt of his aggression. The sickening realisation gave him a dilemma to consider. His instinct was to get rid of the man, for he felt sure he was totally responsible for the death of his honest gamekeeper Jacob.

However, sacking him, would undoubtedly cause him to return home and take it out on his wife and the family would suffer financially once more, which was an intolerable thought to Henry. So, when Albert turned up for work the next day, Henry sent for him to come to his study.

Albert strutted in as confident as a crowing cockerel. His very demeanour infuriated Henry.

"Sit down" he commanded with a stern face. Albert went to speak but Henry immediately cut him short. "I don't want to hear it! I have brought you hear to listen to me! I have no interest in what you have to say." He paused for his message to sink home into Albert's arrogant skull and compound Henry's absolute authority here. "Let me make this absolutely clear. I do not believe your cock and bull story about yesterday's odious goings on. You might fool those imbeciles who call themselves police but I am no idiot." Again, Albert went to speak. "Do not treat me as one!!" Henry shouted, slamming his fist on the desktop. "I have never known a boar behave in the way you have described. I do not know what was going through your head or what you aim to gain from this absurdity but it will not wash with me!! I believe you have not only killed an innocent and valued animal but you have taken the life of a decent, hard-working man. Worst of all, you have lied and show no remorse whatsoever for this heinous act. This is totally reprehensible behaviour and if I had my way, you would be thrown in a cell and left to rot." Henry could hardly bring himself to speak his next words but he did so to try to protect Peggy. He spoke slowly now with an immense air of gravity, "I have given this a great deal of thought. You deserve to be sacked from this employment on the spot. However, I understand from the staff that you have twin children and so, I do this for them. You may remain here at Stapley Manor and continue your work with the pigs. You can start by clearing up the mess from yesterday. I shall be watching you like a hawk and if you step a foot out of place, you will be gone. Do you understand me?" There was silence for a brief moment whilst Albert considered suggesting that he instead be given the gamekeeper's job but decided better of the idea. As he prevaricated, Henry's impatience gave way, "Answer me!!"

It took all of Albert's control not to step forward and take a punch at his boss. Thinking better of it, he mumbled his agreement and left the room. Henry raged inside and stood from his chair to pace the room. He had never felt anger like it. He felt so sure that this obnoxious man was responsible for Jacob's death but he could never prove it nor did he believe he would ever get to the truth. He feared for dear Peggy and what her day-to-day life must have become. Not for the first time, he thanked God that Albert had never discovered their affair. He reflected on those heady lustful days of time spent with the gentle, caring, sweet girl that she was and found it hard to regret their time together. Yet, it was true that their union had caused such hurt to Elizabeth and of course, he regretted that bitterly but he could never regret the outcome of the love that he and Peggy had felt for each other. Elise was the pride of his life and he must do all he could to protect her as well as Peggy and Elizabeth. It was better to keep a close eye on Albert here, under his constant supervision, than to release him into the unknown and spend his time looking over his shoulder to protect his family and wondering what vile behaviour he could be up to, endangering the welfare of Peggy and the twins. This was the least he could do to protect them all.

What Henry was struggling with was, why. Why would Albert want to kill Jacob? Was it a spur of the moment spike in his temper, of which he knew very well he possessed? Or was it predetermined with vengeance? If so, for what reason? Again, this he may never now discover. What was clear, was that he had created a plausible scenario, in which to kill Jacob. He needed someone reliable to again fulfil the role of gamekeeper, to watch over him. He would have to settle to find such a person. The thought of 'replacing' Jacob did not sit well with him. He would be sadly missed, not only as a competent employee but as a dependable and devoted member of the team at Stapley Manor. He would also pay a visit to Jacob's grieving mother. That would be a very difficult duty.

Albert too had a storm of anger raging within himself, a feeling common to him. He strode from the building after Henry's plain speaking and headed towards the piggery. If it were not for wanting to finally achieve his plan, of securing the coveted job of gamekeeper, he would have happily used his fist against Henry's jaw, to release the peak of anger, which fizzed within his own chest. He had to use all his determination to rein himself in, but gave way instead to thumping or kicking every tree he passed, on his way to the piggery, until his knuckles grazed with blood and his foot pained him. He had no doubt in his mind that he would find an opportunity to get his own back on Henry. He promised himself he would. No matter how long it took. Who the hell gave him the right to speak to him like that? How dare he silence him in that manner? Bloody nerve of him! Once he was gamekeeper he would get better opportunity to really reap revenge. He would have plenty of time to think of something! He smirked.

Finding the dried bloodied mess, which he had created the day before, horror suddenly struck him. Albert stared, as though expecting to find the dead body of Jacob still there. Of course, it had gone. The missing corpse instilled a kind of disbelief within him and he seemed thereafter to remove himself from the responsibility of the carnage he faced. It was as though he was able to disconnect from the murder he had committed, almost a case of 'no body, no crime'. He slowly set about doing what was necessary to clear the area and resurrect a previous 'normality'. He then went inside as usual for lunch, as though he had finished a regular morning's work.

Three days later, Henry was dressed head to toe in black and in sombre mood to attend Jacob Prowse's burial, accompanied by a number of deeply shocked and sorrowful residential staff who wished to pay their last respects to their colleague and friend. Elizabeth had intended to also attend but had woken in the morning with an intolerable headache rendering her nauseous. Henry had left her in the care of Alice who was well used to dealing with these occasional distasteful bouts from which her mistress suffered. She would prepare a feverfew tea for her mistress and take care of Elise whilst Elizabeth recovered.

Old St. Eadburgha's Church was not full, reflecting Jacob's meagre social life and small family but just before the ceremony began, the congregation was generously increased with the arrival of those from Stapley Manor. Henry had not previously met Jacob's mother but the grief stricken elderly woman sitting on the front pew, barely able to breathe between sobs into her lace handkerchief, was surely her. A young gentleman sitting next to her held her close, with his arm comforting her about her shoulders. He too was crying unashamedly; unusually so for a man. Henry assumed this to be perhaps Jacob's brother, although he could not at that moment recall him speaking of anyone, other than his mother.

The service was heart breaking. A life taken too soon 'by accident'! Henry found himself shaking his head in quiet disbelief. His peripheral sight caught a movement to his left, slightly towards the back of the church. It was Albert. He had obviously come to the service straight from home. Henry felt angered at his temerity, yet he would probably have felt the same had he not attended! The man simply annoyed him! He wondered what was going through his head but whatever his thoughts, he hoped he was steeped in guilt, though, this he doubted very much! By the time the coffin was carried away from the alter, towards the church door and the graveyard, Albert had disappeared.

When all was done, the congregation, by invitation of Jacob's mother, was heading towards the neighbouring coaching inn, the Crown and Trumpet, for refreshments. Along the short walk, Henry, caught up with Mrs. Prowse, making it his business to speak privately with her. He introduced himself graciously, before offering his deepest condolences. Mrs. Prowse was clearly honoured to have Jacob's employer, the master of Stapley Manor, attend the ceremony and was visibly flustered at his humble approach. There was no suggestion of her holding him accountable for this dreadful 'accident' and she took in every syllable of his sincere and kind words, memorizing everything he said, so that she could relive them time and again later, to bring her some comfort.

The gentleman who had been with her in the church, caught up with them as they entered the inn and ensured that a seat was found immediately for his dear friend's mother. It was the least he could do to make sure that she was cared for now that Jacob could no longer do this for himself. He had come to know Mrs. Prowse really well over time and he had even come to look upon her as a mother figure in his own life. He had been visiting her house to visit Jacob every week for years. She had always been so very kind to him and so welcoming. Anything he could do for her now, in Jacob's memory, he believed would be a privilege. It would be comforting for him to continue to go visit her, almost as though Jacob was still there. He couldn't believe that he would never see Jacob again. The sudden thought swept over him like a deep wave sucking him under a strong current and he felt overwhelmingly distraught. Sinking into the seat adjacent to Mrs. Prowse, he put his head in his hands and continued to sob uncontrollably. Mrs. Prowse held his hand tightly and crooned soft words of understanding, audible only between the two of them. Eventually he calmed down. Henry brought to the table three glasses of brandy. Mrs. Prowse ensured that her companion took a sip of his, before she did the same. Remembering her manners, she introduced her son's dear friend Frederick, to Henry.

The three chatted for some time before Henry felt obliged to move away so that others could speak with her, passing on their sympathies just as he had done but not before something interesting came about in conversation. Mrs. Prowse made a point of telling Henry, that Frederick lived with his wife Mabel in the village, in Primrose Lane. Of course, her unconvincing comment was not lost on Henry but he was not one to cast aspersions on others for the way they choose to live their lives. However, he was more intrigued about a connection he was slowly putting together. His immediate recollection of carrying Peggy to her front door and meeting her sister Mabel, gave him an uncomfortable feeling, for fear of Albert discovering a link.

Time passed by and over the months Henry relaxed about Albert not making more of an association between Jacob and his brother-in-law, Fred. More importantly, Albert clearly had heard nothing from Mabel about Henry's visits to see Peggy, whilst he was at Kilsby. Henry noted that Albert seemed to keep his head down at work and did all the right things to give him no opportunity to sack him.

In the meantime, Henry was still prevaricating about finding another gamekeeper, for he could not bring himself to 'replace' Jacob, as it somehow still felt wrong but he would have to address this matter sooner rather than later.

Biding his time and sensing things had calmed down, Albert prepared to take his chance to speak to Henry about the position of gamekeeper, which he knew, had still not been filled. First though, he needed to be deemed indispensible. He created a fool-proof plan, or so he thought, to make Henry beholden to him.

Whilst having his usual morning break one day, in the back of the kitchen pantry where he had been designated a wooden chair and table to partake of a hot drink and a cake of some description left by the cook, he spied a platter with some sliced beef. He helped himself to two or three juicy pieces and secreted them in a rag he had in his pocket, thinking that they might come in very handy if he were to execute his plan later that day. At the end of work, he knew that Beauty would be taking a nap as always in the barns at the back of the house. With strategic planning, he used the promise of the beef to lure his master's loyal dog away from the estate buildings and led her away and up the hillside, far from the estate. Reaching the shepherd's hut, as he had planned, he tied up the dog with the rope he had brought for the purpose. The dog barked as he left and Albert smirked with achievement, as he walked home.

Next day, when Albert reached Stapley Manor, there was a certain distress about the place. The staff explained to Albert, that their master's dog had gone missing. Albert was summoned to Henry's office and he responded with guilty dread but pleasantly surprised when his master simply instructed him to go and find the dog for as many days as it took to find her. The opportunity fell right into Albert's lap and he used the time to enjoy his freedom away from work and take a titbit of food for the imprisoned dog. He had at least the decency to leave her a bowl with water which he had taken in a bottle and which he thereafter relied upon the rain to refill. The dog's bark upon seeing him gradually reduced to a whimper and cry, as she grew weaker. Each day end, Albert would sorrowfully report his lack of success in finding Beauty and Henry could not understand how this could happen. She was a loyal dog and would never have strayed. He was therefore convinced that the dog had been taken. Concluding then that it looked necessary to employ a gamekeeper if they were at risk of intruders, he suggested that, for the moment, Albert should take the position of gamekeeper. This would inevitably come with the use of a protective rifle.

Albert had succeeded! Yet he was not yet ready to bring the dog back home, for that would look too contrived. He waited some months before he brought back Beauty, who was by this time extremely thin and nervous as well as clearly pregnant presumably from a stray dog. He led her to Stapley Manor but did not announce her arrival. No, he was too clever for that! He already had the job he sought so would feign innocence and allow her to be found by someone else. He left her lying in the barn and walked away.

At this time, two year old Elise, was dearly loved by both Henry and Elizabeth. Those early weeks of readjustment for Elizabeth now seemed a distant memory. She could not ignore the natural instinct within her to protect and provide for this tiny babe who had been placed in her care and was totally dependent upon her for her safety and wellbeing. It was easy to acknowledge that the little child quickly came to respond to Elizabeth's presence and would turn her head towards her voice, hold her arms up to her familiar shape to be picked up and even bless Elizabeth with her first smiles. How could she not adore this baby? She was truly heaven sent to them. The hurt Henry had inflicted upon her, eventually subsided and she found it in her to accept his contrition for hurting her so badly. Between them, they had agreed, that Elise would never know that Elizabeth was not her true birth mother and their secret would go to the grave with them both. Jointly, they saw Elise grow and together they celebrated as she achieved all her childhood milestones, her first words, her first steps, her first tooth.

She had such a strong resemblance to her father and people would say she was the apple of his eye. It was true to say that once Elise had learnt to walk, she would follow her father just about everywhere. Wherever he was to be found, so was she. Elizabeth had to remind him not to spoil her so but he just could not help himself. He did it knowingly and with so much love. He lavished encouragement upon her and bragged at her every small achievement, as though no other child had ever succeeded in sitting up unaided or managed to take their first spoon of food independently.

It was easy for Henry to see his own likeness in Elise and laughed at her determined stubbornness, just like him! He found himself looking for nuances of Peggy in her. Occasionally he caught a glimpse of likeness in her young face, something about her eyes perhaps? Yet, there was often something fleeting about her mannerisms, which reminded him so much of Peggy. These were sometimes so brief, that they were gone before he could catch them and as these intangible moments flickered past, he felt an equally ephemeral, warm emotion, which he cherished but never spoke of to anyone.

One early morning glorious day in June, the familiar soporific clop of horses' hooves broke the silence, as the ornate red and green vardo pulled by two heavy horses along the dry bumpy cart track, headed slowly towards the sunrise. Once a year, during the summer months, the Romani fair came theatrically to town. The slow trail of caravans would make their way to the same grassy arena just outside of the town of Evesham where they would, with certain precision, set up camp for two weeks. It was always a spectacle of intrigue but not always a welcome one. Whilst there were those, especially the children, who welcomed the thrill of commotion brought in by the band of gypsies, there were those in equal numbers, who were openly disapproving.

As a first job on arrival at Evesham, as with any time they set up camp, the gypsy men would set to task on erecting the impoverished stands for the fair, in the adjacent meadow. The entertainments were basic but the activity fuelled excitement in the town and surrounding villages, providing an impoverished income for the troupe. True to say, however, that for village folk, a sense of dread accompanied the arrival of the Romanies. Stories of child abduction, criminal activity and mistrust, were rife. Local crime was often attributed to the gypsy presence and often committed by locals with deliberate intent for the gypsies to take the blame. An atmosphere of suspicious tension followed them across the country and was accepted by all parties, as part of their existence.

Their camp, was set up on the banks of the River Avon with unspoken routine precision, such was the regularity that they did this. A perfectly formed circle was quickly established and in no time, it seemed, a roaring fire became the centrepiece. The sturdy cart-pulling horses were led a short distance away and tied up to graze. If they were lucky, they might receive a cursory grooming but if not they would be ridden into the shallow end of the river where at least they would be treated to a bath of sorts. The women too would access the side of the riverbank to scrub through a few clothes, beating the saturated fabrics against the pebbles to better cleanse out the dusty filth. The very young children treated the area around the fire as a playground and ran off energy charging about, making their own meagre entertainment. The adults took on a shared responsibility for the children and within their own codes of acceptable behaviour, shared in their upbringing.

Rosanne and Django Mullick had settled themselves in and planned their usual round trip to various places looking for daytime work. Each visit they would call in at the same places, where they secured work last time. Django had a way with mending pots and pans, sharpening knives and was willing to have a go at repairs of any sort. He would never turn down work, even if it were outside of his capability. That in itself, got him into trouble, more than a few times. Rosanne had an altogether different way of working. Her beguiling manner and persuasive chat was alluring to most, male or female. Yet she most of all, had success with winning over the men. Not surprisingly, for she could use her swaying hips seductively, use her buxom figure unabashedly and without doubt, she had the darkest eyes of a temptress. Django knew, she would never – ever – be disloyal to him and he would watch her, with certain pride, in the way she could cajole from them, exactly what she wanted, especially from the men, without ever compromising her allegiance to her husband.

During the quieter moments along their travels, Rosanne and Django would make crafts of all sorts, ready to sell. Django took on the making of laundry pegs and spoons from scraps of wood. Rosanne, was adept at lacework but if by chance in the late summer, she could 'obtain' bunches of lavender, she would transform the fragrant seed heads into pockets of fabric to tempt her customers to ward off evil spirits or as good luck charms, depending on what she sensed her customer would most wish to hear. This was not all, however. Rosanne only used her wares as a way of entering into dialogue with folk. Once she had their immediate attention, she could then lure them into what she was best at: Fortune telling. This was far more lucrative and true to say that for this, she had a genuine talent. It was a gift she had inherited from her paternal grandmother. She grew up with this wily old woman who tutored her in the skill of reading palms to foresee the future. Rosanne needed little tuition, for she seemed to have a natural gift and a persuasive, almost hypnotic charm, which enchanted her believers. This, for her, was an easy skill, which needed no materials and could be accessed at any moment to furnish her with coins. Of her many tasks and talents, this was her favourite, for she loved to get to know people, to understand how they tick and if she could, to help them. Never, however, would she foretell of death. She saw that as a divine right and not hers to impart but sometimes on those occasions, she would feel sad to know that such grief would visit a person, soon.

For four or so years after she had met Henry at the Mill House and read his palm predicting the arrival of a baby girl, they only saw the master of the house, once again, despite calling each summer to seek for work at Stapley Manor. On that occasion, Rosanne warned Henry that his dog, may one day leave him. Henry could not imagine this happening since he was the most loyal of all canines!

However, this, the following summer season, when Rosanne and Django rode up to the manor house once more, they chanced to see a tall man walking through the orchard, hand in hand with a small child. Rosanne recognised the man instantly and so they slowed up the vardo and Rosanne called out to him. Instantly grinning his welcome, Henry and the little girl approached the colourful caravan. The little girl was fascinated with the horses.

"So, I was right then?!" Rosanne called out, self-satisfied.

"Indeed you were!" His proud smile spoke volumes. He hesitated a little and added, "In fact, I might even allow you to read my palm again!" Henry happily began to regale her with the story of a long awaited child and the utter despair of his wife, when he suddenly stopped short of the actual unconventional arrival of Elise upon the doorstep. He would rather she believed that the baby was naturally theirs by birth. Few people knew the truth and even then not the entire truth, for nobody except Henry and Peggy and later Elizabeth, knew of the baby's birth mother.

Rosanne smiled at the little girl and then looked up to Henry with a whimsical smile and added, "Her birth mother did the right thing!" Her comment took Henry's breath away. "You know?" he asked incredulously. "I am a gypsy. Of course I know, Sir."

"So, what else do you know 'Madam Gypsy'?" he asked, laughingly thrusting his palm forward for her to read. "Well Sir, I will read your palm ... but might I first remind you of a promise you made to me, should my last prediction come true?"

"Ah, yes... my promise!" Henry recalled, jovially. "I have for some time reflected on that," he smiled. "Well?" asked the gypsy. Henry bent down to pick up his darling daughter, kissing her cheek as he did so. "This is Elise. My beautiful daughter! She is now two years old."

"Do you have children, he randomly asked?"

"Yes Sir, we are blessed with a fine son, Manfri. He is the apple of my eye, so he is!" She smiled proudly and added, "His name means Man of Peace and you cannot deny he is his father's son!!" She gestured to a small child outside of Henry's vision in the back of the vardo, curled up under a blanket sleeping peacefully. His thick black hair as sharp contrast upon the white pillow.

Henry nodded and smiled. "And do you think he would like to settle down one day, with a family of his own?"

Pulling her long black curls around one shoulder, she laughed, explaining, "Sir, he is but five years old... but I can tell you, he is in my eyes a black blooded gypsy like my husband here. He has the gypsy culture through every bone in his body. So perhaps one day he will honour us with grandchildren, yes! I hope he has many!" She looked at Henry thoughtfully, as though searching for the words to explain, "But settle down? I doubt that! He will have the same wanderlust as his father Sir." she laughed. "We are travellers Sir, we follow the sun, we work, we move on."

Henry was curious that Rosanne should only refer to her husband rather than them both as having wanderlust and he suspected there was reason behind her comment.

"...And you Rosanne, you are not black blooded too?" She smiled at his intuitive interpretation of her words.

"No Sir, I am not. My mother was a town girl and ran away from home as a young lass. She lived on the streets for a long time, scavenging for scraps of food. Fortunately for her, my father came along and rescued her from near death. She believed it to be destiny and told me many times how she loved him instantly. So, I am born into the gypsy way of life but ... sometimes, I crave my deeper roots..."

Henry, nodded his understanding, and returned his thoughts to her question. "Your prediction... it gave me hope. It made me think of things differently and so when Elise arrived, it was not in the way we had imagined. Yet knowing you had foreseen her in my life, I knew she was truly meant to be my daughter. Elise has brought us such joy and without doubt, she brought my wife back from the brink of darkness."

"My reward to you is to offer you to visit my land as often as you wish. I will pay you well for any jobs you may undertake here and I would welcome you to read my palm whenever you pass by." He smiled benignly. "But in addition, I have decided to leave you something in my Will."

"I thank you Sir... but I do hope that I shall have to wait a very long time for that!" She laughed.

"Well, surely you shall know it before I!" he said cleverly. "In fact, you might recall... your prediction about my dog? You said..."

"Yes Sir, I remember this of course!" she interrupted.

Their thoughts both simultaneously revisited that time when Rosanne and her husband visited Stapley Manor as they did each year, for which services Henry paid generously. It was on one of those such visits, that whilst reading Henry's palm, Rosanne had foreseen the loss of his loyal dog. Henry's heart plummeted to hear her tell this but it was too painful to harbour and he tried to discharge it from his mind, as though if he didn't think it, it would not happen. Incredulous then, that during that past year, Beauty did, shockingly, disappear.

Henry described his loss to Rosanne and Django and how he was naturally bereft and on a daily basis he had instructed his hired help, Albert, to search for her. He related how hours passed into days. Days passed into weeks and how he eventually had to resign himself to the thought that his treasured dog was forever lost. The gypsies were saddened to hear Henry's story and listened intently to his words with deep empathy.

Continuing with the tale, Henry spoke of how almost four months had passed, when one day his driver came in, shouting for his master to come quickly... They had raced out to a disused barn where Henry found an emaciated Beauty, lying amongst disused machinery whimpering. Beneath her matted coat, suckled three squeaking new-born puppies. Henry described the joyous reunion. And how Beauty's tail thumped against the floor as she lay, wagging as frantically as he had ever seen, when she recognized him.

Henry still wondered how come she had left home in the first place and wondered how long she had been there! It was anyone's guess but Henry was resigned to never being able to know these answers, yet the fact that she came home, was all he cared about.

Thrilled to have her back, Henry believed she had made her way home from wherever she had been, in order to give birth in safety. However, it troubled Henry deeply, to find that the poor dog had clearly suffered some cruelty with the bloodied scars across her body and what looked like rope marks around her neck where she had presumably been tied up. She had clearly

82

suffered cruelty in the time she had disappeared but he tried not to think on such abuse since he could not fix it in retrospect and so concentrated on caring for her wounds as tenderly as she deserved and he would be sure to have Beauty resume her rightful place in front of the fire, with her puppies, as she was used to. It was true that she had undoubtedly changed from a trusting, relaxed creature, to a timid, nervous one, was testament to her abuse while she was away from Henry's watchful eye. She now did not like to be closed behind a door, nor did she like unexpected noises. She continued to raise her young and was especially protective towards Elise, who adored her. There were curious moments too, when Henry noted that Beauty was especially on guard or at least uncomfortable when Albert was around. In all the years Henry had owned Beauty, since a puppy, he had never heard her growl. Yet, since her return, the sight of Albert made her hackles spike up and she would make a low throaty warning, which at one point resulted in a moment of teeth bearing. Henry was astonished and noted a look of awkward embarrassment on Albert's face, as though the dog was going to tell what he had done. Henry reassured his dog and gave Albert a knowing look, strongly suggesting he came nowhere near the dog again.

CHAPTER 8

Whilst Elizabeth had absolved Henry of his guilty adulterous act some eight years ago and forgiven his contrition, she could not forgive that he had accepted the outrageous challenge to face the repulsive Albert in a duel for that same misdemeanour. Suddenly, somehow, this obnoxious man had discovered Henry's affair, the truth of which had lain dormant for a decade but she thanked God that he did not seem to have knowledge of Elise! Albert was far from a gentleman. In fact he was nothing but a gamekeeper, employee. How degrading it was, that Henry, her fine and upstanding husband and true gentleman, should be called out by this employee. She could not see this challenge as brave. No, to her, it was the most egocentric thing Henry had ever done. She would never be able to forgive this act, which risked not only his life but the house and grounds too and with that, the security for her and their daughter. It seemed so uncharacteristically selfish of her husband and she didn't understand why.

It was only once Henry had gone, that she realised the full impact of leaving Stapley Manor with an almost nine year old Elise and facing the degradation of accepting the paltry home of the pompous man who enticed her husband to his end, in exchange for their stately abode of decades. Elizabeth and Elise were now caused to live in a pauper's cottage, which the imperious Albert and subservient Peggy Turner had vacated.

The day of the house swap was upon them. Elizabeth woke to a surreal world. She must surely be dreaming?? How could it be that Henry was dead? How could she possibly be moving from her home of twenty years? She doubted she had had an hour's sleep. It seemed only moments ago that she finally dozed off. She had cried and cried all night and still not made any sense of the past few days. Henry had taken his butler and closest friend Noah, to be his duelling second. It was he who checked Henry's pistol, paced out the distance and called the men to fire. It was also Noah who came back to Stapley Manor, with heavy heart, to bring Elizabeth the news. She had gone over and over in her head how he had told her that Henry did not fire at Albert but took the gun to his own head. They were all astounded. It had made no sense to them at all. The same question resounded in her head. Why? ... Why??

The household members of staff were all in shock too. They would never work in the employ of anyone as kind as Mr. Carter. They did their best to support Elizabeth in the packing up of the house and were willing to transport her to the cottage and make an effort to set up something of a home there. The women cried and the men kept a stiff upper lip but largely fell silent. They would not be remaining at Stapley Manor for it seemed disrespectful to Mr. Carter and they had no desire to work for Mr.Turner in the circumstances. In any case, they were not sure what he would pay them with! At least in time, Mrs. Carter would surely receive money from her husband's estate once his last will and testament was read and she would be able to move on to something more fitting of her standing in society, than the earthy cottage she had been temporarily donated as part of the duelling deal. For the moment, they just had to get on with that harsh blow.

It happened that as the day progressed, the exchange of belongings from one house to the other, for both parties, was achieved. Elizabeth had absolutely no desire to be confronted with Albert Turner and so she instructed her staff to do something for her, possibly for the last time: To ensure that their paths did not cross.

Darkness fell. Elizabeth and Elise sat that first night by the small fire in the one room of the cottage. Elise held her mother's hand while they both wept. Mostly the tears were for the loss of dear Henry but undoubtedly it was also for the loss of their beautiful home and the cruelty of Albert Turner.

Even for the Turner family, there was no excitement. No joy to leave the cottage where the twins had been born and spent all their early years. Their mother had packed their frugal collection of worldly goods and chattels in an organized fashion but portrayed no sense of enthusiasm and her face was passive. It was strange to be taking up residence in the biggest house in the neighbourhood, yet there was no sense of deserving, except from Albert, who was crowing like a cockerel, yet being ignored by all the family.

It was thus, that Albert and Peggy took up residence in Stapley Manor, with their two children. Albert had thrashed Peggy on several occasions before they moved, just to teach her a lesson about respect, loyalty and most of all obedience. Yet, he magnanimously agreed for her to stay with him for appearances sake, as well as to look after the children and of course himself with all aspects of life he saw as a requirement of a wife's role. Taking up this elevated position of grandeur at the manor house, he needed to appear every part the gentleman and she must behave in such a manner befitting the lady of the house. In accordance with new house rules, she would now become known formerly as Margaret, since Peggy was now simply too lower class for their esteemed new elevation in society. Peggy cringed at this absurd notion but for fear of his idea being beaten into her, she nodded her acquiescence. Ironically, as it transpired, nobody took heed of Albert's bombastic new rule because as the months went by, few came into contact with this ever increasingly remote family. Even Albert himself forgot in a short time, about his ridiculous decree.

Assuming the role of master of this grand edifice, Albert took energetic, leaping strides up the elevated steps leading to the front door but was shocked that it did not swing open by the respectful butler as he knew should happen, nor was there any greeting by a subservient footman. Entering the bare and cavernous hall, he was instantly staggered by the silence as well as disappointed, calling out irritably through the echoing reception rooms, only to discover that the house did not come with staff, as he had expected. He had held elaborate ideas of grandiosity and of acting the tyrant master of his new empire as he had always aspired to. It seemed that in his haste and greed, he had been remiss in omitting this stipulation from the contract at the point of the duel agreement. Once the staff had heard of the successor to the property, they would rather have gone hungry, than work for Albert Turner.

The children were each allocated a room. They settled their shabby belongings and were then given the chore of picking some vegetables from the garden for dinner. They should have wanted to explore the corridors and rooms and staircases together but Nancy May seemingly had no enthusiasm. This was most unlike her and Giles was beginning to suspect she was unwell. It was no fun to do this on his own so he simply crept stealthily about the place by way of orientating himself. The house was silent, empty and impersonal. There were no staff, no animals. Nobody spoke. Their few household belongings barely furnished the basic rooms. Footsteps echoed. Giles was set to task making the fires in the parlour, kitchen and bedrooms. He did at least find this fun and it kept him occupied for a while.

Meanwhile, sitting on a window seat, Nancy May gloomily peered out across the near gardens towards the pond. It was a dank, dreary, misty autumnal day. She could not rid her mind of the grotesque images she had seen just a week or so ago. She knew she could never feel that this was her house. It would never be her home. Her father had gained it by theft. He had wilfully stolen a life. It felt bad. She was beginning to piece together the recent events to make sense of it all but had no desire to share this with her twin. He wouldn't understand. He would not believe her. Even if he did, he would never connect the despicable thing that his father had done in order to gain his pleasure, be that wealth, property, superiority, power, she did not know what this house signified to him. She longed to be back in her familiar home. It was small and impoverished, but secure, despite her father's harsh treatment. She loved her mother and still could not understand what it could possibly be that she had done that was so bad. The only bonus of being here at Stapley Manor, she suddenly realized, was the ability to be further away from her father. She could probably hardly ever see him if she organized her time wisely.

Nancy May had learnt to play her father like a flute. She portrayed herself to her father as angelic. She never gave him the opportunity to punish her. She had a clever knack of getting away with things, never by blaming other people but just never allowing herself to get caught for things she knew she should not do and always appeared to do as she was told. Most importantly, she did her utmost to keep out of her father's way.

Giles, on the other hand, was sadly not quite so smart. It irritated him that his sister got away with adventures. Nancy May was born with a free spirit and a sense of jeopardy and hated to be controlled and cooped up. Giles envied her wayward streak but was too careless and always stumbled into trouble. He often bore the brunt of his father's slipper or belt and resented that his sister, did not. It was true, however, that he had no idea how brutal his father was.

Never could Nancy May ever forgive her father for wanting to kill another man in cold blood. The man did not even try to defend himself. Perhaps by putting the gun to his own head, he was knowingly taking away Albert's pleasure of killing him. She also wondered if perhaps this man was a true God fearing gentleman, who did not wish to kill another human being but had been put in this ridiculous position of defending his honour (or someone else's), for whatever reason. Nancy May at that point, found huge respect for this man. As far as Nancy May was concerned, the dead man was the true hero. She had seen it with her own eyes and would never forget it. He was so courageous to stand there and take that bullet, knowing it was his last moment. It was almost as though he wanted this last gesture to take away any possible heroism from her father. It was perhaps intended to belittle him. Sadly, she believed that this was lost on her father, for he continued to be as bombastic as ever, in what he perceived as his success.

Peggy realized she would have even more work to do than previously. She suspected it might be some time before they had staff to help with the upkeep and she had no idea how her husband proposed to pay for any such support. She knew her place and it was not hers to enquire as to his plans.

It was such a huge house and they only had their own furniture plus anything unwanted which Elizabeth had left. Elizabeth had had the presence of mind to take with her, those precious pieces she would need to move forward in life with and the rest of what was worthwhile, she sold to give her enough funding to live off for the foreseeable future. She had no desire to be the generous donor of household goods, for the comfort of Turner, whom she considered despicable. She did, however, pity his wife and young children, not much older than her own Elise.

That first day, arriving at the manor house, Peggy stood looking at the front of Stapley Manor and a thousand thoughts went through her head. She struggled to unscramble them. In that single moment, she had memories both sweet and sad. She bore grief too. With a brief glance upwards, she swore she could see Henry's handsome face looking down from an elevated window, smiling directly at her but of course, she knew it was just a flashing memory.

Remembering then, how it had been a dank November day when late one morning, she sensed the nearness of giving birth. She had had some dull backache, which seemed to be increasing and the baby felt very low in her belly. She went to her sister and feigned a random offer to go to Stapley Manor to help out for a special occasion. She would be away for a couple of days. She knew she could depend on her sister for support but hated that she was lying in order to conclude the secret she had been carrying for months. Nobody but herself had known for sure about the baby, although there had been a couple of instances when Peggy thought some of the local women may have guessed she was again with child. Peggy did her level best to avoid any suspicion by carefully wrapping herself with layers of clothing to disguise her increasing rotundness. Mabel agreed without question and stoically took on the care and responsibility for the twins, proud that her sister had a job to fulfil, which made Peggy feel all the more guilty for her deceit.

Peggy began the slow, heavy walk to Stapley Manor. Light fog swirled overhead and snow threatened in the greyness. Over the past few weeks she had been conjuring up a tenuous mental plan but had had little opportunity to make any real arrangements, other than gathering a few pieces of some wood and placing them at the back door of the Mill House. She truly hoped that she had started her journey with enough time to make herself as comfortable as possible. Her priority would be to make a small fire to keep her warm, in preparation for the gruelling hours ahead of her. She carried a small bag in which she had placed some carefully chosen items in anticipation of the birth and prayed hard that she could do this on her own. Approaching the drive to the big house, she was enforced to slow her pace with fatigue and dreaded that anyone should see her, for she could not easily defend her reason for being there. The pathway was extremely muddy and she was slipping in her lightweight shoes, which leaked with damp cold until she could barely feel her toes. Wrapping her shawl tighter around her against the chilling wind, she longed to get to her chosen shelter for rest.

Just in the nick of time, as she saw a carriage leaving the front of the house coming towards her, she reached the overgrown pathway, which led to the Mill House. As quickly as her body would allow, she was able to make her discreet way to its back door. She forced open the door and stepped into the derelict space. Dropping her bag to the floor with a heavy sigh of relief, she looked around to really appreciate the impoverished surroundings in which she now stood. It was so very different from the last time she spent the night here and she longed to feel the comfort and security of having Henry with her, as she did then. She had not imagined it to feel like this, so empty and lonely and scary. Hugging her own arms around herself for comfort and warmth, she realized just how dismal this plan was. There was no choice and she must be brave. With sinking heart and aching back she knew she had to begin getting organised. Taking from her bag some precious matches, she must firstly make a small fire. She remembered how important that was nine months ago in making a glow of warmth for comfort. She brought inside the small collection of wood she had gathered and was proud she had thought ahead to do this. Taking it as a sign from the heavens that someone was looking after her, she was grateful for the camouflage of the thickening fog, disguising the smoke. That done, she fetched some water from the stream outside, placing a small vessel of it upon the fire, to boil. A hot drink would be good. Watching the flames take hold and appreciating their frugal warmth now, she removed her shoes and placed them on the hearth to dry. Taking a small pile of clean rags from her bag, she placed them within reach, knowing these would be essential later on. Then, taking off her coat, she lay it upon the fireside bench and lay down to rest a while. She sipped at her hot water as though it was a fine liquor and tried to imagine she were somewhere else, other than here.

By the time the sun was going down, it had become uncomfortably dark. She waited until absolutely necessary then took a couple of tapers from her bag and lit them from the fire. With tears in her eyes she recalled Henry doing this very task and she suddenly missed him dreadfully. The dingy cast of flickering light was bleak and ghostly and the silence within the walls heightened the country noises outside and made her tremble and once again wishing she were anywhere but here in this damp, mouldy, derelict accommodation. The guilt of bringing a child into the world in these circumstances, made her weep with shame and she resumed her seat on the fireside bench and closed her eyes against her discomfort and thought of Henry. It now seemed an eternity ago that they had lain here together on that unexpected magical night. She breathed deeply as though to take in his scent one more time, yet knowing her efforts were futile. She tried to conjure up the look in his sparkling eyes, the nuances of his movements, his voice replaying his reassuring words, reliving their precious time together and finally, she drifted into fitful sleep.

With no sense of how long afterwards, she woke suddenly, when her waters broke, leaving her shaking with reaction and anticipation. Wiping herself with some clean rags, she did her best to keep herself calm and suffer her intermittent pain stoically. She stole a moment to stoke the fire, wash out the used rag and hang it to dry by the fire. She managed to complete a few tasks to prepare for the birth as best as she could between pacing the floor, bearing her painful spasms for hours as they increased in intensity and regularity. She was scared, so very scared, not for herself but for the dread of being discovered. In the dark loneliness, she worried too if something should go wrong. She had not before thought of it, until now but in those last hours, she recalled the story of one of her mother's sisters, who died during childbirth. The thought of leaving her two children behind, without a mother, was just too cruel. She knew she must never scream for help. Even if there was a chance that someone could hear, which was unlikely since the Mill House was so remote, no one must know about this child, for she would be shunned from her community and find herself homeless and without her beloved children, should Albert ever discover her infidelity. She prayed she could do this on her own. With muffled screams and exhaustion, she endured the peak of her labour, until after hours of isolated fear, her little girl was born in the pale light of dawn. Relief, joy and sadness overwhelmed her in equal measure. A little later, clearing away evidence of the birth and feeding her new born, she tried to come to terms with now having to give her away. She wept endlessly.

The next day was more than difficult. She had very little food to sustain her but she ate the stale bread and pie she had brought in the bag, saving the precious apple for later. Her baby suckled immediately and took her first milk well. She was such a placid little thing, unlike her first two children who rarely slept. For this she was extremely grateful. Wrapped in a precious white linen cloth, which Peggy had brought especially for this purpose, Peggy held her baby close, rocking her gently and softly singing to her. She was the prettiest baby, with a strong look of her handsome father, yet at the same time, Peggy could see similarities with Nancy May when she was newly born. How sad she was that these two half sisters would never know each other.

They would never build a sibling relationship, share toys, laugh together, celebrate birthdays or find comfort in each other. Her melancholic heart felt it was breaking. Looking down at this wonder of nature, she had a huge desire to hold these precious few moments in her mind for ever, for they would be gone too soon. With a huge surge of love, Peggy simply did not know how she could possibly part with this beautiful child. She had been born from love and now she must surrender her and walk away, never to hold her again. Yet the chains of a mother's instinct seemed to forbid her and her instinct to nurture and protect this tiny life was equally strong. The child deserved a good life however, and so, with great resolve, she must gift her baby back to her father, in the knowledge that she would be loved and cherished.

The fire was all but extinguished and the room had been returned to its former cold, empty space, as Peggy left through the back door of the Mill House, just as she had arrived. Her baby, recently fed for the last time by Peggy, was now asleep and swaddled in the white linen, cradled inside her bag. Every step of the gruelling walk to the front door of Stapley Manor, Peggy felt painfully tortured, as though someone was physically ripping out her heart. Still foggy, she hoped not to be seen. Approaching the grand front door, then reaching the top step, she gently withdrew the tiny babe from her bag and tenderly kissing her forehead for the last time, she said a quiet prayer asking for her forgiveness and with a final squeeze of motherly love, she laid her precious bundle on the top step in the shelter of the doorway. With a final glance behind her through streaming tears, Peggy left the scene as quickly as she was able.

Isolated in her grief, never to be shared or consoled, she compelled herself to walk away. Every forced step, a calculated, grudging, reluctant decision to leave her baby behind, was against all natural instinct. Her heart ...... painful with the wrench that only a mother could feel when torn from her child. Barely able to see through obliterating tears, she moved forward following the path, nurturing her anguish. Reaching the cover of the bushes edging the pathway, her legs collapsed involuntarily. No longer able to take another step, she propped herself against the stone wall, then slowly slipped to the floor in utter despair, sobbing, bitterly lamenting her decision. Regrets spun in her head. She tried to look into the future and see her consequences but her mind would not allow

it, for deep in her soul she knew that nothing in this world could ever forgive her for what she had done. She punishingly believed herself to be wicked but prayed that her decision would bring this child a better life than ever she could give her and she hoped that both her child and God would forgive her.

Through the lifting fog, she suddenly sat alert and squinted her vision towards the house, listening with as much acuteness as she was able. A sound. Her baby. Crying. It stopped and she paused motionless, hearing only her staggered breath. It came again. Instinctively, with weak legs, trying to raise her sore body from the ground to return to her child. She could bare this no longer. Her head throbbed with distress as she scrambled to her feet and began a few hurried paces to return to her baby's cry. But then another noise came. Voices. She stopped. Her pert hearing, straining. A door slammed shut. Silence. Gone! Her baby was gone!

Pulling herself back to the present day, Peggy blinked back the painful tears of reminiscence and reaching the top step at the front door of Stapley Manor, where she had last held Elise and laid her just hours old, she saw a baby girl in her mind's eye and wondered how grown up, how pretty she will now be. She imagined her to be like her father no doubt and with beautiful long dark hair. She felt a huge sense of loss for what might have been, had life dealt her a different card. The memory left her with a sense of loneliness and heartache. To give up this tender young baby, only hours old, was the most difficult, heart-wrenching thing she had ever had to do. She was resigned to whatever regret her future might hold, having imagined giving up her baby in her mind's eye during her pregnancy but when it came to laying her baby down on the step for the last time, never to hold her again, the pain was tortuous. She sobbed for what seemed like days.

Thus, this house was already haunted, with many bittersweet memories. She could never see this as her home, without Henry. If only things had been different. She had loved him so much and how best could she prove it but to give away her baby girl to another mother, for the joy of her lover. Henry knew that their secret was safe between themselves. Yet, in reality, there was still one other person who knew. Rosanne.

CHAPTER 9

Thanks to Henry's generous financial bequest, Elizabeth and Elise had by now moved from Primrose Lane into a beautiful home a little way outside Evesham, in the quaint, white-cottage village of Harvington. It was by no means as grand an affair as Stapley Manor but Elizabeth was a pragmatic soul and satisfied with her lot. She was able to make a comfortable life for herself and more importantly, for Elise.

Elise had always shown a keen interest in animals and this cottage came with a considerable acreage of peripheral land which might, one day allow for a smallholding if Elizabeth felt so inclined.

After her initial meeting with Mr. Foster, Elizabeth felt much relief from the knowledge that they would continue to be financially secure. She was so touched to hear that Henry had generously reserved an amount of money in trust for Elise. In time, she would disclose to Elise how much this fund would be, so that she might plan its best use but for now, it would remain private between herself and Mr. Foster. It did, however, intrigue Elizabeth to hear that there remained two outstanding issues from the will. Grateful for the settlement of generous funds thus far, she continued to wait patiently for further advice. She had no idea what information, could possibly await her but assumed it to be something relatively insignificant.

Almost a year passed by, when unexpectedly, Elizabeth was again summoned to speak with Mr. Foster. She was shocked to have to revisit the awful details of the night of the intrusion into their home, by Mr. Albert Turner...

"As it is already clear, Mrs. Carter, your house was lost to you as a result of the duel, which Mr. Carter had agreed to, with his employee Mr. Albert Turner. The duel was to take claim of Stapley Manor and its land." Elizabeth dipped her head and whispered her affirmative response.

Mr. Foster continued, "It seems that the duel arrangements were made in haste, were they not, as is often the case and it has come to light that the Mill House was excluded from the agreement, simply by accidental omission. However, I have had to seek expert advice on this point Mrs. Carter, as this discrepancy is crucial to one of your husband's wishes. On the one hand, one could argue that the Mill House, stands upon the land which was inclusive of the agreement, on the other, it is a specific item which was NOT itemized in that contract but WAS specified in your husband's Will and therefore, in this case, a fortuitous exclusion!" Elizabeth had no idea what the man was talking about. "Sir, forgive me but I fail to see your point!"

Mr. Foster looked up from his spectacles and continued, "Mrs. Carter, your husband was very specific about leaving the Mill House to Elise. The result of my research has concluded, that we CAN consider it an exclusion to the duel agreement and as such, your daughter is eligible to claim it." Elizabeth was quite taken aback. This bequest seemed rather strange to her, as it was to her knowledge, of no particular significance to Henry, nor was it of any great financial importance but she tried to focus again, as Mr. Foster continued.

Setting aside the previous papers, he concentrated now with certain gravity, on another clutch of parchment. "There is something more, Mrs. Carter but I am unable to disclose this at the present time. In fact, issues such as these, may take years to be resolved, so I would implore you to be extremely diligent in your patience and I shall reveal all as soon as I am able."

Once again, Elizabeth was discharged from his company without any opportunity to question the solicitor's pronouncement.

Mr. Foster had had great difficulty over the next few years following up his thread of concern about the correctness of the duel rules and their outcome. Firstly he needed to take a witness statement from Henry's butler, Mr. Noah Fielding but after he had left employment at Stapley Manor following Henry's demise, he moved away and he had been very difficult to track down. After considerable time, he was found to be living in Wales, where he had returned to his roots, in a remote backwater, to retire. His statement eventually confirmed that he saw his employer and good friend, bring the pistol to his own head and fire. Indeed, he could swear upon the Bible, that Mr. Carter, took his own life.

That task completed, the case rumbled on further with legal discussions between the lawyer and his learned colleagues, about the fairness of the conclusion of this particular duel and its consequences. It was agreed that strictly speaking, with the evidence of one witness, the duel should be called null and void since Mr. Turner did not kill his opponent. However, they all felt that they needed more evidence than just one statement, to confirm the accuracy of the outcome. It was decided to revisit Mr. Fielding, to see if he could cast any further thoughts on who else might know of Mr. Carter's intention to take his own life. Perhaps a diary may have been later uncovered, for example?

CHAPTER 10

By late afternoon and into the evening, the fair became a bustle of sound and colourful vision. Music struck up, enticing curiosity and excitement. The fire was stacked and a magical vibrancy overtook the usual calm of the countryside. Lanterns were lit beneath the trees and laughter pervaded the flamboyant scene. Children screeching with joy and in a corner, men gathered, tankards clinking and voices becoming ever more boisterous.

As the sun began to lower in the summer sky, the first few folks gathered with intrigue, a guitar struck up a fast rhythm, quickly accompanied by a shimmer of tambourines which served to quicken the pace and the flamboyantly dressed Romani ladies began their entrancing dance, fan flicking dramatically to the beat, in a frenetic collision of colour.

Nancy May and Giles arrived at the fair to be immediately immersed in its enchantment. Tonight was the last night at this venue and the crowds were larger and more boisterous than usual. It was a glorious summer's evening, the sort that with the setting of the sun, darkness never really comes. The fragrant perfume of freshly cut hay lingered in the air and the birdsong continued until the nightingale sang. Neither of them could remember a time when they had missed the event and it had become a traditional occasion for them both, wrapped in childhood memories. In the early years, it was Nancy May of course, who had escaped through a back window of the cottage and against her father's vehement forbidding. The excitement was therefore twofold. Firstly, the thrill of hiding behind bushes to peer through and secretly observe the spellbinding activity of a place that fascinated her, simply because it was forbidden. Secondly, to be successful in defying her tyrannical father and risking the beating from him, should she be caught. Giles was never so brave and did not settle until she was safely home again.

Tonight still held the same magical fascination.

Almost running the last few steps with excitement, Nancy May and Giles spotted the boxing arena... They dashed over towards it immediately. They spent a good half hour joining in the roars and shouts of the crowd as two burley men fought each other. Crushed together in the crowd of spectators, Giles jumped up and down thrusting his arms in the air to cheer on his spuriously chosen man. Nancy May looked about the crowd and suddenly caught her breath as she glimpsed sight of the most handsome young man she believed she had ever seen. Standing to the side of the boxing arena, Nancy May concluded, he seemed to be in charge of the event. Making her way surreptitiously towards his direction, she drew up as close to him as was possible without drawing attention to herself, as though the crowd had jostled her into position. She tingled with excitement when his body was caused to brush her arm and since he was seemingly unaware of any such contact, she found an excuse to nudge even closer so that she could better feel his strong arms against her.

Finally, with a sickening crack, one of the boxers fell to the floor. He lay still for a moment, then someone lifted his head, revealing a blooded nose, then dropped his head back on the floor with as much care as one would handle a dead sheep. The crowd jeered as the fight came to an abrupt end and with a surge of momentary booing and hissing, they disbanded to go and find other amusement. Giles too was ready to move on. Nancy

May went to turn away alongside Giles, but somehow, in the next moment, she was on the floor wincing in apparent pain. Of course, Giles immediately crouched down to see what had happened and offered assistance but his attempt to help was met with her glaring eyes for, as she had hoped, the unknown swarthy young man, also stooped to help. "What happened? Are you alright?" His deep richly accented voice came with concern. Naughtily, she looked provocatively up at him, doing her best to pout seductively, just as she had practised many times alone in her bedroom, in case such a moment should arise. Looking up into the deepest, dark eyes in the world, Nancy May realised her mouth would not work to answer but instead, she felt two strong arms wrap around her, lifting her from the ground and against his tight chest. Pushing past Giles dismissively, he carried the willing prize effortlessly for some moments. "Was this really happening? My God! Who was this man?" Thoughts saturated her whirring mind, taking no notice of where he was taking her. Too soon, with a sudden bump, she was placed on a wooden chair at the side of a green vardo. Giles was nowhere in sight. Her instantly spontaneous plan had worked but right now she felt a little ashamed of herself, for faking injury.

"Where is my brother?" she asked out of instinct more than concern.

"Oh, your brother is he? I'm sure he will find you – eventually" he added, laughing softly. She looked around her, realising they were rather cut off from the fair, tucked away in the gypsy encampment.

A slight panic overtook her mind, "Oh I am sure I shall be fine, she said, attempting to stand up, feigning a slight limp." I can manage I am sure. I must go find my brother, he will worry for me."

Taking her by the wrist, he pulled her gently back towards him. "I could not possibly let you go yet my lovely. Come, sit here a while and let me get to know you!" Part of Nancy May's mind wanted this fairy tale introduction never to end and yet something in her wanted her legs to get up and run as fast as she could.

He poured two glasses of ale and thrust one into her hand. "Oh I don't..."

"Of course you do!" he insisted. He looked at her then gulped down his full tankard and gestured waiting for her to do the same. Shaking a little, she began to sip at the distasteful liquid. "No..." he said laughingly, take it quickly!" She tried again and gagged a little. He laughed again... "Come," he said, "Let me see how well you dance!" and held out a hand, enticingly.

Giles finally jumped into action to search for her. How dare this stranger just step in like that and pick her up! That was HIS job to take care of her, like he had always done - nobody else's! As if that wasn't enough, the bold fellow had gestured with his intimidating eyes to make sure he didn't follow. The silent message was clear and in that moment Giles froze. Why did he let him get away with that? He just stood back mesmerized and let it happen. By the time he had pulled himself together, they had disappeared. Giles darted about in the crowd, pushing through the circles of entertainment, but could not trace their steps. Desperate and chiding himself for the idiot he took himself to be, Giles looked around the fair for what seemed like ages but couldn't track where they had gone. He asked those who were in charge of the various events or stalls and described the man who had taken Nancy May but rarely did he even get a response, let alone anyone who looked like they could care a jot. It was almost as though he was invisible. Despite his inner panic, he was also cursing his minx of a sister for being such a dramatic thespian. He knew her so well and doubted that she had hurt herself at all. This time, he suspected she had probably gone too far with her games and he worried that, she had now got them both into trouble!

In despair, he flopped down on his backside in the middle of the hubbub. On the floor, with his legs crossed beneath him, he looked around him in the hope of spotting his sister. He was so cross with himself! To cap it all, it was usual that they would have made a plan should they ever get separated for any reason – a safe place to meet - but tonight, tonight of all nights, they had not done so. Even if they had, he wondered if she was free or able to have done so. He was not sure if she had in fact really hurt her ankle. She was such a good actress and could easily play wounded for attention and by the glance she gave him, that was exactly what she wanted! The gypsy fell right into her plan! Then again, maybe her idea had backfired! Maybe now she could not escape! All the stories he had ever heard about these travellers, suddenly came to his mind and drove him more crazy with fear. Right! That decided his next move! He would go to each and every one of the caravans and knock at each door until he found her. Surely she would be screaming for help if she were trapped?!

The crowds were thinning out now as the evening was drawing to a close. Giles jumped to his feet with intent to execute his next plan. Moving into the next field, he stood for a moment behind some bushes. Best that he listen first. He could hear his heart hammering against his ribs. There were no signs of danger. No disturbing noises. Nothing unusual. Slowly, he walked forward towards the nearest vardo. Empty. As was the second. He noticed a glimmer of light coming through the folded doors of one of the furthest vardos. Holding his breath, he took some steps towards it, then, "Oy!! What do you think you're doing?" came a deep, sharp voice. Shocking Giles back into the moment, he spun on his heels.

Trying to sound brave despite his shaking voice, "I, I am looking for my sister!" He took a deep breath, "I think she may be here, with one of your travellers."

"You've no right to be here. This here is private to us! Now get the hell out of here before I pick you up and throw you into that river." Not knowing where his courage had come from, Giles turned full face to confront the man further.

"No! I am not going until I find her! I am certain she must be here." Pointing towards the lit vardo, he asked, "Who is in there? I need to know! I think she might be in there!"

"Well haven't you got a nerve! Think you're a big boy then do you? 'Tis none of your business who be in there! Now like I said, get the hell out of here!"

Just then, from out of nowhere, another voice rumbled from behind him, "We got trouble here then Damien?" and with a sudden jolt, Giles was picked up from the rear by the scruff of his neck and physically lifted off his feet and manhandled away towards the river. Struggling and kicking to free himself, Giles attempted to fight back but his efforts were completely worthless. With a sudden push, he was freed from the vice like grip and he landed splat on the edge of the riverbank. A guffaw of laughter from both men added insult to injury for Giles but their final message was unmistakable! Giles would not be welcome back anytime soon, if he wished to keep all his body parts!!!

Unseen by Giles, the evening was ending with the dying embers of the fire and chords of a guitar, strumming a slow ballad sending soporific waves across the early evening air. Giles however, was walking slowly home, with a heavy heart and troubled mind.

Eventually arriving back home, he was frantic with worry. Skirting past his father who had collapsed on a rug by the fire as he often did, he ran upstairs to check in on Nancy May's room in the desperate last hope that she had run on home ahead of him. He had looked everywhere else and was just about the last person to leave the fair. His heart sank in despair to see her bed had not been slept in. Crumbling to the floor and in that moment, his heart felt like it had been ripped out and trodden upon. Head in his hands he whispered to himself, "What the hell do I do now?"

Plucking up the courage, he struggled to his weary feet and felt along the dark passageway to his mother's door, rapidly knocking to waken her. Sitting up in bed with a start, her hair in a pink bonnet and a greying chestnut brown plait falling over her shoulders, shock written across her face to see her son by her bedside. He babbled through his desperation at not finding Nancy May. Fear struck her hard. She flung herself out of bed and rooted for her wrap, pacing the floor and asking Giles a thousand questions. He assured her that he had looked everywhere but Peggy's mind was just fixated on the fact that he had last seen her in the arms of a complete stranger, who it seems was a gypsy.

Under her absolute command, they were to prepare immediately to go back the long distance to the fair to find her. Exhausted as he was, Giles tried to insist he go alone but Peggy would hear none of that. As quickly as was physically possible, she pulled on some clothes and they set off silently in the moonlight all the way back to Evesham. They knew they must be back before Albert awoke or else all hell would break loose.

Reaching the fair, exhausted with desperation to find Nancy May, they approached with caution. Peggy was especially fearful of the gypsy reputation and did not wish to put themselves in danger but her motherly instinct was not afraid for herself but for her darling daughter.

It was now early hours of the morning and everywhere was tranquil. The fire embers still smouldered, filling their nostrils with the familiar scent of burnt ashes and a calm serenity surrounded the caravans. Peggy and Giles had had time to make a plan of action as they tramped across fields and tracks as fast as their energy allowed and looked to seek out in the dim light the most ostentatious vardo, in the hope that they were about to knock on the door of the most influential gypsy. Just as they reached the circle of brightly coloured caravans, they startled a dog, causing both their hearts to jump and race frantically. The sudden ferocious barking alerted what seemed like all of the inhabitants and doors began to flick-flack open. Voices shouted threateningly. More dogs joined in the cacophony of barking. On seeing the suspicious couple, one burly young man came out of his home, staggering half asleep towards them, yelling questions. Trying to keep calm, both Giles and his mother spluttered their apologies but also their desperate plea to find Nancy May.

Peggy spoke with a trembling voice full of emotion as well as fear. "Please do not be angry with us. We are sorry for disturbing you but we must find my daughter." She began to cry as she spoke. "She was here earlier and we need to find her. She did not come home and we fear for what may have become of her." Hoping the gypsies did not suspect they were being accused of hiding her, she tried to reason with the man, "Please, we hope you may be able to help us know where she has gone??" Gesturing towards Giles, she continued, "She was with my son: Perhaps you recognize him? They were together and she hurt her foot? Do you know where she is??" Giles attempted to add into the plea but Peggy put her hand on his forearm and gave him a glance to be quiet, feeling one voice at a time would be more productive and seem less accusative. She continued, "I think one of your young men may have tried to help her, so perhaps he might know what became of her?" She had really hoped that this would not sound too condemning as though she suspected them of taking her but unfortunately, that was exactly how they did take it. It was as though they were ready and fired up to be defensive. There was no chance that they were going to look for her or ask around the group to see if they could help. No, they gathered outside of their caravans and formed an impenetrable, forbidding semi circle.

The intimidating band were together aggressive in their response, "What are you suggesting?" "Clear off out of here…" "Be gone, before we set the dogs on you…" "There's nobody here but us…" " You've got no right to be disturbing us…"

Feeling the sense of antagonism, Peggy saw Giles get ready with his fist and thought that this could only end badly if she did not diffuse the situation quickly. "Please, I am begging you as her mother, I am desperate to find her. I do not wish to cause trouble but I fear for her safety… if she is not here, I had hoped you could help me find her." Again they used threats to get the pair away from their enclosure and slowly encroached on the space between them and Peggy and Giles who found themselves stepping backwards as they begged. Eventually, Peggy pulled at Giles's jacket sleeve and implored him to leave with her. There was no use in trying here. Not like this. They were getting nowhere. She could only hope that by the time she reached home again, her beautiful daughter would already be in her bed as she often did after one of her escapades. Should that not be the case, however, she would come back tomorrow when daylight may make things feel far less threatening. She silently prayed that that plan would not be necessary. As a last hopeful, parting shot, Peggy begged one last time, imploring them that if they did find out where her daughter was, to bring her home to Stapley Manor. Apologising once more for their intrusion, she coaxed an infuriated Giles away from the ever escalating, inflammatory situation.

They walked home exhausted and in near silence. At first, Giles had wanted to stay there until dawn to see for himself if she was there. He was so certain that she was! Peggy however, had all her hopes pinned on her having returned to her own bed and that their paths had somehow, simply not crossed. She was also very afraid that Albert would have woken to discover them gone and there would be another almighty fractious row to deal with then and if she survived all that, she had no idea how to break the news to her husband, of Nancy May's disappearance. He never needed an excuse to give Peggy a beating!

It was fully daybreak when they reached Stapley Manor, footsore and exhausted. The first chords of birdsong had long since been heard. Opening the back door, Peggy breathed a huge sigh of relief to find Albert exactly where they had left him hours ago, face down on the rug in front of the now dead ashes of fire and so they stepped quietly around him towards the flight of stairs and Nancy May's bedroom.

Albert stirred in his drunken stupor and glimpsed Peggy at a distance. "Where the 'ell 'av you been?" He slurred. Taking her utterly by surprise, Peggy stopped dead in her tracks, catching her breath as her heart jumped high in her chest. Giles, a few steps ahead of her turned, as did Peggy.

Giles braved the moment. "Father, I ... I er, er, thought I heard someone outside and woke Mamma. We went to investigate... but all is well."

Albert looked from one to the other of them, then snapped, "You're lying!!!!"

Gulping down fear, Giles tried to sound reassuring, "No Papa, I think it must have been a fox ...after the chickens..." Giles had hoped this would be sufficient to quell the tirade they both expected. Albert scoffed with mistrust and went to get up from the floor but once almost upright, his legs caved beneath him and stumbling forward again, crashed hard upon the stone floor, face down. Motionless.

Peggy and Giles looked at each other, then back to Albert who lay entirely still. "Quickly, go and check on Nancy May, before he comes to!" she ordered Giles, "Come straight back here" she whispered loudly as an afterthought. Peggy remained statue still on the stairs, looking down on her husband.

A moment or two later, Giles returned, "Mam, she is not there!" Her hand flew to her face and Peggy gasped with utter horror. Involuntarily, she sank to sit on the stair.

"No!! Are you sure?" A futile response, which even she did not know why she had asked the question. It was just hopeful, wishing she had misheard Giles's words. Giles assured her he had looked properly. Nancy May had not been in her bedroom since she left to go to the fair. "Oh dear God!" she silently prayed and sobbed again.

Tears still streaming down her face, slowly, slowly, Peggy got to her feet again. With a sense of duty more than concern, she and her son stepped ever closer to Albert. Like petrified stone he lay still on the floor, face down. Deep red blood was trickling from somewhere, pooling beneath his head. He lay motionless in the accumulating sticky crimson fluid. Peggy stooped to touch him. Trembling hands, she held her breath. Not a sound. She tentatively shook his shoulder but there was no response, so she tried to roll him over but he was too heavy. She snatched her hand back to her face. Glancing up to her son, "I, I think … Giles, I think he's dead!" she whispered with incredulity. Giles looked from her to his father's body sprawled across the grey rag rug. He too bent down as though in prayer but could not bring himself to touch his father's still body. They stayed thus for some time. They knew not how long.

Leaving his body where it lay, they sat together, in stunned silence and fatigue. The clock fingers had moved around its face twice and so with mute communication, they again set off towards the fair in the hope of having a more profitable dialogue with those gypsies they saw hours earlier. It was as though they were in the middle of a horrific nightmare. They should be grieving for Arthur but found that they had no feelings with which to do so. There was no sense of sorrow or loss between them and it felt shameful. At the same time, they were drenched in despair for the loss of Nancy May. Even now, they considered her disappearance as a loss. Their hope was slipping out of their grip. Giles kept reminding themselves that he at least knew who he was searching for. He would recognize the man who lifted her up and took her away. He would know him anywhere. The thought of once again encountering the gypsies was terrifying but he needed to be a man and face up to them. He knew Nancy May would mock him if he did not do so. He wanted Nancy May to be proud of him, so he must find the courage! All they needed was to see the gypsies altogether and he could pick him out of the crowd. That thought, kept him going for the long walk back into the town but as the sun was beginning to lighten the sky and they approached the edges of Evesham, the scene seemed somehow different now. It was quieter, emptier. A sick feeling came across Peggy and she ran towards the fields where they had visited last night.

Getting closer, she began to scream, "NO, NO, NOOO!!" Reaching the dead fire in what had been the centre of the arena, her legs collapsed from beneath her and she bent and rocked back and forth on her heels, her head in her hands weeping bitterly. Giles stopped short of his mother and stood completely still gazing about in disbelief. They had gone. Completely gone! All of them, gone! He could not speak. He could not move. He could not take in what he was seeing. His mother's distressed wailing seemed remote to his hearing. How could this be?? Where was she? His dear beloved sister, the one he relied on for everything, had disappeared. He felt numb with disbelief. Focusing eventually on his distraught mother, he went to her side to try to comfort her. Putting his arms around her shoulders he pulled her towards him but there were no words from his lips. He had none to offer. What could he possibly say to console her?

Somebody passed by, a woman. Peggy looked up in hope. "Excuse me dear," she wept through her words, "Please, do you know where they have gone?" The woman looked at her not understanding, "The gypsies," Peggy continued, "Where have they gone? Please tell me where they have gone?"

The woman looked pitifully upon Peggy and shrugged her shoulders apologetically, "I do not know. They must have left before sunrise, as they always do."

Peggy made the most awful sound of distress that seemed to come from her very soul, "Noooo! Dear God, nooo!"

Arriving back at Stapley Manor for the second time in only a few hours, Giles's feet bleeding and Peggy's badly blistered, they were totally exhausted and bereft. They wearily took each painful step at a time up to the front door, mother clinging onto son, supporting each other. Peggy had no idea how she had the inclination let alone strength to walk back from the town. She just wanted to flop onto her bed, go to sleep and never wake up. To leave this living world was all she wanted. She made her way slowly up the stairs and mindlessly opened her bedroom door... to be confronted by a ghostly pale Albert standing in front of her, staring right back at her, congealed blood from head to shoulders. She screamed harder than she thought possible, before blackness fell upon her.

CHAPTER 11

Albert had, over the years, sunk low into despair. He had no job, no esteem, no joy, no friends and doubted now that he ever did! His wife spoke not a word to him unless she was forced to and the house he so desired brought him nothing but misery and shame. On reflection, he also found that he was conscience-stricken for killing a man who did not try to defend himself. He could not rid his mind of the duel and its consequences. He was also ashamed that he could not keep his wife from looking elsewhere and had no care or respect for him. He felt embarrassed to have the ever-deteriorating reputation within the village and knew only too well that folk scorned him, not just for taking the life of a well loved man but for the arrogant man he had always been. He had once heard someone say, about him, "How the mighty hath fallen" and they were so right.

Stapley Manor could never be thought of as his home. He had grown to hate it. It was as though he could feel Henry laughing at him in every room and once the light had gone from the day, he swore he could see or even hear Henry's voice, taunting him. The place had quickly become dilapidated and he had no money, wisdom or inclination to fix it. He had only ever known labouring or game keeping. Any practical skills he had accrued from his younger years, paled into insignificance, against the size of challenge presented by this house and land.

Almost inevitable then, that Albert should take to the bottle. He had in the early days discovered Henry's cellar with enough alcohol to swim in. Still in the heady months of euphoria in claiming the manor house, he took to treating himself throughout the day. From the beginning, he failed to realize the importance of creating funding to run the place. It had never once occurred to him that he might need to support its upkeep. He threw orders to his family as though they were servants and so for a good while, vegetables could be picked from the gardens, fruit from the orchards, Giles kept the fires roaring in the grates, Peggy did her best to keep the place looking as fine as she could. Nancy May kept her distance but tried to help her mother in daily tasks. It was not what any of them had expected of living in such a prestigious residence and all except Albert craved for their old home.

As time went by however, Albert's addiction to imbibing alcohol clogged up his mind and he became numb to anything of any importance. His shouting became worse and Peggy dreaded his salivating lurid attentions. She had learnt that if he drank just a little more, he would render himself incapable and so was guilty of encouraging him to that point which made them all safer. This done, she also knew he would waken the next morning with a bear's head and they would all need to pay for that.

However, Albert had never been the same, since that night she found him in her bedroom. It was as though he had returned to childhood. He was lost. They did not know if it was the bang to his head when he fell, which had turned his senses or the trauma of his daughter's disappearance, which had rendered him senseless but whatever the cause, it brought a mix of feelings for Peggy. On the one hand, he proved to be no longer a threat to her and never tried to force himself upon her ever again. On the other hand, he sometimes did not seem to know who she was. From time to time, he thought Peggy was his mother and spoke like a child. He would cry like a baby and want to go to his room to play with Giles's old toy car, the only toy the boy had had as a youngster. Peggy had to attend to his personal care, which often times disgusted her but she forced herself to do this out of necessity and not love. It had become a more than occasional occurrence that he had become incontinent, either because he was distracted or enraged about something or even asleep. Peggy often times had barely enough clothes to keep him dry and his laundry was a constant chore. As exasperating as this was, she never once chastised him or lost her patience, for that was pointless but there were many times she hid away, and cried.

It was the mood swings which were the most difficult to deal with, never knowing whether she was going to engage with Albert as a little boy, benign and child like or Albert the drunkard with a volatile temper and flailing fists. She was just as likely to find him laughing hysterically in dialogue with an imaginary person, as she was to find him sitting in a corner sobbing and cowering from his hallucinations. Other times, unprovoked, he might erupt into a blaspheming row with a non-existent other person. These were the most scary times and at first, naturally, she would try to show him that there was nobody there, that these people were in his imagination but she soon appreciated that this was just making hard work for herself and it was wiser just to go along with his confusion. It caused both of them less distress. This sometimes proved harder than it sounded for there were the instances when this tack became tiring beyond words. When he repeated a question over and over again, she knew it was best to answer the same thing repeatedly and not snap back with an impatient reminder she had just told him the answer to his question. He didn't understand or couldn't remember, so best she tried to distract him onto something else. It was exhausting.

As time progressed, she found that she needed Giles's physical help more and more to assist her when he fell over or became awkward. She quickly realised he still had the instinct to throw a fist or slap her and if he was not in the mood, he would fight her from helping him bathe or dress. She had to cajole him as one would a child and bargain with him offering rewards of a cake or such like until he co-operated. When her bribery failed, she would frequently come away from his room with bruises. On one occasion she felt sure he had succeeded in breaking one of her ribs. Without sufficient funds for nutritious meals, Peggy had to scrimp for food. Making something out of nothing, as she put it. She had managed to make a watery broth and some bread, which was as hearty as she could make but it still did not suffice for Albert. That evening, as she approached him with this meagre offering, he glanced mockingly at the impoverished effort and became enraged, knocking the whole tray into the air with one fierce swipe, blaspheming. Shocked and scared, Peggy stooped to pick up the shattered bowl and as she did so, he kicked his foot powerfully upwards directly into her midriff. With a shriek of stabbing pain, she fell to her knees, whereupon, he repeated his action several times over.

Peggy never came to terms with her daughter's disappearance. She continued to believe that Nancy May had been abducted by gypsies, that fateful night, almost a year ago. Not a night went by, when she did not pray to God that she would be returned to her, or at the very least God would watch over her and keep her safe. It was all she could do to get up each morning and feed herself, let alone cook to feed her son and husband. Giles thought she may blame him for Nancy May's disappearance but she did not. Not once did she reprimand his careless actions for losing her. Truth be told, she knew only too well what her daughter could be like once she had a plan in her head, no matter how spontaneous. She knew she could cleverly manipulate a situation for her own spurious fun and she also believed that if she really wanted to, she would have been able to escape the clutches of anyone forcing her. She was such a smart girl. She had all her life run close to the edge of danger, be that one adventure or another but mostly she seemed to get the greatest self-gratification, from avoiding her father's wrath. The riskier, the better. So there were only two possibilities in Peggy's head. Either she had been overcome with such extreme force that she could not escape the strength of her abductor, or she had not wanted to! Peggy could better imagine this scenario. It almost made Peggy feel better to imagine, or indeed accept, that this was more likely to be the case. Perhaps this was just another of Nancy May's exploits. It would not surprise Peggy at all, to know that her daughter had found herself in the best of all heroic acts. She had always had a romantic notion of life and never really understood danger because she had always been lucky enough to escape without major consequence. What worried Peggy most of all, was that Nancy May would not realize until it was too late, the gravity of her romanticism.

Giles too fought with his dark thoughts. On a daily basis, the loss of Nancy May was always with Giles and at times almost too much for him to bear. Not only because he missed his soul mate terribly but because he carried such heavy guilt about losing her. He could not forgive himself for his stupidity that night at the fair and by going over and over again every moment of that last night, he punished himself far more than anybody else was capable of doing to him. If only he could turn the clock back, there were so many things he would have done differently. His sense of bereavement was mixed. He missed her annoyance, the way she always knew best but he was cross too that she always got away with things yet at the same time, had a cute way of rescuing him from trouble too. He wished he could again hear her giggle – so infectious that he would laugh too without knowing why! Sometimes he would panic if he couldn't bring the sound of her voice to his mind. It was only by recalling one of her reprimands that brought relief of her sound and then he would smile. He missed her wisdom and felt the irony of knowing she would know how to find him, if he had disappeared! Again, a pang of utter distress and guilt swept over him. He simply felt lost and had no reason to laugh without her. He had gone over and over again in his mind the details of that last night at the fair. He wondered if he had done things differently, ignored the gypsy's threatening glance not to follow them – he should have insisted on staying with her. Or perhaps if he'd stayed in the environs of the fair longer, he would have found her. Most of all, he should not have left at all and stopped the troupe moving on until he had searched every vardo!!

Giles could not help but believe, that she had been held against her will and taken without her consent. Otherwise, surely she would have found a way to escape and make her way home. There was however, a niggle at the back of his mind, that this was the ultimate in adventures for her and what she had found herself mixed up in, was preferable to the mundane life she left at home. That saddened him immensely, for it suggested that she did not miss him or their mother, as much as they pined for her. Heaven knows where she was now. He would persecute himself trying to imagine what she would want him to do. She was the brains of the pair and he was born without imagination. If only she could send him a signal, a message of some kind, he might know what to do to find her.

Albert asked for Nancy May on occasions but fortunately his memory lapses and confusion were so severe now, that it was relatively easy for them to fob him off with one excuse or another as to why she was not there at that moment. They often said this was lucky for her, for if he had been of sound mind, they hated to think of the consequences which would greet her when she eventually did return –and they very much prayed she would return and soon!

CHAPTER 12

Times had become desperate. Giles had done his best to keep chickens so that there were at least some eggs to be had and at worst, they would kill one to pad out as many meals as possible. The vegetables in the garden had long since been used and without the ability to replant, the garden had sadly become overgrown with weed. It was exceedingly disheartening to Peggy who, with Henry's approval, had started to establish the foundation of such a beautiful kitchen garden. Despite her knowledge, Albert allowed her no time or money to regenerate the much needed food source. The established fruit trees were initially a godsend to get them through and Peggy had the skills to ensure nothing went to waste, preserving what she could for a later date by using the larder ingredients frugally. The previous servants had left what turned out to be a substantial store, presumably as a result of their hasty departure, so the flour and basic spices had been such a bonus, though months on, these were now almost totally depleted.

Neither Giles nor Peggy had any money but Peggy felt sure that somewhere her husband would have secreted some coins, for his own gratification. She and Giles took it in turns to search for it, whilst the other occupied Albert to keep him from suspecting their rummaging. They had come to Stapley Manor with very few belongings, so one would have thought, it would not be difficult to find a hiding place. Their hope was that if they could just find some coins, it could be enough to get them on their feet, maybe buying more hens to sell the eggs or a cow to sell the milk. It seemed a fairly reasonable plan. If this failed, Giles would have to resort to begging for food, or worse still, thieving! They were at their wits end now. Of course, they had for long enough discussed the option of Giles going out to find work but that had not felt like a good idea for either he or Peggy, as they both feared for Peggy's safety if left alone with Albert. He was simply too volatile. It seemed a much better idea to try to sustain a business of some sort in the grounds of Stapley Manor but without money to stimulate this, they were lost.

They had exhausted all the options they could think of where Albert may have hidden some money, until by a weird fluke one morning, Giles unearthed an unexpected chance discovery. It was feeling quite autumnal now with the weather turning rather chilly. Giles had found enough logs in the woodland to make up the fires so at least a few rooms in the house could be kept warm. Having set up the essential one in the kitchen used for cooking, he prepared to light one in his father's room. As he dropped the logs onto the hearth, he noticed one of the side bricks move loosely. Trying to fix it back into position, it refused to go back into place. Giles removed the brick altogether in order to reposition it but noticed an obstruction. Raking it out, he sat back on his heels in disbelief. With a surge of excitement, he held in his hand a small but weighty leather moneybag. Untying the string which bound it, he poured onto his palm a small collection of copper and silver coins. His mouth fell open with unexpected astonishment and he felt the pulse in his neck rapidly throb. Quickly pulling himself together and in fear of being caught by his father, he hurriedly replaced the coins in the grubby bag and stuffed the purse into his trouser pocket. Desperate to share his find with his mother, he quickly made the fire and once it burst into a roaring blaze, he ran downstairs to his mother with the excitement of a young child who had found treasure. This, could be their lifeline. Biding his time to ensure Albert was not in earshot, he dragged Peggy to one side by the elbow to reveal his findings. Secretively, he nervously pulled the bag from his pocket, breathlessly whispering his story. Relief and joy found them both almost silently hugging and jumping up and down with reprieve. Tears ran down Peggy's cheeks, "He's had that moneybag for years", Peggy noted. "I haven't seen it in a very long time! He never let me go near it!" Giles whispered, "We need to count it!"

Pointing to Albert who was sitting in the half broken chair at the kitchen table, "Shh! Not here. Give it a few minutes and I'll tell you to go fetch some eggs. Go count it in the barn. I'll keep him busy."

Moments later, under the contrived instruction of his mother and with heart–racing excitement, Giles made his way with hurried steps to the barn. Glancing behind himself with frequency, as though expecting to be caught out like a thief, he quickly found himself a secluded area on the dirt floor behind some rotting bales of hay. Flopping onto his knees caused a couple of roosting chickens to flutter up and cluck their annoyance at the unwelcome intrusion. Once again Giles removed the treasured purse from his pocket and pulled loose the cord, hurriedly tipping the contents onto the hardened soil, shaking the last one free. Scooping the coins back up one by one he added up the total worth as he did so, then checked his addition once more. This was wonderful! He did not believe he had ever seen so many coins. Enjoying the weight of them in his sweating hands, he held them tightly in disbelief. He simply could not comprehend such a lucky find yet somehow there was guilt lurking beneath his joy and he felt a child-like naughtiness creep over him. Distracted with the thought, he counted the coins one more time before replacing them in the bag and knotting the cord securely, he replaced it in his pocket.

Standing to leave, he remembered the masquerade errand and quickly foraged for a handful of eggs. Trying to look casual, as though someone might suspect him of burglary, he made a great effort to steady his breathing and walk more casually back into the kitchen, hoping not to encounter his father.

The day had come for Giles to set off early to market and began his walk into Evesham in the early autumn sunshine with a sense of hope. Such a glorious time of year and for once, he was in better spirits. It was agreed that with careful speculation of the newly discovered funds, Giles had enough funding to consider a sensible purchase at the market. With that newly found confidence, he strode out until he reached the market, with more hope in his heart than he had felt in some considerable time.

Market day was always busy and for some reason it seemed especially so first thing. The weather was still surprisingly hot for autumn and the animals needed to be kept as cool as possible. The sooner the better they could arrive at the vast sheds for auctioning and then on their way to their next destination, whether it was onwards for breeding or more gruesomely for the butcher's block! By the end of the morning the stench could be smelt for a mile or so around and carts were being pulled in and out to transport the animals. It helped to know where one was going, for the chaotic melée of activity could easily be overwhelming to the first timer. Giles, was one of those! A complete novice, trying his best not to show his naivety.

Since he had never before set foot inside the animal market and had no idea how to bid for an animal, someone had advised him that it was dangerous to fidget if you were an onlooker, since the slightest nuance of movement could be taken by the auctioneer, as a signal of intent to buy. A nervous twitch of an eyebrow could effectively place a bid for a great deal of money to buy a creature you do not wish to purchase. So with much trepidation, Giles, approached the entrance to the market. He watched the regular farmers and tried to take on some of their experience. He did not hold back asking questions. He needed to learn.

Two frisky brown and white heifers were brought into the ring. They looked identical with their chestnut red bodies and beautiful white faces. They had the most doleful eyes with flamboyantly long eyelashes. Giles stood to one side to watch the spectacle unfold in front of him. The air held tight with anticipation. Farmers crushed up against one another, craning their necks to better see. Then the bidding began. The auctioneer gabbled words at high speed and Giles did not understand a single word. Each speedy phrase was interjected by a curious hiccup sound, which Giles found comedic yet everyone else seemed oblivious to the ridiculous noise. The process was brisk and Giles could barely keep up with what was happening. He caught sight of some of the bidders each with their own particular signal to offer a bid. A slight lift of a finger, a nod, a nudge of an elbow. These young cows were led by a young chap, sporting a ragged jacket, flat cap and stick in hand to flick the young cows' backsides, keeping them in line. He made sounds to the animals, which Giles had never before heard. It was like a special language communicating to the beasts what he wanted them to do. These were pretty creatures, Giles thought. No sooner than they were in the ring than the frantic bidding was over and they were led out, having been purchased.

People shuffled about swapping places, some leaving and some moving forward. Giles moved inwards towards the centre of the arena. The next ones came in. Black this time. Two bulls. Huge beasts. There seemed to be a great deal of interest in these. The crowd surged forward a little further. Bidding seemed more frenetic this time and longer. Finally the auctioneer's gavel was slapped down and this seemed to indicate a conclusion to the bidding.

It had not, until that moment, occurred to Giles, that this was a place for men. It was only when his eyes settled on a particular face that he realized he was looking at a beautiful young girl. He instinctively looked around to verify for himself, that she was in fact, the only female he could see and considered how brave she was to be there. He was transfixed by her beauty. Her long black hair, curled slightly about her sweet young face and although she did not exactly smile, her eyes seemed to sparkle with excitement as she concentrated on the small flock of sheep in front of her. She held in her hand a rolled up piece of paper, which she occasionally used to signal her bid to the auctioneer. She seemed keen to buy these creatures. Excitement seemed to shine from her face. Her mouth impassive, yet seductive. She licked her lips. He glanced towards the back of the arena, which was now full, then back again, to the girl. She was alluring. Captivating. Bidding was, as before, rapid but short. She was not successful and remained in her place, quickly referring to the rolled up piece of paper in her surprisingly delicate hands. Again, onlookers shifted positions. Giles lost sight of her.

Next up, came a fine beast of a male sheep. Excitement in the outer arena bubbled. There was quite a bit of jostling for position and squeezing in around the barricade. Then, a sudden quiet whilst an introduction was made. Giles was not skilled enough to interpret all that was said but it was plain that this was an important sale. This creature certainly deserved attention as it was led around the arena, as though he thought himself the proudest ram in the world. He was tethered by a rope around his neck and occasionally stopped and turned so the viewers could appreciate his every side. The bidding was on-going, fast and furious. Giles had never seen such a huge tup and wondered what sort of money he would sell for. It was as though this was the sale of the day. At one point the bidding had to stop as an argument flared up between the bidders. Once the two men in question were separated, proceedings recommenced with no less excitement. The bids, seemingly came down to two onlookers. One was a balding older man in front of Giles. The other was someone unseen from further forward in the arena, just out of Giles's vision. Suddenly the gavel was slapped down and the bidding over. A furore of muttering erupted with some jeering and much disappointed grumbling.

Giles looked around to see the girl but it seemed that the crowd had swallowed her up and she had gone. He even wondered if she had been in his imagination! In any case, he decided he had seen enough here. He left the sheds, slowly wandering into the fresher air and headed over to some pens containing an array of ducks, geese, hens and some rather odd looking birds he believed to be turkeys. Trying to decide which to purchase and only then considering how he was going to get them home, his thoughts were suddenly interrupted by a rumpus nearby.

There was an argument building in intensity behind a cart, just to Giles's left. As the voices became raised, he picked out the notes of a female voice. Intrigued, Giles found himself wandering over and as his instinct had suggested, it was between the young woman he had seen earlier and the same balding much older man who had been bidding in front of him just moments earlier. Between them, stood the prize ram, held by the young girl at the end of a piece of rope. The man was attempting to snatch the rope from her tight grip but she stood her ground impressively. In that instant, another man approached. Giles at first thought he was coming to the girl's rescue but was shocked when he spoke to her mockingly and tried himself to release the rope from her hands.

"What would a bit of a wench like you be wanting with a fine beast like this eh little girl? I doubt you'd be able to handle a big chap like this ...so I think we should take him off your hands and we'll look after him for you eh? You give him to me see and I'll throw you a coin or two then you can be off on your way."

The girl held fast to the tup as though her life depended on it, "No I will not! I've paid fair and square for him. Too bad you lost the bid but I am not parting with him now! Move out of my way!!" Her grit and determination made Giles think of his sister and he could easily imagine Nancy May being just as single minded as this young woman! The two men were not for giving up however.

"See here, let go you wench!!" spat the older man. The younger man moved behind the girl and started to try to peel her away from the beast whilst the older man tried to take the rope. Her strong willed resistance was weakening against such powerful male strength. She did not scream or screech but did her best to fight back with lesser strength. Giles could not bear to see such injustice unfold before his eyes and stepped in.

"Hey!!" The shock of the sharp interjection was enough in a split second to draw the attention of the two men and allow the girl to take a faster hold on the rope. Coming up behind the older man, Giles shouldered him out of the way releasing his grip on the rope. In the next moment, he had swung a balled fist straight into the jaw of the younger assailant, throwing him backwards against a wall. Nobody could have been more surprised at his wilful strength, than Giles himself. Perhaps it was the months of pent up anger, imagining he could do just that to the gypsy who took Nancy May but wherever the strength had come from, it was impressive and achieved a moment's grace. Giles gestured for the young girl to move away with her sought after beast, which she did immediately. As suspected the enraged younger man was not ready to give up and spontaneously came back for more, swinging his fist this time. There was a short exchange between the men before a final opportunity for Giles to grab his neck and throw him against a wall, threateningly. Growling between his teeth, Giles spoke just a few words quietly into his ear. Whatever it was, no one else would ever know but it was sufficiently menacing to have him back off. Both men skulked away wordlessly. Giles straightened himself up and turned to find the girl.

He caught sight of her in the near distance, leading the ram away towards some carts and ran after her calling out, "Hello!" He repeated a little louder, "Hello!!" She turned around and paused. "Hello!" he said again a little more softly, along with the biggest smile.

The young woman, returned the beaming smile, "Ah! Hello... Samson!" She added, teasingly. "I suppose I ought to thank you!" A soft laugh from Giles and took the compliment of a referral to the strongest man he could think of.

"I don't need thanks, just to know you are alright?" Catching up with her now, he walked alongside her, just as far as the cart where she stopped.

"Of course I am fine!" she replied as though that was a silly question. "That happens all the time!" she added.

"Really?" he asked.

She looked at him as though he was mad, "Of course it does! I'm a girl – unless you had not noticed! They don't like it when I win a bid. I regularly have to deal with that kind of argument. I only lost once, right at the beginning but it made me tougher! I'm not for giving in!" Once again, he thought of his dear sister and smiled.

"In the beginning?" he questioned.

"I have just started setting up a small holding, so I'm learning on the job. I had not realised how possessive the old men would be! They just don't like it that I'm a woman! What would I know?!"

"You're brave!" Giles offered her the compliment wholeheartedly.

She shook her head and smiled, "No. It's just a case of 'needs must' and anyway, why should it matter if I'm a girl? But I've been rude, Samson!! I should say thank you properly for coming to my aid! I am not used to such kindness! Fancy yourself as a bit of a bruiser eh?" She laughed and he did too.

Giles, without invitation, made a fist of helping her to load the heavy ram into the cart. As they lifted the back gate of the cart, she glanced back at him, "So did you buy today?"

"It's my first time here today. It's all a bit overwhelming. I need more guidance I feel, before I waste my money!" I'll maybe come back next week to buy something." Taking his chance, he added hopefully, "Will you be here then?" She laughed charmingly, seeing where this interest might be going, "Mmm maybe, Samson," his nickname had seemingly stuck!

Not having bought anything with the precious few coins in his pocket, did not disappoint Giles. He had learnt much from his first visit and his head was full of the thoughts of the mystery girl whose name he did not yet know. He was already looking forward to next week with rare anticipation. He would be sure to take a cart to bring home the purchased animals, for he felt sure he would be buying. He would return now to prepare a pen for some ducks and he decided to build a chicken coop ready for some more hens. That, he believed, would keep him busy until next week.

When Giles returned home to Stapley Manor enjoying thoughts of the day's excitement bringing him the best joy in a good while, his light-heartedness was soon dampened as he opened the back kitchen door, to find Peggy in great distress.

She had had the worst of days. Things had gone drastically wrong and it felt so much worse without Giles there.

CHAPTER 13

Nancy May woke to a soporific rocking motion of her restricted bed. Slowly attempting to open her eyes to the daylight, it took moments to retrieve her memory and understand where she was. With a gasp of horror, she sat upright, her head throbbing sickeningly and drool trickling from the corner of her mouth.

"Why are we moving?" she questioned but nobody was there to hear her. Looking up from her hands she could now appreciate the tiny enclosed space she found herself in. She banged on the side of the caravan and shouted "Why are we moving?"... "Stop! Where are we going?!!" Her frantic words came with tears of panic. She screamed again, "Please, STOP!! I want to go home!! Why are we moving? Where are we going?" She threw herself at the door and fought to open it but it would not budge. "Why have you locked me in?" She shrieked. Her legs were threatening to collapse from under her and she sank to the floor fearing the swaying motion might make her sick. "Oh God no!" she whispered ashamedly. Although the memory of last night was still patchy, she already knew full well how she had behaved like some sort of trollop. Her self-loathing was simply too much and her stomach lurched uncontrollably as she vomited into her lap.

Dear Lord she felt abysmal. What had she been drinking? Why had she behaved like that? The shame and embarrassment came in equal parts and accumulated into deep regret. This time she had gone too far. Her father would be furious with her and no doubt beat her to a pulp when he got his hands on her. What was going to become of her? She must find a way to escape and make her way home. She would rather face her father's fury than face whatever future was now in store for her. By the time they reached their next destination, she had again fallen asleep crying.

Manfri finally opened the door and woke her with a jolt. He stood back as the smell of vomit assailed his nostrils. He looked at her in both shock and disgust, "What the...! Get out and get yourself cleaned up. Then clean up this mess. The river is there," he said, stating the obvious as he pointed vaguely behind him, "and you can clean your clothes while you are there. I'll find some more from my friend's wife. There's plenty of us here to keep our eyes on you, so don't you have any thoughts of running off!"

"Where are we?" She asked him weakly.

"Malvern" he replied vaguely and without hesitation, as though that really had no bearing on anything right now. His response had no real impact on Nancy May as she was still so far from home, he might as well have said Timbuktu! She was feeling so unbelievably unwell and so sorry for herself, that she simply followed his instructions and wearily made her way to the nearby river. There was a clutch of older Romani women chatting and scrubbing clothes against some rocks and she walked towards them. They stopped their babble and watched her sit beside them with incredulity.

One asked, "So your Manfri's secret then eh?" The women laughed.

Another jibbed as an aside to the others, "He could have done better than her me thinks, scrawny wench!" The women again erupted into laughter although one, who was somewhat younger than the rest, with a ratty dog at her feet, had a distinct irritation about her which if Nancy May had seen, could have taken as jealousy. Nancy May, however, was in no mood for their opinions and began to strip off her stinking outer clothes. It was then that she noticed her lace-trimmed drawers were wet and she felt another surge of heat rushing to her cheeks as she blushed with excruciating embarrassment. Unwelcome tears poured down her forlorn face as she set her mind to getting herself clean. She tentatively dipped herself into the lapping cold waters at the edge of the riverbank then held her breath as she plunged her head into its sparkling shallowness to rinse her hair, flicking it back defiantly as she finished cleaning herself. It served to resurrect a little of her usual spirit and seeing the approach of a woman bringing clothes, she stepped out of the water and rang out her hair.

"Here!" the young woman cast the clothes on the floor in front of Nancy May.

"Thank you" Nancy May said gratefully.

To her surprise, the young woman gave her a half smile in return and said, "You'll be alright you know. I'll help you settle in! My name is Josie."

"No you don't understand!!" replied Nancy May in panic. "I don't want to 'settle in'! I want to go home! ... Will you help me get back home Josie? Please?" she found herself begging.

Josie stepped a little closer, "Your name is Nancy May, is it not? I know you feel like that now but by this time next year you'll feel differently! It gets into your blood, this way of life and by the time you have a choice, you wouldn't want to be anywhere else than here with us!"

Nancy May could barely believe her ears. "No! I want to go home now! I will escape you know!" She was still mentally catching up on Josie's words, "What do you mean by this time next year?"

"We keep moving on after every fair but we go back the same way each year. We'll be back to Evesham this time next year. You'll see!"

Nancy May fought against every word in disbelief, "No!! I don't belong here! My mother will be distraught at my leaving and my brother... he'll try to find me! He won't give up on me!"

"In my experience, he'll try looking for a while and then, yes, he WILL give up on you!"

"No!! No, he will not! You don't know him like I do! He's my twin! He'll keep searching until he finds me!"

Trying again with a natural reassurance, Josie continued, "Look, why don't you think of it as an adventure! You might be homesick for a few weeks but it will pass. You'll adapt and who knows – you may even learn to love this way of life" Try it!!"

Nancy May flopped to the floor shaking her head in disbelief and crying. "Come" encouraged Josie. "I'll show you how things around here work." Nancy May felt slightly comforted by the kindness of Josie and was cajoled enough into pulling herself together, at least for the moment. She reluctantly dressed and followed her back to camp.

Josie fed her some breakfast. They were lucky to have such luxury today, as usually there was nothing more than a bowl of gruel for their morning feed but today, as they were in Gloucester, they had a connection with a bakery, where some of the men went each year to repair the ovens and spruce up the baking tins until they shone bright again. In return they were given bread for each day that they were in the area.

Nancy May did not think she was hungry but as soon as she reluctantly bit into the still warm loaf, she realized how good it was to have food in front of her. She had a jug of warm milk from a tin container over the fire and began to feel so much more like herself.

She was just beginning to feel better when Manfri stepped close to her, seemingly out of nowhere. "Feeling better?" He asked kindly.

"Yes I am thank you but that doesn't mean I'm happy at all! I am angry and I've told you, I want to go home!"

Looking down at her from his tall height, he smirked a little, "Well, you should have thought about that last night when you...." He looked around and remembered he was within earshot of others.

"Why did you take me away?" she asked earnestly.

He looked at her agog. "Take you away? Ha!!" He laughed.

"Yes, you've kidnapped me and I want to know why!"

He was fully laughing now at this seemingly hilarious accusation. "You kidnapped yourself!!" He was finding this hilarious! "Has anyone ever told you how entertaining you are?!"

With all the feistiness she could muster, she stood up and took an angry swipe at him. Of course she did! Whenever did she allow anyone to laugh at her?

He caught her arm effortlessly mid air. "I wouldn't try that again dear girl, if I were you! You won't win, you know!" Nancy May tried again with her other hand. Again, he blocked her effort. He held her close, trapped between both his strong arms, yet his grip although constricting, was not cruel. She looked directly into his black eyes and ignored a frisson of something, which passed between them and realized her attempt to physically get the better of him was futile.

"You captured me and I want you to take me back! My brother will be looking for me!"

He took her by the hand and led her to a nearby grassy slope. She did not resist. Without force, he suggested she sat next to him, which she did without fuss.

"You seem to remember last night quite differently to the events I recall!" he began. "Shall we go through this together?" He smiled and she didn't know if she wanted to hear what he had to say, because in truth, she knew her memory was considerably fuzzy. She shrugged her shoulders in agreement. He smiled again. He had a beguiling smile, she fleetingly thought, then dropped her eyes for fear he could read her mind.

"You hurt your ankle. At least you acted as though you had – but you hadn't really, had you?" He paused and raised his eyebrows in question. Again, she shrugged, knowing he was absolutely right. "You even fooled your brother too didn't you?" He did not expect an answer. He knew he was right! Nancy May was inwardly cringing. You should never try to dupe a gypsy, you know! We have ways of working things out, quicker than most! And I have to tell you – we don't like being taken for fools, because that we are not!!"

Nancy May swallowed her pride. "I'm sorry for that" she replied. "Perhaps I got a little carried away with myself!"

He laughed heartily at this, "Oh, you certainly did that alright!!"

Nancy May immediately regretted her apology. "What's that supposed to mean?" she snapped.

"As pretty as you are, my little temptress, you deserved to be taught a lesson! You wanted my attention, so I thought it only right to give it to you in bucket loads! To begin with you were rather out of your depth but with a little persuasion you got the hang of things... " Teasingly, he added, "In fact, you REALLY got the hang of things!!"

She looked at him in horror. "Oh, my life! What do you mean? What did I do?"

"Let's just say you were quite amorous!"

Her head fell into her hands with absolute shame but just as quickly he returned her glance to him, "You don't mean I ... we...?" she couldn't bring herself to finish her sentence.

"I know gypsies have a bad reputation for all sorts of things we are accused of but I can assure you that our code of conduct is firm. No matter how you might tempt me, my little one, I would never pursue you in that regard. Especially not when you had had a belly full of ale!"

Still confused and upset, she retorted, "But you still took me away! You kidnapped me, for heaven's sake!"

He did not like to still be accused of this and thought she deserved to know the entire truth. "You do remember your brother coming back for you, don't you?"

"He did?" she was taken by surprise that she could not remember this.

"Your mother too!" he added an extra punch of guilt.

"My mother?..." Oh her poor mother – what she must have put her through! She must have been so very worried and upset. "Well, why didn't you tell her where I was? You should have sent me home with them!"

"I don't think you would have wished your mother to see you in that state! You had your head in a bucket by that time and no legs worthy of walking on. You begged me not to let them know you were there!"

"I don't believe you!" she snapped back.

"Well, there are plenty of folk here who would testify to my telling the truth!" he reminded her.

"Well you would say that! You're all on the same side. Of course they would all agree with your story. You're all in it together!" Her voice became more panicked.

Giving a deep sigh of frustration, he gritted his teeth before he began again.

"At first, I was happy to go along with your attempts to attract my attention and to be honest I thought you might have shown me a bit of fun, so I shrugged off your lapdog brother and yes, it's true, over the generations, we gypsies do back up each other because we've had to stick together. We are a close knit bunch; a big family. So, of course they would see off any unwanted intruders, just as they did with your brother and mother."

Before she could interrupt, he continued, "Soon after they were 'encouraged to leave' however, you realised you were out of your depth with your game and I suppose I was annoyed at your withdrawal, so I decided you needed to be taught a lesson. You're a sweet girl but you went too far teasing and one day that will get you into real trouble if nobody makes you understand that behaviour like that, is foolish. I admit I encouraged you to drink and that was wrong but I did try to stop your advances and suggested it was time for you to walk home. You insisted you stay with me in the vargo. Ha! I didn't think that was a good idea! I am not so unscrupulous! Suddenly the alcohol had got the better of you and you passed out. I laid you outside with a rug over you, alongside the caravan for shelter, to let you come to your senses and I went to bed. I was sure you would wake in your own time and make your way home."

The fact that he had covered her up, touched Nancy May. Nobody, least of all a stranger, had ever looked after her in that way. Her throat constricted just a little.

Manfri continued to explain his perspective. "We all planned to be up at sunrise and on our way, as we always do. It wasn't quite daylight when I started to pack away, so I can only presume that as we achieved our morning river ablutions and prepared the horses, you must have crawled back into the vardo. I found the discarded rug – and no you! So, of course I presumed you had come to your senses and crawled home in disgrace! Naturally, I locked up the vardo before we set off. I genuinely didn't know you were in there."

Nancy May vaguely now recalled feeling the early morning chill and with a shiver deciding to go inside the caravan, where she could warm up, just for a few moments. She must have fallen asleep. Feeling stupid for this alone, she still did not excuse Manfri for kidnapping her. "But you must have heard me bashing on the walls of the caravan??"

He reflected on the journey. "Ah, that was you?" He smiled at the awkward realisation. His mind drifted back to the instant when he thought he heard a noise. "I'm sorry about that! We were well on our way, passing through Worcester, when I thought I heard banging, though to be fair, I did not hear your voice. We were trying to stay in convoy. It was market day and there was a great deal of clatter around the stalls and carts with people shouting. I assumed it was an irate person trying to get by, slamming a fist into the vardo. We get a lot of that - people irritated by us. Our route was constantly challenged and I had to keep focused on finding my way through the hubbub of chaos and keep the troupe together. I wasn't even sure the noise was coming from behind me! By the time we were through the pandemonium of the town, the noise had ceased, so I just assumed it was my imagination. You must have fallen asleep again" Finally he confirmed convincingly, "I am not a kidnapper!"

She listened intently. Some of what he said triggered memories and although she could not remember it all, she knew in her heart, he was telling the truth. She felt utterly disgusted with herself. 'Shameful' didn't come close to describing her inner abhorrence. Yet, he had encouraged her to drink alcohol and 'teach her a lesson', so in her book, he was still not without blame!

She looked up at him, "So now what?

Here she was, apparently in Malvern, many miles from home. Her mother and brother would be distraught at her disappearance. Then, the very worst of all thoughts occurred to her yet again: Her father! Oh dear Lord! He could possibly kill her for this latest prank! She thought on this for a moment and decided that 'killing her' was a worrying and realistic consideration! She knew only too well of what he was capable! However, she believed that she might be spared this extreme punishment but knew unequivocally, that he most definitely would beat her and quite probably, throw her out of the family home. Perhaps she would be better off staying with the band of gypsies?

She looked around her, hopeful of some kind of divine intervention. A sign maybe. What was she to do? All that occurred to her was that it was going dark. She could not start to walk home now!! The troupe had already set up in readiness for another fair and Manfri would have to go and take part. She had little choice but to stay with them rather than run away into heaven knows what kind of danger but that was up to them. Would they let her stay with them for one more night?

"Will you take me back home tomorrow?" she asked Manfri hopefully.

"You know I cannot do that, Nancy May!" Her tummy flipped to hear him say her name. She didn't even remember telling him.

"But surely you could take me back and then catch up with the troupe? They will be here for days will they not?"

"They depend on me here. You don't understand what you are asking of me!"

"Then can I stay with you tonight? I am too afraid to set off walking home at this time of the night and..."

"I will absolutely not allow you to walk home in the dark! That is a ludicrous idea! Whatever are you thinking about!"

"Well, I have to get home somehow and sometime! If I can stay here overnight, I can be gone by first light."

Manfri didn't much like the idea of her plan in many respects but he had no better ideas for the moment. With a deep sigh, he offered his considered reply, "You can stay safe in my vardo – just for tonight, mind! I will be working at the fair and will check on you when I've finished. I'll sleep outside, don't worry."

It wasn't a perfect scenario but it was the best option available and she was surprisingly grateful. Tomorrow she would begin to walk home and take her chances on any kind of danger, which could befall her, either en route or on arrival back home.

They walked back to the circle of colourful wagons in silence and he made sure she had food and water before he left her.

Rain was setting in and Nancy May was grateful for the cosy shelter, food and water.

The fair finished early that night for the increasingly heavy rain had reduced numbers of visitors significantly. Manfri arrived back at the vardo, soaking wet. His plan to sleep outside seemed ridiculous, especially with the last clap of thunder. Even the front bench was soaked without any cover, making that option for sleep, out of the question. Without further concern, he unlatched the green wooden door and climbed inside his vardo. Nancy May had kept the tiny stove burning, so it was welcomingly warm inside and his clothes immediately began to steam.

Half lying on the bed, facing the door, Nancy May flinched with embarrassment to have Manfri's unexpected presence in such close proximity. Not knowing how to react to such an unpredicted intrusion to the tiny space, she immediately feigned sleep, secretly permitting her a private moment to lay back and luxuriate in his every movement. Shocked at herself, she allowed her barely opened eyes to soak up the vision of his black curly hair plastered to his head with raindrops running down his handsome, tanned face and down his neck, disappearing beyond his collar. His saturated shirt clinging wet to his strong torso, enhanced every ripple of muscle across his back as he bent to add another log to the stove. Without thought or inhibition, he ripped off his white shirt, revealing his glistening body and she became entranced by the sound of his steady breathing, as he removed his wet trousers. Knowing she should not be looking, she still could not avert her eyes. A curious, unaccustomed, warm ache permeated her lower abdomen as she watched him take a ragged piece of cloth to ruffle dry the worst of his wet hair. Without further hesitation, he gathered a blanket around him and lay on the bench at the end of the caravan. Almost immediately, he was asleep and his breathing steadied into a calming rhythm. Nancy May however, lay awake for hours.

CHAPTER 14

Peggy could not wait to tell Giles all about her day from hell with Albert, whilst Giles was at market. She had been hanging out some washing on the line in the yard and taken five minutes to sit in the autumn sunshine before returning to the house. Deciding to make herself a drink, she called to see if Albert would also like one. There was no answer and at first she assumed he had fallen asleep in his chair, which he often did. She went through to the other room where he liked to sit in his armchair in the bay window but the chair was empty. Looking from room to room, she became a little agitated, calling out for him with still no reply. Wondering if he had maybe gone outside for some air, she checked around the back of the house and a sense of panic overwhelmed her. Calling louder and hurrying her pace, she darted about looking here and there. The garden was vast and becoming overgrown with no one to tend it. She noticed that the long grass had been disturbed in one direction and so she followed the barely visible path, which had been recently trodden. She heard his voice call out but could not decipher his words.

Calling him again he shouted back, "Stop there!" Peggy instinctively stopped in her tracks.

His voice came again, "I know you're there! Come out!"

Peggy responded, calling back to him, "Albert, it's only me! Where are you?" She could hear him mumbling as he sometimes did. She tiptoed forward towards the sound of his voice. He was in the walled garden. She entered slowly through the red brick archway. She instantly heard the sickening click of a rifle engaging. "Dear God" She prayed out aloud. "Albert, it's me, Peggy. What are you doing?" she added hesitantly, her heart racing inside her chest. Seeing a movement behind some overgrown bushes, she bravely stood her ground. "Albert, it's me. Look! I'm here! Nobody else is here, Albert! Just me!" Albert stood tall and to her utter horror, he was pointing the rifle towards Peggy. Her heart hammering, she tried to reason with him and spoke softly, "Albert, It's me, Peggy. What are you doing? Put the gun down. There's nobody else here. Just me."

Shouting now as he jabbed the point of the gun towards Peggy, "What are you thieving? Hey? What's in the bag?" Peggy calmly replied, "Nothing Albert. Nothing. Look, see, I don't have a bag!"

Exasperated, Albert took a couple of steps towards his wife. He had a strange dream-like look about him. It frightened Peggy. "You've hidden it! Where have you put it?" Was it a chicken, or a rabbit, 'eh? I'll find it you know! You've been stealing from Mr. Carter. Nobody steals from this estate. Nobody gets past me! Drop the bag on the floor! NOW!"

Peggy didn't like this one bit. She was scared. His mind had obviously returned to his job as gamekeeper and his imagination might take him to actually use the gun. She had known that Albert's rifle was still in the store room from when he worked there, presuming that during the rapid exit of Elizabeth's staff, it had been overlooked but she had not for one moment considered that he might take it to use it. Intuitively, she decided the safest way to deal with this was to play along with his imagination. Picking up an imaginary bag off the floor, she mimicked its weight. "Yes Sir. I'm sorry Sir." She placed the invisible bag in front of her feet and stepped backwards.

"Right now clear off before I put a bullet through you. Go and blag from somewhere else but don't even try to come back here or..." He pointed the gun to the clouds and pulled the trigger. The sound made Peggy flinch tight with horror, as he continued his threat, "I warn you, the next one will be through your head."

Peggy exited quickly and hid behind the stone wall for a moment or two, her heart banging rapidly. She heard him talking to himself and then disengage the rifle. Waiting a few minutes longer, she called to her husband again and walked slowly towards him, doing her best to present a smile. Hoping her risky plan would work, "Hello Albert are you coming in now?" I saw someone running away? You did a good job of getting rid of them!"

Albert however, seemed completely confused now and flopped to the floor discarding the rifle to one side, as though the past few minutes had not happened. He did not even seem to hear her words but looked up at her with child like eyes. "Hello Mam" he smiled.

By the time Giles returned, Albert was in his bedroom asleep in a chair.

Hearing his mother's story and seeing her utter despair and consternation, Giles worried deeply for her safety. This could not go on! Imperatively, he took charge of the rifle and hid it upstairs securely, where his father could not access it. Then, over a hot drink, he tried to calm his mother's shattered nerves, as they sat and chatted. He suggested that from hereon in, if he planned not to be in or around the vicinity of the house, they should ensure that Albert was secured in his room. How they did this, was another matter but it was the only way Giles could feel reassured to leave his mother alone with him. He promised however, that he would not leave her without knowing she was safe.

Such a plan sounded easy but it proved far from it. On each occasion, it depended on Albert's mood as to how they could cajole him into cooperating. The easiest moments were those when Albert regressed to childhood and could be easily persuaded to go to his room to play with his toy. His was the only upstairs door they could lock. In his aggressive moments, they had to bide their time and leave him be, giving him space to cool off. Other times, it came down to tricking him into going into the parlour, which was the only other door they could successfully barricade. This was usually successful with the temptation of food or alcohol. Of course, these interludes were never of certain duration and they discovered that part way through any certain plan, Albert could suddenly turn and take on another personality.

Giles was out in the yard one day, building chicken coops when a thought occurred to him but it was a long shot and risky. His aunt Mabel and uncle Fred had been struggling in so many ways over the past few years. Fred had become reclusive following the sad loss of a good friend of his, some years ago. At the time, he couldn't speak or eat for weeks and became a shadow of his former self. Giles knew no more than Fred's friend had been involved in a shooting accident at work and his death had come as a great shock to uncle Fred. Aunt Mabel had coped with his unusual grief for years and had done her best to put food on the table since Fred was rarely up to earning money. Mabel was finding his depression difficult to cope with and she herself sank into despair. He wondered if allowing them to come live at Stapley Manor would be an all round solution. The sisters could offer each other mutual support and perhaps give uncle Fred a new purpose in life with helping out around the place. Knowing help was around for his mother, should there be an incident of any sort, would reassure him. The problem would be how to do this without incurring his father's wrath or increasing his difficult behaviour. The house was large enough to easily accommodate them and he felt sure he could find a way to make it work.

Peggy agreed to the idea, Mabel and Fred jumped at the chance to live in the big house. Albert's confusion was in this instance convenient, as fortunately he did not recognize them (as sometimes happened with Peggy and Giles themselves) and so they became accepted as hired help, which appealed to Albert's snobbery.

Giles now felt more relaxed about spending the day away from his mother. In fact, he was positively excited to be going to the farmer's market but that motivation was not just about buying animals! All week he had been thinking about the shepherdess and hoping that she would be good to her word and be at the market today. Despite carrying an awkward shaped wire crate in which he hoped to bring home some more birds, there was a lively spring in his step and he seemed to be in Evesham in no time at all. A number of wagons overtook him. Some bounced lightly along the rugged road, rattling their way past him, he assumed empty, whilst others drove slower with their heavy loads ready to sell.

Over the past week, he had considered how he might start to create a little business and concluded that he was not prepared yet to buy anything bigger than birds. For one thing, he could not afford a means of carriage to transport them home! Plus, he needed to learn more yet before he took anything bigger into his care. As last time, he approached the market and became part of the whole confusion of bustling activity. He loved the hubbub of the atmosphere and felt more confident to perhaps have a go at bidding this time. The event was again frenetic and exciting and after watching the sales of some of the bigger animals, he felt he was beginning to learn a little about what to look for in a beast. He kept his ears open, listening in to conversations between farmers and trying to absorb their experienced comments. By the end of the morning, he had been successful in purchasing four ducks, which the seller had fitted expertly for him into his wired cage. Giles had a euphoric sense of pride and achievement as he began his walk towards the exit of the market, amongst the vibrant pandemonium around him. Reaching as far as the bridge, and admiring his purchases, he reflected on his morning with a little disappointment that he had not seen the beautiful girl. With a slightly downcast shrug, he thought, "Perhaps next time!"

The following week, he found himself walking the same route, with his wire basket. This time however, he proudly took with him some eggs to sell: An assortment of hen and duck eggs. Even if these raised a few coins, they would be put to good use. His aim was to use some more of his father's money to increase the number of birds in his collection. Following the same routine as last time, he visited the animal sales and realized he was beginning to get the hang of what to look for in a good beast, be it sheep or cattle. He started testing himself. Half a dozen sheep were brought into the arena to be paraded. He knew, that if he were intending buying, he would of course have looked closely at them first in their pens but looking from a distance, he found himself analysing each animal – did it have a straight back? That would be preferable. Was it bow legged? It should not be so! Were the hooves clean and healthy? And the udder? No scabbing? He felt so proud of himself!! He really had learnt quite a lot! Next for sale were two beautiful calves. He needed to listen to what was being said about them, so he could learn more. They both seemed healthy enough to Giles with a nice dry shiny coat but the men standing around him did not seem to rate these two young beasts. Giles had to listen in hard to what they were saying above as the noise of the bidding was raising.

"Nay I looked at 'em before and that'un was layin' on his own like, so I didn't care for the look of 'him. I can see now he's got a bit of a big belly on him. I wouldn't touch 'im like." The other man agreed. Giles had learnt a useful lesson.

There were a few stalls for selling cheeses and milk and eggs and these seemed to be doing a busy trade. He was keen to try to get a few coins for the eggs he'd brought. Giles had nothing to lose, except for a few eggs and a bit of pride if he failed. So, not having much to sell, he thought he would simply stand to one side and mimic their techniques. Seeing a half broken wooden box on the floor, he placed it in front of him and rested his cap upon it, into which he reverently laid the eggs.

Taking a deep breath and trying to look confident, he called out, "Eggs for sale! …Lovely fresh eggs for sale! …Come and buy!!" People came and went and passed him by. He continued to call out. "Freshly laid this morning!" he lied, to pull attention, though it did not work. Suddenly he found himself shouting, "Cheaper than anywhere else!" and there were a few who turned their heads towards him.

"How much?' someone shouted. "If you buy four, I'll give you one free!" he replied. "I'll have them all", came another voice he instantly recognized.

"Hello Samson!" she said beaming a smile as bright as a summer's day.

"Hello!" he stammered a reply. Feeling silly to be caught doing a bad job of selling, he flushed red.

"I think I owe you for your help a couple of weeks ago, Samson." She laughed. "We need some eggs anyway. My mother will be delighted!"

Giles didn't know if he was more excited to have sold the eggs or to be standing in front of this beautiful girl again and have her strike up a conversation with him. She threw some coins into the hat he had rested the eggs in and he clumsily thanked her for her generosity.

"Are you buying today?" she asked with genuine interest.

"I hope to be!" He replied, nodding towards the poultry area.

"Want some company?" she offered, taking him by surprise. Although totally taken aback, he tried not to show his excitement too much and tried to be casual.

So, shrugging his shoulders as though he was not bothered if she came with him or not, he answered glibly, "Yes, of course, if you want to..." She smiled, knowingly.

Today, there was quite an assortment of birds. What a noise they made! He had wondered whether to buy a cockerel. This seemed to make good sense to him and started scanning the pens to find one. However, they came across something, which attracted the attention of them both. A wooden box of fluffy downed chicks chirruped busily in the early autumn morning sunshine. Their soft plumage of speckled shades of brown, was so alluringly tactile. Another box had similar birds but obviously a little older and bigger. Giles had no idea what these were but guessed they were perhaps young ducklings. The young woman watched Giles and correctly assessed his ignorance.

Sensitively, not wishing to belittle his integrity, she commented, "What sweet young turkeys these are, Samson. They look good and healthy too. See how their plumage is fluffy and clean and they seem so alert too. Might you be interested in these? You will need a bigger space for them to run about than your chickens. Have you got a small field you can fence off, perhaps?"

He nodded suggesting that would not be a problem. She bent down to pick one up, trapping their feet between her fingers expertly. Having had them identified, Giles thought he might wish to bid for some of these. He reckoned if he could buy say half a dozen of these, he could fatten them up and sell them at a profit but keep just one back for the Christmas table. His mam would like that! The lovely girl seemed to know what she was looking for and Giles found the confidence to admit to his own lack of knowledge and ask her opinion on choosing which ones to buy. She showed him how to look at the chest feathers of the slightly bigger birds and pointed out the feathers on the lower part of the male's chest, had black tips. Impressed with her knowledge, they chose between them, enough chicks to sensibly fill the cage. Giles had asked the price and naively was ready to accept, only being able to afford but a few but the girl stepped in and bargained with the seller, managing to almost double the quantity for the same price. Giles was astonished at her know-how and self-assurance and was very grateful for her intervention in gaining a significantly better deal. Relying upon the seller to fit them in the basket for him, with such expert handling, Giles admired such skill and thought how he could never manage the wriggling birds as adeptly as he did. Making the most ridiculous of all bird noises, they were now packed into the crate and Giles needed to set off home.

The two new friends walked back towards where her cart was left standing at the gate to the market. Giles carried the wire basket and they chatted amicably as they went, as though they had known each other for some time. Listening to Giles's personal story about needing to find work to keep his family from starving, she suddenly had a thought. In the most spontaneous way, the words were out of her mouth without any real consideration.

"This may not be much but as it happens I am looking for a 'Samson' to help out now and then in my smallholding. There are fences to be mended, a barn to rebuild and sometimes I need helping out with the animals. The job is yours if you want it." She flashed him a smile and quickly added, "It might not be what you want and I can't pay much but there will be a few coppers in it and you might learn a few things along the way to help you with starting your little farm."

He was bowled over by the surprise of her offer and wanted immediately to accept but something pulled him back from being too swift. "It sounds perfect" he stalled, "but where do you live?"

"Harvington" she replied.

His eyes were suddenly crestfallen, as he had to make the hardest of decisions to turn down her offer. "I so wish I could" he began, "but it's just not possible! I live in Broadway!" It's simply too far, as I have to walk!" They continued walking in thoughtful silence until they reached her cart.

"Well maybe there is a solution!" He looked at her questioningly, without any idea what that might be. "Meet me here next week and I'll see what I can do." With that parting comment, she got up on the cart and snapped the reins to signal to the horses to pull away. He watched her go off into the distance and had the most extraordinary mix of feelings, many of which he did not recognize.

The week could not pass quickly enough for Giles. Peggy saw something about her son which had transformed his demeanour. He had returned from market that day, with a certain excitement about him. When she tried to probe, he was very reluctant to talk, which was not at all like his usual self. He was non-committal about the events at the market but she knew something had passed for him to seem so happy. She knew better, though, than to push him further. Digressing from her intrigue, he showed her the young turkeys and explained his plan. Peggy was impressed and very proud of his efforts and apparent success at market. For the rest of the week, alongside his regular work to help his mother in the house, Giles took great care of his birds, as instructed by the seller and with his new friend's guidance. He needed to nurture them all until he could sell them for a profit, not just to maximize on the sparse coins they had but to impress the young girl. Until he had heard her next proposition, he would play his cards close to his chest and not divulge his excitement to his mother.

He had only been at market a half hour or so, when he felt a tap on his shoulder. A familiar wide smile greeted him as he turned around. "Hello!" came her sweet voice simultaneously.

His heart flipped a little in response. "Hello... how are you?" he beamed back at the beautiful girl.

"I have some good news!" she said, jumping up and down on the spot. "But first, let's go see what we can buy!"

They spent some time together perusing the beasts, which were on offer for sale today and the shepherdess chose a fine bullock. There was fierce bidding for this lovely young bull but with a final bid, she succeeded in winning. With enormous excitement the two new friends went to collect him and load him into her cart. Giles had already proudly sold some eggs and collected his latest purchase of a cockerel. Curious beyond words he waited patiently for her to return to the subject she had promised and discover what was the 'good news' she wished to share.

"Hop in!" she invited him and she began to roll the cart forward with expertise. Surprised at the casual invitation, he settled as comfortably as was possible on the hard bench and looked at her in anticipation.

"Can you drive a cart?" she asked unexpectedly.

"Of course!" he exaggerated. It was true that Giles had driven one before but he was hardly proficient, though he would never admit this to her and was certainly not expecting what happened next!

"Swap seats then!" she took him by surprise.

The exchange was done before he could panic and took the reins more easily than he anticipated. They jogged along in quiet ease for some time.

Eventually, The beautiful young girl spoke again, "How about, if you take me home and we unload the bullock and settle him in?" Samson readily agreed.

She continued, "Then, you can ride Spirit back to Broadway and come back on Monday to start work for me? You can borrow Spirit each weekend to get you home and back. Mother said she will work out some accommodation for you but it'll be basic mind!" she added in a very business-like manner. I would expect you to put your hand to whatever work needs doing. It seems I need the help and maybe you could use the experience and some coins?" Without much of a pause for breath, "Have you somewhere to stable Spirit?" she added, nodding towards the horse's mane.

"I would be honoured to look after him! I think that plan would work very well!!

"Do you accept my offer then?"

"I accept your offer gladly!" he replied. They whooped in celebration and shook hands across the bench to seal the deal. "Very good, Samson, we are agreed!"

"I don't even know your name!" he countered.

Throwing her hair back seductively over her shoulders, she replied, "You can call me Ma'am!!" They laughed!

CHAPTER 15

Elizabeth could never think to take herself another husband, for the love of her life had gone forever and no other could come close to making her as happy, as her time with Henry, her beloved soul mate. Of course, both she and Elise missed Stapley Manor a great deal as the home where Elise was brought up and where Elizabeth and Henry had spent many happy years together. The place was steeped in wonderful memories for her to cherish but she was beginning to find herself able to let go of the past and just be comfortable, living day to day. Perhaps one day she would find it in herself to forgive him for leaving her.

Elizabeth often had time to reflect upon their life together and whilst most of it could be described as idyllic, there was that interlude of sadness and betrayal. She considered the concept of betrayal, to be on both parts. Yes, it was true that Henry had once been unfaithful, with life changing consequences but she had come to consider herself guilty too for pushing him away both physically and emotionally. She had not been able to deal with her own disappointment of not conceiving a child and punished herself for disappointing Henry, month on month. She felt inadequate and failing in her duty as a wife to provide an heir but it was more than that, she wanted that certain proof of their love for each other which they were unable to evidence to the world. This may have seemed illogical to those dearest to her but it was of immense meaning to her. At least Henry's indiscretion, had a positive outcome with the arrival of their now beautiful daughter, Elise, whom they had both loved more than life itself.

Elizabeth also had mountains of time now to wonder about Elise's birth mother. She still wondered who she was and where she was now. How did they meet? Had she loved her husband or was their attraction simply physical? Henry had remained throughout his life, true to his adamant decision in the beginning that he would never divulge the woman's identity. As frustrating as that was for Elizabeth, she respected and loved all that Henry stood for – his discretion, his determination to honour her privacy and to keep her safe, none of which was any great surprise to her. She wished she could tell this woman now, how grateful they were for her gift of a child and that they had given Elise the best that was possible, whether it be in her education, her home comforts or with more love than she believed she could possibly find anywhere else. One thing still did hang worryingly in her mind and that was Henry's comment that if her husband had found out about the baby, he would kill her, then him. There was a certainty about the way he said this. It was literal. Henry could not have been a more gentle soul and as a husband, his kindness was exemplary. Never would he have lifted a hand to her. Never had he threatened her. To live in fear of being beaten or abused in any way, was almost unthinkable to Elizabeth and she wondered if this woman had led such a life. She pitied her, if this was so.

Elise, however, hated boredom. During her teenage years, she pleaded with her mother that she might take control of the pastures around their cottage and turn them into farm land. Her mother thought she had lost her mind! Whilst most girls of her age and wealth would think of nothing else but finding a handsome, well-to-do husband or buying pretty ribbons and gowns, her daughter was never happier than taking care of animals and coming home covered in mud and smelling of rural countryside. So for the last four years, she had conscientiously bought and sold a number of sheep and also cattle, gradually increasing her herd. She had learnt to help them birth, brought them in from the cold during the worst of the winter months and market traded them to build up funds. She faced ridicule from neighbouring farmers and land owners, who thought it ridiculous that a young girl should try to compete, even in a small way. Elise had more about her than to let their jibes penetrate her confidence and quietly she held her own, in facing their mockery and taunting. Her mother could not have been more inspired by her efforts and realising she was proving her determination, she gave Elise a small allowance, to support her keen efforts. She grew really proud of her daughter's endeavours to develop what was becoming a successful business. To cope with increasing need, Elise had, with her mother's approval, taken on hired help to repair one of the barns and she also depended on this help, for driving the animals to or from market. She had found a young man, who seemed to be an honest, courageous, kind sort and desperate for work. It seemed he lived in Broadway village and was as keen as any other she might employ. Their chance meeting seemed like God's will that he had come into her life. He had some carpentry skills and so the building of the barns would be within his capability and he seemed a pleasant soul, grateful and willing to work hard. Besides, he was good to look at!

Over the following months, Elise took the small business she had created, from strength to strength. With the help of this hired help, the barn was fully repaired and secured for Elise's growing cattle herd and in the fields she had a small herd of sheep which she hoped would produce lambs come the spring. Her efforts to grow vegetables was producing sufficient quantities to sell at market in Evesham at a small stall on Saturdays and generally she seemed to glow with a sense of wellbeing. Elizabeth watched her with interest. There was a definite connection between her and the young man and she was pleased she had found someone to share her farming passion with but there was more than that to their working relationship. They laughed at the same things and seemed to almost think in the same way. They shared ideas and intuitively worked out solutions to problems with ease. Elizabeth liked the young man and was happy to have him join them at the dinner table. He was courteous and funny and although he didn't speak much of his home life, she got the impression he cared a great deal for his mother. It was not her place to pry but she got the impression that his parents were quite dependent upon him.

Samson never wished to overstep the mark with his new employer. It was a comfortable relationship and he would consider them to be the best of friends, yet he had no real idea what she thought of him. She was so hard to read. He loved being in her company and strived hard to please her, like a child looks to his parents for approval. There was one occasion, when he dreamt about her – well, it was about them! It felt so real - and when he woke, he realized he wished it was real. The memory of the dream hung around him all day like a fairy tale and he could barely look her in the eye for fear she might guess what he was thinking. He swore he blushed when she spoke to him. He wished he could dream the same dream again, over and over.

They would complete their respective jobs in the morning and if they were out in the fields, they would stop work at the same time and sit together to eat their bagging out – whatever had been prepared for them by Elizabeth's kitchen maid. Their chatter was relaxed but even the silences were comfortable. They seemed to laugh all the time. It was never about anything in particular, yet they seemed to share the same sense of amusement.

CHAPTER 16

Significant time had passed before anyone from the solicitor's office, was sent to Wales, to again interview Noah Fielding. It was reported that, sadly, he felt he could add no more to the enquiry, as no paperwork had been uncovered pertaining to Mr. Carter's intent.

Fortuitously however, one further revelation transpired during this interview. It was a throw away comment by Mr. Fielding, which caught the interest of the legal messenger and notes were taken which he felt might help the cause. It was that he believed that he saw someone else present, at the scene of the duel. At the time he dismissed what he had seen and even considered it may have been in his imagination but the fleeting glimpse of a young face in the long grassy slope above them, had later haunted him. It was only when he was helping Mrs. Carter to move from Stapley Manor, that he began to piece together his thoughts about that image, which continued to lurk disturbingly in the back of his mind. The area, where the duel had taken place, was necessarily remote but it transpired that the closest few homes would be along Primrose Lane. He had pondered much on this in the days following the tragic event and he had calculated that the only children nearby would have been Albert Turner's twins. Mrs. Carter had stipulated that she did not wish to encounter the new arrivals at Stapley Manor, so all the transition was carried out by her then staff, with Mr. Fielding as butler, orchestrating timings. There had been an uncomfortable moment for Mr. Fielding, when he had chanced to see Mr. Turner and his son exiting their cottage for the last time. In that moment, Mr. Fielding believed he recognised the face of the young boy, as that of the same one of the child in the grass that fateful morning...

Back in the Cotswolds, hope reared its head and despite many years having passed since Albert Turner and his family took up residence at Stapley Manor, Mr. Foster prayed that the son, still resided there, or if he did not, he could be traced. Failure to close this case had rumbled on embarrassingly long but he was not for giving up without fulfilling the wishes of his deceased client Mr. Carter, according to his last will and testament.

The solicitor's envoy rode up in a carriage, one cold but sunny midmorning, asking for the son of Mr. Albert Turner. Fred answered the door to explain that he did live there but was away working at the present time. A message was left for Giles to present himself at the solicitor's office, as soon as possible. No more detail was given and of course, Peggy worried if it was in connection with their darling missing Nancy May.

During the night, the weather had turned significantly wilder in Malvern. It had rained heavily and incessantly throughout the long hours, with blustery winds and bouts of thunder and lightning. Such a storm would normally have spooked Nancy May, yet here, where she lay, listening to the rain battering the roof and feeling the wind buffeting the sides of the vardo, she had never felt so secure.

Certain irony, that here, she found herself stranded miles from home with no certain way of getting back, removed from her familiar existence and with a man she barely knew. Yet, in some way, she felt safer than she had done in years, without the constant fear of her father's exploding temperament. How could this be? What did this tell her about her life? Had she always felt so insecure within her family? She hated that her mother was so vulnerable to her father's demands and that she took the back of his hand more often than was right. Her bruises were always excused and she knew her mother had spent her life protecting her children. Bless her! Tears trickled down Nancy May's cheeks as she considered what a stoic woman her mother was, to have survived the years of misery she must have endured! Nancy May conceded to herself, that she had never really taken the time to ponder on her upbringing in this way but lying awake in this strange situation, she allowed herself certain truth and clarity of mind, to delve into her deepest conscious thoughts and be honest with her own, uninterrupted reflections.

Admitting to her conscience, that she did not know if she was at risk here or not but cocooned in this tiny wagon, warm and protected from the elements, she felt a greater sense of belonging than she had had at home, for all these years. She lay awake mulling over her strange circumstances, trying to make sense of her confused emotions.

She had always been one for risk. Her adventures had often caught her unawares and ALMOST got her into the worst of dilemmas. Yet somehow, she always managed to just escape trouble by the skin of her teeth. She wondered now, if perhaps, her adventurous spirit was a mechanism to allow her to feel she could 'run away' from that which she hated. A subconscious escapism. Perhaps this latest behaviour was some kind of deep-seated wish to be kidnapped from her life and be taken away from what she hated, even feared. That notion of being 'taken away', removed her from the guilt of wilfully, 'running away'.

Hearing the nearby sploshing of footsteps in puddles, jolted her to the present. Somebody was about already and it was barely daylight. She lifted the fabric at the tiny window to see the dank and dreary day awaiting her. One of the gypsy men was carrying water back to a neighbouring wagon. She sighed. She had not slept at all. She stretched as far as the small bed would allow. On the upside, it had not been a tortuous night. In fact, in the cold light of morning, she had found it to be reassuringly illuminating, since with the dawn of this new day, she seemed to have concluded, that if she was to be true to herself, she did not wish to go back there to Stapley Manor. That said, she found herself feeling deep regret and guilt for considering leaving her mother and knowing her disappearance would be painful for her. Leaving Giles too, would be akin to cutting off her own limb but she hoped he would forgive her for her selfishness, for she knew he would grieve for her absence too. Yet, her mind was clearer now and she had a sense of decisiveness.

Wiping the remnants of tears upon her face, she lifted herself from her bunk feeling resigned. She did not know where the day ahead would take her but this seemed the right time to change her life. She could go anywhere, do anything with just a few coins in her pocket, a heap of courage and a bucket load of determination in her heart.

Distracting her from these focused thoughts, she heard Manfri stir and yawn. "Good morning, my little run away!" he greeted.

Her heart swelled at the gentleness with which he spoke to her but being Nancy May, she contested, "I'm NOT a run away!" Thinking better of her manners, she half smiled and added, "but good morning to you too!"

"Did you sleep through any part of that storm?" He cared enough to ask.

"No... but I had a comfortable night, thank you. I'm glad you took shelter in here – it would have been impossible to sleep outside!"

He laughed at her 'generosity', "Well, I'm glad you approved of me sleeping inside my own vardo!" There was more than a note of sarcasm in his voice.

She was sorry if she had made him angry, "I didn't mean..."

"I know! Forgive me - that was not necessary!" he raised his hand by way of apology and got up from his bench bed to leave the caravan. Nancy May appreciated the privacy and quickly pulled on her day clothes to make her way to wash in the river, in the steady rain. At least the air felt fresh and restorative after the storm.

Manfri came back some time later with warm bread. He heated up some milk on the stove for her and they sat inside the vardo, in comfortable companionship. He advised her that many trees had fallen overnight and he had heard tell that the vast fields that they had driven through the day before, were now badly flooded, as a result of such torrential rain. He recommended that she should not try to walk home today and gave her permission to stay just as long as it took for the roads to be safe again. They would be pitched here for at least a week. Such honest counsel touched her. Manfri looked kindly upon her and said his conscience would not allow him to send her off to walk so many miles across the countryside to return home, when he knew full well that any attempt to make that journey on foot, would be fraught with dangers. Seeing the question yet again in her eyes, he explained kindly once more, that he could not leave the troupe to return her to Broadway. Equally however, he reiterated the offer for her to remain with the travellers for a few more days, until they were due to leave. There was a clumsy agreement for her to share his vardo, which ironically, made her face redden. In other circumstances in society this would of course have been totally unacceptable as an agreement and no doubt, her mother would be shamefully abashed at her acceptance. However, these circumstances seemed to break all rules and since she had got herself into this mess, it was a little late for her to start thinking of propriety! Besides, who would ever know, once she had returned? With no other option available, she was forced to accept Manfri's detached offer for her to remain a while longer. It was agreed that he would share his basic food and in exchange, she would do some work to repay the travelling community for their tolerance. It was an amicable, business-like agreement, for which she was grateful.

Josie was a sweet girl and over the next couple of days, readily helped Nancy May along the way with the routine of camp life. She seemed pleased that Nancy May had had to stay over a few days and the two young women had a natural rapport. Apart from Josie, it was quickly apparent that most of the troupe, were indifferent to Nancy May's presence. They were polite but also private and did not encourage her in dialogue. Some were probably suspicious of her intrusion but would never question Manfri's decision to keep her with him. Josie and Manfri were the only ones who communicated freely with her and accepted her willingly. There was, in addition, only one other, who did not fit into either group. The woman who sat at the riverside on that first day and made it quite clear she was not happy to see this stranger amongst them. It was more than that though! It was annoyance that the newcomer should be seen to come out of Manfri's vardo. Josie had suggested that Nancy May keep her distance from Kezia, as she was a 'wilful demon' who would stop at nothing to keep Manfri for herself. It transpired, she had for many years made clear her 'intentions' for Manfri. They had grown up together and both sets of parents had always believed that the two would, one day, marry. Manfri had other ideas, however. It was known amongst the troupe that they had shared teenage kisses but Manfri had never made any promises to her yet she jealously craved his full consideration at any and every opportunity. Worse still for Kezia, the more she pushed him, the more he resisted her attentions.

Over the past few days, Kezia had been watching with envy from the periphery of the circle and jealously observed the ease with which Nancy May and Manfri shared each other's company. Admittedly, she saw no specific closeness but she had no idea what went on in that private space at night. What was more annoying to her, was that Manfri had paid her no attention whatsoever since this young woman had come on the scene and her imagination ate away at her as the hours went by.

The troupe were discussing how they should have been moving onwards in two days time but there was great concern about their route in the current worsening weather. Nancy May was listening to their dialogue, mentally preparing to part company but with no fixed decision about where she would go. On the one hand, there was a certain comfort in considering her return to the familiar territory of home yet returning to Stapley Manor and her father did not fill her with joy. What was certain however was the sense of sadness she felt, to be leaving the gypsies or at least to be leaving Manfri and Josie. Both had been unexpectedly kind to her and she knew she had done nothing to deserve this. They had offered her a sense of unfamiliar safety and Nancy May shocked herself to consider them to be friends. She had not, even at this age, ever really had friends. She had previously never needed more than Giles and so it felt special to have someone else to care for her welfare. It felt good and she would miss that, so hearing that the departure might be delayed, did not at this point concern her too much.

Some of the men, including Manfri, had gone out into the nearby woods to forage for food. Nancy May had heard some gunshots and turned cold at the sound with a flashback to that early morning a decade ago. Yet, the women sitting around her were gleefully hopeful of the mens' success. Food for their bellies was a priority! By evening, Nancy May was helping to cook a rabbit stew in the pot over the fire outside. She had helped prepare the vegetables and was charged with keeping an eye on the pot to ensure a thorough cooking, mixing it occasionally with a long handled wooden spoon. It was almost time to eat and with one last stir of the pot, she decided to take the chance to relieve herself, before the troupe gathered around the fire to eat. She was feeling very proud of her proactive contribution to the evening meal and looked forward to the moment when they all came to taste the food, of which she had to admit, the aroma from the pot was deliciously tempting.

Kezia's insidiously cunning mindset did not miss a beat and watching Nancy May walk away from the pot, she took her chance. Nancy May's short absence, would be just enough for Kezia to make her move. Heading stealthily towards the fire, she grabbed the fire cloth used to lift the pot from its swinging frame. Flicking her eyes around the vicinity checked nobody was watching, with quick dexterity, she unhooked one of the two grapnels, which held the handle in place. Simply resting it in place over the fire, would not draw attention to its precarious poise. Replacing the cloth where she found it, she darted away before anyone could suspect her and waited in the wings of the circle for the certain disaster waiting to befall the young interloper.

Nancy May returned and called for Josie to come assist her. Josie in turn, yelled out for the troupe to gather for their meal and in no time everyone had congregated ready to eat, each keenly holding a bowl and spoon. Josie grabbed the cloth and passed it to Nancy May so that she might lift off the pot from the fire and set it aside for serving. Kezia watched with intent, her heart beating with anticipation, trying to hide her smirking grin. Just as she planned, Nancy May bent forward to reach the handle and mentally counting to three, stretched across the low fire and lifted the pot.

The inevitable happened! With a screech, the pot swivelled uncontrollably away from its handle so that Nancy May could not save it from spilling over to the ground, losing its contents across the stony earth...but what was worse, was that her bare hand had instinctively shot forward to rescue the scalding vessel and burnt it badly. A roar of annoyance rose up from the small crowd with foul language emanating from all quarters. Kezia, no matter for her hunger, could not stop herself from laughing. She did however, notice Manfri shoot her a suspecting and disgusted glance, which panged in her heart, as he ran forward towards Nancy May. Kezia's chest constricted further as she saw him sweep up Nancy May in his arms and run with her towards the riverside and out of sight behind its bank.

Nancy May was distraught, not just with the physical pain but with the shame of what had just happened. Her embarrassment, disappointment, guilt, was overwhelming. She wept pitifully.

Settling quickly at the waterside, Manfri held her tightly against his broad shoulders and calmly plunged her hand into the cool trickling water. Safe in his charge, she felt momentarily comforted. "I'm so sorry! I'm so, so sorry, Manfri! I've let you down... it was just an accident! They'll all be so cross with me!" she sobbed her words through one entire breath, the pain of her skin in the water stinging badly. Without looking at his face, she could feel against his tight chest how angry he was and she just wanted, ironically, to run away!! Moments later after holding her hand beneath the water he spoke surprisingly quietly. She had expected a tirade or even a beating, yet this strong man did neither.

"This was no accident." He said softly.

"It was, I promise you!!" she quickly defended herself. "It slipped! I couldn't help it!!"

"It was no accident!" he reiterated more assertively. "That hook had been dislodged! The handle wasn't fixed properly! It's the oldest trick in the book – you wouldn't have seen it."

"What?... What do you mean?" Nancy May was confused.

"I take it you left the pot unattended?"

"Well, yes, just while I ...."

"Exactly!" He shook his head slowly, "I know exactly who did this!"

"Who?"

"Kezia!!" he told her reluctantly.

Manfri slowly escorted Nancy May back to his vardo. She held her badly burnt hand cradled in the other for protection. Tears still visible across her cheeks.

"Hurt yourself, did you?" Kezia called out sarcastically.

"Don't you dare speak!" Manfri threatened through gritted teeth and she truculently turned her back on him with a sneer.

Once inside, Manfri poured Nancy May a small strong brandy, which she accepted graciously. Within moments there was a knock at the wooden door and a middle-aged gypsy woman climbed in carrying a bulging Dorothy bag. Nancy May had seen her at a distance a few days ago and mesmerised at her beauty. Her black hair curled down her back and her white lace blouse accentuated her generously proportioned shapely figure, masked only by a black and red shawl, which hung about her shoulders.

'This is Rosanne" he introduced the woman, adding, "She is my mother. Let her look at your burn." He firmly coaxed Nancy May.

Nancy May looked into the eyes of this attractive, motherly woman and could now see the resemblance to Manfri. Rosanne smiled kindly and took her hand gently in hers to inspect the damage.

"My dear, this is nasty!" she saw a flash of fear strike Nancy May's face. "We'll get it fixed, my dear, don't you worry."

Turning to her son, "Manfri, you did the right thing bathing it quickly in cold water but it needs more attention. Go and ask Josie to fetch either some honey if we have it, or an egg." Manfri shot from the vardo as instructed.

Muttering some soothing words to Nancy May, Rosanne opened her Dorothy bag and rooted through its contents, pulling out some white cotton strips and a smooth wooden instrument which looked something like a blunt knife. Nancy May did not hear her indistinct words but was somehow lulled by her tone and began to relax into her gentle care.

Everyone was still standing around, verbally chewing over the incident and watched Manfri's quick actions. Some called after him words, which were unjustly accusative, pertaining to the clumsy wench he had introduced to the band. He ignored all name calling and concentrated on his task.

A short time later, Manfri and Josie arrived back at the vardo and were surprised at the amicable, calm scene that met them. Josie needed no further instruction from Manfri and without any honey to hand, she had quickly prepared a whisked mixture of egg white in a jug for Rosanne's needs. Rosanne was proud that her protégée was learning fast and smiled her appreciation, not lost on Josie. She tenderly smoothed the white mixture across Nancy May's very red skin, which made her patient wince. Firmly wrapping the area in the white cotton strips she had ready, she then poured into a small cup from a small bottle, a reddish brown mixture, which Nancy May instantly recognized.

"Oh please, no!" she begged.

"Take it!" returned the instruction.

Nancy May held her own nose as she had been taught by her mother and swigged the bitter, foul tasting tincture in one gulp, trying not to wretch. Its distaste sent a reactive shiver down her spine but she nodded a thank you to the kind woman in appreciation of her care. Josie passed her a spoon of jam to follow, ridding the taste, for which she was truly grateful.

"Good, now get into bed and rest if you can. This will be very sore for some days. I'll check on you tomorrow." Rosanne cast a smile at her young patient and left the vardo. Josie stepped forward and briefly reassured Nancy May as best as she could. She too left, leaving Manfri who took up a seat beside Nancy May.

"You move on the day after tomorrow... I don't..." began Nancy May with a concerned frown.

"Don't worry about that for now." Manfri interrupted soothingly. "Get some sleep and let your body repair. We'll see how you are tomorrow."

"I still feel so bad about what happened! I was so pleased it smelled so good and...!"

"Well, don't worry about that either, they'll get something else to eat – there's bread and eggs at least!" He then realised she hadn't eaten either! "Can I get you something to eat?"

"No thank you. I'm no longer hungry! Besides, I think that would be the last straw for your family to see me being fed!!" They both raised a smile.

"I'll leave you for now. You'll be tired and the laudanum will kick in soon. I'll check on you shortly."

Nancy May thanked him for his kindness, which she truly believed she did not deserve. She had never known such attention from anyone other than her mother and brother and felt humbled after all the trouble she had caused.

As Manfri left, the tiny space suddenly felt empty and she had a pang of homesickness. Images of her mother and dear Giles, flooded her mind and she wept hard for them. She knew she was responsible for herself as an adult and could easily admit that this situation was entirely of her own making or more accurately her stupidity but what happened earlier, was not her fault. She had been trying to do something good and felt proud of her achievement, yet the whole thing had backfired and she felt totally unrewarded, even punished! Her hand and arm hurt badly but the laudanum eventually took over. By the time Manfri returned some two hours later, she was fast asleep.

Manfri slept in the vardo alongside Nancy May, just as he had done since the first night. He was a little concerned for her wellbeing this particular night and kept a watchful eye on her. She slept fitfully and did not seem aware of his presence. Once morning came, Rosanne came knocking at the door and was a little concerned for her young patient. Nancy May was still drowsy but on Rosanne's request, she pushed herself up to sit against a pillow to permit Rosanne to untie the dressing. The area was looking quite angry and Rosanne was not comfortable with this lack of progress. She bathed the area in warm water and repeated yesterday's egg white treatment, which she had brought with her, then finished by wrapping fresh bandaging. Nancy May was not hungry and Rosanne was reluctant to repeat the laudanum. Instead, Rosanne had Manfri prepare a hot restorative caudle, which Nancy May managed to drink.

That evening, Manfri had taken a break from watching over Nancy May and Josie had taken his place, he went to sit by the camp fire to take time for himself and rid himself of the pent up stress – even anger, he felt for all that had happened to render this lovely young woman so poorly. He sat quietly in the cool night air, with a glass of cheap brandy and looking into the orange flickering flames, he reflected on recent events, right from the moment he first saw Nancy May and the shock of finding her in his vardo, until this latest horrendous incident and his confused thoughts about a girl he barely knew. He was furious with Kezia, the girl he had grown up with and had shared childhood dreams as many youngsters do and he pondered on how he knew her through and through. He was very well aware of her feelings for him and had always made it clear to her at least, that his feelings for her were not reciprocated in the same way. He had not lied. There had indeed been a strong attraction to her within this close-knit community but it was unquestionably physical and no more. He did not believe that this was sufficient to take them through life together and he wanted more from a lifetime relationship. Kezia was a beautiful dark haired Romani, with a fiery nature and quick-tongued temperament. He knew immediately, this incident had her name all over it and he could not forgive her for this latest stunt. Yet, nothing he could say to her now, would make Nancy May immediately well, although venting his feelings, would certainly make him feel better! This was such an unforgivably wilful, premeditated, vicious act, that she needed to know how strongly he disapproved of her callousness and stupidity. He had not seen her since the incident and was glad he had not, for his fury might have proved equally hot headed and stupid.

One of his best and oldest friends, Lash, saw him sitting on the felled log and walked slowly over to sit by him, greeting him with a friendly acknowledging slap on the back as he stooped to take up a place next to him. They sat for a while in silence, sipping their drinks. Eventually, Manfri spoke.

"It was Kezia."

"I know", came the quiet reply.

"The girl is really ill, Lash! The burn has become badly infected. I just hope my mother can work her magic and pull her through." There was a lengthy pause. "God, I'm cross with her – she's always been jealous!"

"And does she have reason to be this time?"

Manfri looked at his intuitive friend. "Maybe!"

No more was said. There was just an unspoken, sympathetic understanding between the two men.

The next day dawned and Nancy May didn't fully wake. Manfri became increasingly more concerned for his 'little run away' companion. She seemed to be becoming troubled in her sleep and was hot to the touch. He sat with her for some time, bathing her forehead with a clean rag dipped in cool water. She was beginning to thrash about in her little confined bed and muttering incoherently in her sleep. She was a fragile, vulnerable sight and she made his heart sore to watch her. He held her arm and hand gently so that she did not incur further distress to the burnt skin as she writhed about. Her pale skin was soft and smooth. He saw her true beauty for the first time and a soft pain bruised across his chest. All that day, Nancy May worried those who were caring for her. They each took it in turn to look after her. The rest of the troupe were getting things ready and packing up ready to leave the following morning, as soon as the sun was up. Manfri stayed awake all that night caring for this beautiful young woman, astonishing himself that he did not wish to leave her side.

The day came for the band of gypsies to leave and head to their next destination. Fortunately, they were headed only as far as Cheltenham. Manfri had no other choice than for him to take Nancy May with him on the next leg of their trip. Nancy May was in no fit state to agree to this but she needed care and of course it was the responsible thing to do. Cheltenham was in fact nearer to Broadway than Malvern, so it made sense for them to take care of her and nurse her back to wellness, before she attempted what would in any case be, a shorter walk home.

Arriving in this town of gloriously regal architecture, once again the gypsies were met with a mixed welcome. Indifferent to this commonplace reception, they set up camp with its fair, as usual alongside the River Chelt. This 'market town' was beginning to change these past few years, with the building of fine Regency terraces, crescents and villas. This was fast becoming one of the more fruitful sites to work the fair, with growing numbers of tourists frequenting the town to drink the medicinal waters. Others came to enjoy the fashionable activity of strolling along the tree lined Promenade or shop in the fashionable Montpellier, for trinkets and souvenirs. It was becoming popular for leisure time to be spent in parks or gardens, where bands of musicians entertained and the fair in consequence pulled in visitors, who were keen to spend their 'treat' money. The population was growing fast as more families settled in the preferred residential areas, especially military families, encouraged by the prestigious Proprietary School for Boys being established in 1841. Manfri had even heard tell that incredulously, there was talk of the establishment of a Ladies College too. How times were changing! Such affluence was the making of a profitable stay in Cheltenham for the gypsies. It had become one of their favourite places to stay and they usually tried to push the limit of time that they were accepted there, into two weeks. The only downside to this site as they saw it, was the occasional odorous stench from the local tannery, which blew on a lea breeze, across the fields. Such acrid stink could only be tolerated for so long and was often the reason for their exiting from the town, which brought them most profit.

By afternoon, Manfri, Josie and even Rosanne were becoming more concerned for Nancy May, as her wounds were clearly infected. Rosanne changed Nancy May's dressing as soon as they reached Cheltenham and declared that the egg white was insufficient to repair her burns. She sent Manfri out on a mission to bring back some honey, which she then mixed with a small amount of crushed opium powder. This was re-applied over the next two days whilst Josie and Rosanne took it in turns to sit with her throughout, bathing her brow and delicate neck line. Manfri checked in on her an inordinate number of times and his concern for her recovery was easily seen.

Thankfully, together with Nancy May's natural resilience, the honey concoction and the care doted upon her by the gypsies, Nancy May's fever reduced over the next two days. She was eventually ready to accept some hot broth, which Josie had made especially to tempt her. She sat, propped up against the pillows which Manfri plumped up for her better comfort and sipped at the delicious food, knowing that she would get better. Rosanne was more relieved than she cared to admit, that the honey application had seemingly worked, for she had never tried this before and had no better alternative.

During one of her visits to check her patient's continued recovery, Rosanne sat chatting to Nancy May for some time. Quite without preamble, Rosanne made a comment, which took Nancy May by surprise and stirred in her chest, an uncomfortable sense of doom. "Tell me, dear child, I see you carry with you a huge sense of darkness in your heart, what is it that you do not speak of?"

'I'm not sure what you mean, Rosanne." She looked at the woman, uncertain of what it was she had claimed to see in her. "I assure you I am fine!"

"It will ease your soul to tell someone, you know! I can see you hold a dark secret..."

"I do not! You are mistaken! I.." Defensively, Nancy May tried to shrug off the accusation but was easily interrupted.

"Do not hide this, my dear! I have seen it in you... You should let it go, dear child!"

Nancy May was astonished at her insightfulness and dropped her eyes, not wishing to give anything further away. Her illness had fatigued her more than she realized and found she had no will to argue.

Rosanne continued to try to purge the pain from this dear girl. She knew she could help if only Nancy May would allow her. "I have a gift, Nancy May and I prefer to use it for good purpose." She made a deep sigh whilst she found the right words to explain. "These past few days... I have seen into your soul, my dear, as I tended your wound and ..." Searching again for the right words... "I saw what I believe to be secret resentment ... and contempt. There is guilt there too!"

Nancy May shifted uncomfortably in her bed but did not respond although she could feel the tears threatening to spill from her prickling eyes.

"Then, there is something in your palm... your palm will not lie to me!" Rosanne added, pausing as she held Nancy May's hand, soothing her skin for some time. Suddenly she added, "Why do I keep envisioning a pistol, Nancy May? Are you in trouble? Is that why you ran away?"

Nancy May flashed Rosanne a sharp look. "I think you are mistaken, Rosanne. Firstly I did not 'run away' and secondly, I don't know what you mean about a gun!" She did not wish to be having this conversation, yet those unbidden tears threatened to overspill her eyelashes and fall down her cheeks, betraying her.

"Perhaps it is something you try not to remember, but it is there... and it troubles you. Will you not tell me? I will tell no-one, if that is what you wish!"

"I have no secrets, Rosanne." She instinctively rejected the notion that she was troubled, then suddenly realised she was even lying to herself. She shook her head as though trying to shake sense into her conscious mind, then with a heavy sigh, looked Rosanne directly in the eye. It took quite a few moments and a degree of courage to part with her biggest secret, long since held private, even from her mother and brother. Now, she was about to disclose it to a relative stranger and she hoped she was to be proved right to do so.

Rosanne waited patiently, knowing this was a significant revelation she was about to hear.

CHAPTER 17

With great hesitation, Nancy May finally spurted out her admission, "I am not sure how you have seen these things in me but it is true, I do hold close something which has haunted me since I was nine years old. I shall tell you ... but I only do this, because you will never meet the person that this concerns..."

It took some time for Nancy May to recount her whole story but although she found it initially quite traumatic to address her deepest kept secret, as she unfolded her inner thoughts, she found the experience quite cathartic. Rosanne proved to be a kind and empathetic listener and seemed intuitively, to know exactly how to squeeze the most out of Nancy May's emotional purging, for her to best profit from the ordeal. Rosanne was left with a clear impression of how Nancy May had lived her life and made her the bold, adventurous, independent young woman she had grown into.

Nancy May had described how her father's mind was changing and he was becoming more difficult, which on top of a volatile personality, gave Rosanne concern. She worried for her return.

Something Nancy May had said, had also rung alarm bells but Rosanne could not be absolutely certain she was concluding correctly. She was very familiar with the place that Nancy May called 'home' but Rosanne and Django had not returned there for some years, since their last visit had not turned out well. All gypsies were used to threats but that incident was especially unpleasant when a man had come out raging and threatening to fire his rifle. There had been no sighting of Mr. Carter, as expected, which made them curious. The estate had a distinct look of sad neglect too. She remembered Mr. Carter fondly: A charming, handsome, generous man, whom she had subsequently been informed, had died in a shooting incident. Could the shooting incident have indeed been the duel, of which Nancy May spoke?

Rosanne reflected then, on the moment she was taken by utter surprise, when some years ago, two officials on horseback, rode into their nomadic community. They had been sent to search for Rosanne Mullick, with some astonishing information. Of course, there was a sense of alarm at their first sight and for some moments, the gypsies were reluctant to allow them to infiltrate their band but with cautious referral to the parchment with legal seal, they reluctantly lowered their defences and allowed them to speak in private with Rosanne. She instantly recalled the benevolent gentleman to whom they referred and was genuinely taken aback and saddened by his death. More so then, was she shocked to be advised, that Henry had bequeathed her a handsome sum of money. Her gratitude to him for this was great and she remained touched by his philanthropic kindness.

In this moment, she could not be sure but if she was right. Was it Nancy May's father who had killed the lovely man she knew as Mr. Carter? The possibility saddened her, especially because she recalled reading his palm on their last meeting and seeing death. On this occasion, she did not share her prophecy but rather wished her reading had been mistaken!

Manfri had made a decision. He could not allow this to eat him up. He must make it his business to find Kezia and clear the air. He struggled to find her. She was clearly avoiding him. He had calmed himself and was determined not to let her ruffle him, at least until he had had his say. Finally, he found her.

She was sitting against some railings by the river, holding on tight to her beloved dog. She was muttering words in his ear, as though the dog understood her tale of woe, a cathartic vent to her grievances. As he approached, he could see she was crying. Without immediate words, he sat next to her, on the damp ground. They were both silent for some time. Manfri picked a piece of grass, peeled it to its core, put it in his mouth and softly chewed. At last, he spoke so gently, that his voice was almost inaudible.

"Why would you do that?" Uncomfortable moments lapsed. "For pity's sake, Kezia, you have been brought up, as I have, to respect our honourable code of behaviour. Yet you perform like this then you show no shame at all! What is the matter with you?" He theatrically thrust his hands in the air questioningly with despair.

She thought for a moment and then shrugged. "I don't know... the gibface annoyed me, creeping round you like you are sweethearts!"

Despite himself, Manfri laughed softly at her expression, "She's not a 'gibface' as well you know it!... Is that what is annoying you? That she's pretty? And you wish she weren't? Besides, she doesn't creep around!"

"Are you sweethearts then?" Kezia couldn't help getting to the point.

"Kezia, you have to stop trying to possess me, following me around like a lost sheep! I am not answerable to you. What I do, is my business and you must get it out of your head that we can be together. I have told you often enough that I am fond of you and we share so many happy memories of growing up as children but that's all: Childhood friendship. You can be so sweet but you have a terrible temper and I could never live with that. I am not your future. You are not mine! You must stop this viciousness, Kezia." Looking at her seriously now, he pressed home the point, "You could have caused her to die! If it hadn't been for my mother... "He looked away, then continued "...Well it doesn't bear thinking about!"

She felt foolish and suitably chastised, yet she was not sorry. She knew she would do it all over again. He could provoke in her, such jealousy. She simply could not accept that he would not look at her as she wished him to, no matter what she did. She wanted to hate him. She certainly wanted to hurt the girl he had let into his life. He was right, she had a terrible temper but worse than that, she knew herself to be vindictive.

"Well, I'm not going to apologise, if that's what you're waiting for! She deserved it!"

"No, Kezia. She did not! Can you not see that?!"

Kezia would not answer but instead made a mockingly dismissive sound between her teeth. "Why don't you get rid of her?"

"Kezia, she would have gone by now, had you not pulled that stunt! She will be with us now for as long as it takes."

This realisation was salt in the wounds for Kezia. Her bitterness had prolonged Nancy May's stay and now she was cross with herself and sulked even more.

"Stay out of her way, Kezia. I don't want to see you anywhere near the girl. And stop being an imbecile or you'll find the only friend you've got, is your dog." With that, he spat out the grass, got to his feet in one swift movement and left without a backwards glance.

Kezia's chin wobbled and she cried silently into her dog's matted hair.

There was no doubt, that Nancy May felt better, lighter, for sharing her story. She felt certain she could trust Rosanne to keep her confidence. There was something about the woman, which exuded reliance. She had even lost that overwhelming sense of homesickness which had hung over her in the past few days and she felt herself relax into the comfortable surroundings of the camp. Day by day she improved and towards the end of the two weeks that the gypsies planned to stay in Cheltenham, she was fit enough to make the journey home.

The gypsy band had begun to mellow with her presence, knowing that it was Kezia who had orchestrated the disastrous event at mealtime and had come to sympathise with her subsequent injury. The whole atmosphere had become rather more tolerant of her or at least less threatened by her 'outsider' company. Some of the women had donated a few pieces of clothing for her to put together a second change of 'gypsy' clothes, helping her at least to look part of the community and less like an intruder. She realised that this was largely their way of protecting themselves and preventing rumour that the girl had been kidnapped but Nancy May was touched all the same, by their consideration and was grateful for their kindness, which she had no doubt had much to do with Rosanne's influence. She had over the past gruelling days, struck a favourable bond with Josie and Manfri ... well Manfri was, she grew to feel, exceedingly attractive!

Rosanne could not get out of her head the last time she visited Stapley Manor and the incumbent proprietor threateningly waving his rifle in the air above his head, shouting obscenities at them. She recalled at the time, being merciful for the cool temperament of her husband in not retaliating, for she believed most would have been tempted to rise to his bait and return not only filthy insults but the threat of a bullet. The raging man presented himself as a vile character, bad tempered with the likelihood of over imbibing: A disturbing concoction! Hearing what she had from Nancy May about her father, she now wondered if this man, could in fact still be the present incumbent of Stapley Manor and, therefore, Nancy May's father? If she was right in her deduction, she pitied the young woman! More than that, she was concerned for her safety upon returning to such a man.

Gypsy codes were strict. Unless the circumstance was exceptional, they never disbanded. Equally, however, they would go to great lengths to protect each other. Rosanne had been watching her son with interest and had seen something change in him, with the arrival of Nancy May. This, however, was more than something visual. Her psychic powers had sensed a powerful aura between the two, as yet unrecognised by themselves.

Rosanne and Django, had a solid relationship. As chieftain, Django was the only one who could permit any change to the usual codes. The couple worked closely to keep the band a tight knit community and as his wife, Rosanne looked after the welfare of the women and children in the group. She had taken Nancy May under her wing as a guest and with their code of generosity and honour, she treated Nancy May with the same concern as she would anyone else. The time had come for Rosanne to speak with Django about Nancy May's return. She needed Django to allow Manfri to be released from the convoy in order to return Nancy May home safely. Django knew better than to pry into her reasons and would refrain from questioning her integrity, for she had never compromised his.

With mutual understanding, the day before they were due to leave Cheltenham heading south, Django spoke with Manfri, giving him permission to return to Broadway to return Nancy May home. Manfri was taken aback at the decision but bowed to his parents' advice and recommendation and was not averse to spending uncompromised time alone with Nancy May along the way. They planned to leave the following morning.

Nancy May was initially delighted with the plan and profusely thanked all concerned. That night would be a special gathering. The fair had been packed away and the gypsies gathered for a night of celebratory music and good food. Lanterns hung in the trees and the aroma of good food hung tantalisingly in the air. The atmosphere was convivial and relaxed and Nancy May considered herself fortunate to have shared such a wonderful experience with these people who had shown her more compassion and consideration than she had ever experienced in life, bar her mother and brother. The balmy night air was intoxicating, enhanced only in part by alcohol and the energy of the dancing brought a seductive glow to her cheeks. As the tambourine rested and a soporific lull embraced the circle of wagons, the violin slowed to a softly melodic tune. Manfri gently took Nancy May's recovering hand, in request that she dance with him. Close. Mesmerized by the moment, she felt his warm embrace and melted into the security of his arms for what felt like blissful eternity. She felt his soft breath against her cheek and her world swirled, as his lips brushed hers.

With immense irritation, the moment was abruptly ruined with the piercing screeches of a female voice. Kezia!!

"Sheebah!!! Sheebah!! She's gone!!!" she shouted frantically. "I can't find her! Sheebah!! Help me find her!!!" The violin scraped to a stop. A tearful, frenzied Kezia rushed about the inner circle of vardos looking hurriedly beneath each one, for her beloved dog. Some folk stepped up lethargically to try to help her whilst others remained seated, rolling their eyes, thinking exactly the same as Manfri: Another of Kezia's selfish tricks!!...

Hours passed and the gypsies had checked everywhere. Nobody could find her. They decided sleep was needed and they would begin the search again in the morning light.

Manfri elected to sleep outside that night, purporting he needed to keep a watchful eye for the safety of the group, should Sheebah's disappearance have anything to do with intruders. In truth, it was more a case of his code of honour being greatly tested, should he have elected to lie in such close proximity with his beautiful 'run away'. Nancy May however, slept well for what she believed would be her last night in this romantically cosy vardo, then woke with the start of the bird's morning cacophony of song.

A plan was hatched to address the problem of the missing dog and work out a plan for a search. The notion of Manfri leaving to take Nancy May home, was for the time being, forgotten. They splintered into groups with firm destinations to search. Some stayed at camp in case the dog should randomly arrive home and a few set about preparing a hot meal for later. Manfri truly believed by now, that the dog had really disappeared, for Kezia was genuinely distracted and upset. If this had been a ruse to separate him from Nancy May or to return his affections to Kezia, she would have by now made her move and not been so pitifully upset. Rather, she had come nowhere near Manfri and only paid attention to him, as he took control of the search. She left with one of the groups which followed the river bank. They spread out and maximized their search. Manfri left with another group, heading into the town, others went to the park. For the time being, Nancy May remained with Josie and some of the older women within the circle of wagons.

Two hours gone and no-one had returned. Concern grew. A waft of stench from the tannery, blew across the fields and suddenly with thought association, Nancy May had a thought. Acting on her hunch, she nudged Josie into action, asking her to come with her.

Josie was curious as to what sparked her inclination. Nancy May had said that the tannery used dog excrement in the removal of hair from the raw hides and it served to mask the smell of the rotting flesh. It also produced the shades of brown colour which was so appealing and when the hides were soaked in a dog excrement and water solution, it enhanced the shine of the finished leather product. It was a bit of a wild card, Nancy May suggested to Josie but she felt there was just a chance that Sheebah had either been taken to the tannery's dog pound or she had followed a scent there, since she had noticed Sheebah to be on heat.

Reaching the periphery of the stinking factory, the nauseating odour made both girls wretch. Wrapping their scarves about their nose and mouth, they needed to check for a sighting of Sheebah, as quickly as possibly and get away from the vicinity. Stepping quietly up to the factory wall, the girls peeped over the top to observe the ongoing, noisy activity. Under a semi-covered outdoor space, huge tables were set up with raw skins spread out before the workmen, clad in apron and tall boots, standing in filthy, bloodied pools, scrubbing down the hides with a cloudy brown solution, just as Nancy May had told Josie.

There was nothing of interest to be found here, so signalling to each other, they crouched down low out of sight behind the peripheral wall and scurried further around the corner towards some fencing. Again, they peered over the boundary, to find another source of stench. Piles of dog dirt covered an enclosed space and two men were unloading a cart full of jute bags of the stuff, presumably collected from the streets. The activity had incited some dogs to bark which confirmed Nancy May's suspicions that they may have a pound with strays. They acted as guard dogs and paid their way with scraps of food to produce the all-important material, for the leather process.

Luckily not alerting anyone, Nancy May and Josie took their opportunity under the camouflage of the dogs barking at the men, to make their way towards their pen. Between them, they scanned the area of moving unkempt canines, to see if they could spot Sheebah. After some moments, they disappointedly confirmed to each other, that she was not there and began to move away. Josie led the way. Out of the corner of Nancy May's eye, she caught sight of a dog curled up in a corner, tucked up against the fence, alone. She caught the back of Josie's blouse and yanked her backwards, almost landing her in the mud.

"What?!" she grumbled, rolling her eyes as she caught her balance.

"Look!!" Nancy May pointed with a whisper.

"Ohh! It's her!!" Josie confirmed.

"Can you reach her? She knows you, surely she'll come to you?"

Quickly checking around them for anyone who may see, Josie called softly to Sheebah. Recognising her voice, the dog looked up and immediately limped towards them.

"She's hurt her leg!"

"Can you grab her?"

Both girls held their breath whilst Josie struggled to lift the injured dog from ground level, up and over the fence. Nancy May helped with the last pull and they landed the dog as softly as possible under duress.

"We'll have to carry her" Josie concluded.

Taking it in turns between them they managed to exit the area undetected and with several rests along the way, finally reached the camp. A roar of delight lifted up and Kezia, who had returned forlorn some time ago, lunged forward to rescue her beloved Sheebah from Nancy May's clutches. Tears of relief streamed down her face and she gave a heartfelt smile of gratitude and profuse thanks.

"She's injured" Josie explained.

"But she's alive!" Kezia replied. "Where did you find her?" addressing her comment to Josie.

"You have Nancy May to thank for that – for all of it!! Everyone had gone out looking and suddenly she thought about the tannery. When we got there, we didn't find her at first, but then Nancy May spotted her in a corner."

Kezia, without reluctance, profusely thanked Nancy May for her kindness. She buried her face in the dog's matted coat, despite her filth and stench. She took the dog away to the river and bathed her, gently revealing a small cut on her leg, which with care she knew would repair.

Moments later, Nancy May watched, with a pang of something close to pain, as Manfri followed Kezia to the waterside and out of sight. Her eyes prickled. Rosanne observed this from the far side of the circle and noted her reaction. She walked slowly over to Nancy May and sat by her.

"That was a clever thought you had, about the tannery!"

"It was just a chance thing really. I'm thankful we found her!"

"Well, it seems the thanks is all for you, my dear, especially after the way Kezia has behaved towards you."

Nancy May simply shrugged but no words would come.

Rosanne surprised her by taking her hand with a squeeze, "It will all work out, you know!"

Nancy May had no idea what she meant by this platitude but accepted the reassuring words with a bleak smile and an almost imperceptible nod.

Manfri caught up with Kezia, who was by then up to her knees in the water, tenderly washing Sheebah's odorous hair, being cautious not to hurt the precious dog's leg further. She saw Manfri approach but chose not to acknowledge him.

"I trust that proves to you what a decent young woman she is? Do you realize the risks she took to do this for you today, when she could have been insisting on setting off home? .... I hope you think on this Kezia and perhaps take note of her generosity of spirit and unconditional kindness. Maybe you might even take a leaf out of her book!" Wordless, she looked up at him from the edge of the river and he held her gaze meaningfully and at length, then turned on his heels and returned to the group.

Striding into camp, Nancy May saw the look on his face and knew immediately that he had only followed her to speak his mind. He came straight over to her and at the same time, Rosanne left Nancy May's side.

"Nobody can be in any doubt now, that you are no threat to our circle. That was indeed a kind and thoughtful thing to do and I am glad you are home safely."

She looked at him, curious at his use of the word 'home' but concluded that of course he was referring to 'his' home and nothing more. In the flash of seconds, which passed as he paused, she realised that this did feel as much like home, as she had felt in years.

He continued, "Why did you decide to look there - at the tannery?"

She smiled and slowly shook her head, almost trying to disassociate herself from what she was about to say, "It was the smell that brought back a memory. My father once worked at the tannery in Evesham. Mother said he was there but for a very short few days, mostly because it took hard graft and he was lazy but the memory stuck with me and I remembered about the connection with dogs...I don't know, it was just a thought!" She paused at the memory... "I was but a small child. He could be so cruel! I remember his exaggerated, gruesome stories that he told deliberately, because he knew it made me feel sick – even more sick than the stench of his filthy clothes when he came home." She turned away her head as though to rid the disgusting memory, closing her eyes against reliving it. She felt a comfortable, caring arm around her shoulder and sank back into it, securely. A tear escaped onto her cheek. With one swipe of the back of her hand, it had gone.

"You are truly remarkable!" She turned her head back towards him. He looked deep into her eyes and her heart melted at his words. What a kind and loving man he was!

Breaking the moment, Manfri stood up and held out his hand, "Come. Let us eat and we shall delay our return to Broadway until tomorrow. Feeling a sense of reprieve, that she had been blessed with one more night with the gypsies, she smiled broadly and followed his lead.

Yet before the night was through, Manfri and Nancy May had each spent hours privately coming to terms with their own emotions surrounding the thought of Nancy May leaving the gypsies and each other. Neither felt inclined to admit to each other their own real reasons but something was pulling hard at Nancy May's heart to stay with this man and she was definitely not yet ready to return to Broadway.

Equally, Manfri was for his own reasons, not prepared to transport Nancy May to her home village and leave the safety of the camp without the certainty that she would be safe from her father. In fact by searching what was in his heart, he too recognised he did not want her to leave at all. So what harm could there be in her lingering a while longer with him? He already knew the answer: One of them could end up broken hearted and he had a strong feeling it could easily be him!

By the time the sun had risen, neither had had much sleep but both had been independently soul searching for a decision, even praying for divine intervention.

Words and logic were not as powerful as emotions and so with mutual agreement they both eventually conceded, without any mention of attachment one to the other, that Nancy May would stay with the troupe until such a time as they chose otherwise. Neither did either of them confess to the other their sense of relief and contentment that came with the reciprocal decision.

CHAPTER 18

The time had come to share with her daughter, the details of her father's last will and testament, as set out by Mr. Foster some time ago. Elizabeth chose her time as planned, to give Elise her father's gift, a few days ahead of her birthday.

"My dear child... You are now rising sixteen and I wish to tell you about your father's generous trust fund. Mr. Foster has given me this to pass to you in anticipation of your birthday. It contains the details of the Trust and will help you prepare for your good fortune." Elizabeth paused thoughtfully. "There is something else too."

She offered the document to Elise and beckoned her, "Sit beside me, my dear and let me explain."

Elise was completely taken aback to hear of such a gift and felt curiously warmed by a strong sense that her father was with her in that moment. She could imagine his benign, handsome face smiling down at her and his protective arms around her. Without distinct words, she summoned up the sound of his comforting, loving voice and she found her own arms wrap around herself in a hug that could have been sent directly from him.

Elizabeth continued, "Next week, we shall celebrate your coming of age birthday and Mr. Foster has been able to unlock a clause and secure a wish, set out in your father's Will. Elise, your father wanted you to have the Mill House on the estate of Stapley Manor. You will remember it well, I think?"

"Oh Mamma!! How can this be?... Yes, of course I remember it so very well. Papa used to take me there often and we called it 'our secret place'. I so loved it there!" Elise beamed at the sweet memory. "We would play hide and seek around its rooms. It's an adorable little house. He said it was very special to him ... and it would be to me too one day!! How curious! I have never thought of that until just now!" Her eyes clouded, yet she smiled at the memory. "Oh Mamma, I am so happy to think I could go back there but surely it will seem strange when we don't any longer own the manor house?"

"It will indeed be an emotional experience for you to return there but allow the happy times to shine though and do not dwell upon the sadness of leaving Stapley Manor. Of course you might find that the house is beyond repair and not worthy of reparation but whatever the outcome, the house is legally yours." Elizabeth knew the risks of her daughter returning to Stapley Manor, only too well. She hoped that if Mr. Turner still resided there, Elise would never come to know the hidden story behind their leaving and Mr. Turner and his family moving in. She had, for all these years, kept secret the truth behind her father's death and it seemed too cruel to drag that up now. It seemed so unnecessary to blemish Elise's understanding of the circumstances of her father's death.

Elise's birthday arrived. It was an overcast, wet day, dank and dreary, just like the one on which she was born – if only she knew it! That did not spoil her day however, for she had wonderful news for Samson, about the Mill House, once they were alone. Her mother had prepared a small celebration, inviting a few near neighbours in Harvington who had welcomed them into the village and become good friends, as well as Samson. It proved to be a special day with lots of laughter and a sense of instant maturity. A significant day in anyone's life: The marking of a stage in life, when one moved from youth to an age of responsibility. Elizabeth had gifted her a beautiful silver chain for about her neck, from which hung a silver locket. Elise opened the locket with gentle reverence and trembled to find inside a thick coil of silver hair.

"My darling Elise, I have treasured this for many years and now I would like you to have it. It is a lock of your father's hair. I hope it will serve to protect you and keep you safe."

Elise shed so many tears she could barely see. She asked her mother to place it securely around her neck and promised never to remove it. From that day on, she wore it with pride in the knowledge that her father was always with her.

After the most perfect of birthday celebrations, Elise and Samson left the house to tend the animals. Over the months, their compatibility grew to be unquestionable. They worked together with ease and were undeniably completely in tune with each other's thoughts. They had immense fun together and had developed the kind of trust, most would envy. Samson rarely needed instruction from his employer, as his intuition for what Elise needed doing on the fields or in the yard, was invariably exactly what she would recommend doing. He did however, love learning from her, about the livestock. She had built up so much knowledge and experience and above all, she was a good teacher. Samson seemed to learn quickly too, which in turn, she found rewarding. They simply pulled together well.

Truth was, that Samson had fallen in love with Elise. He could not imagine life without her. His days at the farm were the happiest he had ever known yet he had been so cautioned by his aunt and mother that he feared to lose everything if he ever disclosed his feelings. However, he could not miss the opportunity to gift her something for her special birthday, thus he had pondered on what that might be, for months. It had to be just right to convey his feelings for her, yet not be so over exuberant as to be presumptuous. Then there was affordability. He would love to make her a grand gesture but this was neither a good idea, nor financially possible.

The week before Elise's birthday, Samson had a chance encounter. He had gone to market and by absolute fluke, had come across a beautiful nutmeg coloured colt. Its long legs and black tail, pale facial markings and gentle nature were stunning. He fell in love with it... and knew Elise would too. It would cost him his savings but he decided it was worth it. He arranged with the woman selling to bring it to Elise's home on her birthday and he would have the money ready. It was easily agreed.

So, after her birthday tea when they went out into the yard, Samson dared to take Elise's hand, "Close your eyes!!" he whispered. She giggled like a school girl.

"What are you doing?!" she chided.

"Shh! It's a surprise! Have you closed them? Tight shut mind!! No peaking!"

"Samson... what is it?"

"You'll see! Hold my hand... walk with me... a bit further..."

"Don't let me trip!" she was still giggling excitedly. He guided her across the yard towards the sheds, avoiding the puddles. With one hand firmly clenching Samson's, Elise's other free hand instinctively extended in front of her as though to stop her bumping into something.

"Right. Stop! Now, open your eyes!"

With a screech of absolute delight, her hands flew to her cheeks, "Oh he's so beautiful!"

"He is for you, Elise. My gift to you."

"No! Surely not, Samson!" She gently walked towards the small creature, tucked away in the corner of the barn and put her hand towards him to stroke his adorable face. "He is simply the most beautiful beast ever!" Turning towards Samson, he could see her eyes were full of tears, "I have never been gifted such a wonderful thing... but Samson, I cannot accept him as a gift. You cannot surely afford this. You must take him back to wherever you found him. I cannot keep him!"

Samson was dumbfounded. He didn't understand this rejection. Flustered by her reaction, he lurched forward to hold her, "Elise, he is yours to keep. I will not return him. I wanted to buy you something special because I..." He stopped short of what he was about to say, realizing he was overstepping the mark as her employee. He knew he was about to make an idiot of himself, just as his aunt had warned him.

"Because what?" She looked him in the eyes, daring him to finish his words.

"Because I want to say thank you for all you have done for me..." he quickly made a fist of an answer.

Seeing how earnestly he spoke, "Well, he is so gorgeous... and I do love him... if you are sure about this?..."

Relieved, Samson smiled his broadest smile and nodded. She bent forward and kissed him on the cheek, which made him flush bright red. "Thank you so much, Samson. This truly is the most special gift ever!"

"What will you call him?"

"Mmm... She patted his mane thoughtfully. He's as cute as 'sugar and spice and all things nice' and the colour of spice too... so that shall be his name. Spice!"

They spent a good deal of time with Spice, then continued with their other chores before they sat down for some more birthday cake and hot milk. Elise took the opportunity to share her good news with Samson.

"Thank you again for my wonderful gift Samson! Spice is such a wonderful colt. He's going to grow into an enviable beauty! You really are the kindest, most thoughtful man I know!" His stomach flipped with joy to hear her speak the words and with

193

that, the inevitable blush, flushed his face. She brought her gaze back from Spice and looked at him, used to seeing his cheeks redden with shyness. "I have a surprise to share with you too!" She grinned excitedly.

"You do?" he looked shocked.

"My mother went to see our solicitor yesterday and the most splendid thing has happened! We used to live in a manor house and in the grounds was a smaller house which had fallen into disrepair. It used to be almost covered in ivy and was a secret place for playing. Well it seems that a clause has been unlocked and although somebody else lives there in the manor house, the Mill House is now mine!! I am so very excited Samson! I have so many happy memories there and I would love to go back and see if it can be made safe enough to live there."

"Gosh! That's such a wonderful thing to happen! I can see why you are so excited! When will you go to look at it?"

"Perhaps the day after tomorrow? I haven't decided yet! Will you come with me? You can drive the trap for me? It will be such fun to go back there. I haven't seen the place since we left years ago – I think I was about seven when we left. It was all so sad!"

"Sad? Why did you leave?"

"My father died suddenly and we had to move out to Primrose Lane for a short while, before we came here. It was simply awful."

"I'm so sorry! You say Primrose Lane? That's such a coincidence. We used to live in Primrose Lane too, before we moved house. How strange! We must have just missed each other!" They both laughed at how serendipity works.

"So will you come with me then? To the Mill House?"

"Of course I will!" 'Samson', as he had become used to being called, felt honoured.

As an afterthought, she smiled broadly and added, "And don't you think it's about time you called me Elise, instead of

Ma'am?", which they both found very funny indeed and Samson nodded as his face turned crimson, yet again.

Despite Giles's recent sense of elation, being in Elise's company, he had suffered some bad nights. Whilst he did not feel unwell as such, he had a very dark, grave feeling about him. He suffered bed sweats as though he had a fever yet when he woke, that was gone. He couldn't quite put his finger upon the problem but he had experienced this feeling before. He reflected on his childhood and with total clarity, the cause suddenly dawned on him. With sickening realization, he knew that Nancy May was ill. When they were small, Nancy May had been out and about in the fields on her own and she had fallen and badly hurt her leg. He had experienced this same sense of disturbing uneasy gloom and went out to look for her and carried her home. In the days that followed, her wound became angry and she fell ill. Giles had that same feeling then, as though they were the same person. He had no wound but he lapsed into a mirror image of her symptoms.

Feeling as he did now, he was certain Nancy May was ill but on the upside, it meant she was alive. He had to hang onto that thought. He chose not to share this sense of dread with his mother, for it would have been simply too much for her to bear to think she was suffering but he could not shake off his feelings of helplessness.

Elise, however, had noticed his dull eyes and worried about him. Eventually, with her coaxing, he shared his fears with her. Of course there was nothing that could be done but it did help Giles to share his sense of grief.

Yet, as days went by, Giles perked up and he felt physically better. Of course this brought him relief, feeling sure this meant that his dear sister was also in recovery. He truly believed it.

Peggy watched her son growing in confidence and was so proud of the man he had become. She thanked the Lord that he did not seem in any way to have taken on his father's ill ways and the only resemblances to Albert, was in the certain way he walked and the colour of his eyes. Other than that, he was nothing like his father.

It was a joy to see Giles so happy in his chosen work, helping out at a farm in Harvington and using his learnt skills to build a smallholding at Stapley Manor. He was bringing home enough money to keep them in food and immediate comforts. Giles was not one for chat these days. Always doing something, in and out of the house and as long as he seemed happy, his mother did not need to pry. So apart from the usual pleasantries and essential chat about either money, Albert, or when he might be next expected home, they no longer seemed to have the opportunity for those long talks Peggy so loved. They rarely spoke these days about Nancy May. Not that she was forgotten, rather more, that their distress of losing her, was so profound, even the mention of her name would send either or both of them into inconsolable distress. They had agreed that there was nothing more that they could do to find her, except pray that she was safe and would one day, find her way home.

In consequence, it was some time before Peggy turned her attentions to Giles's recent change in behaviour and by association, the lady owner of the farm in Harvington who was apparently slightly younger than Giles and by all accounts, pretty at that. This only came about one day, when by chance, Mabel and Peggy were folding sheets in the kitchen and Giles came rushing through with his shirt off, looking for a clean one. Without thought, Mabel teased her nephew about his constant spurious grin and wanting a clean shirt for work could only mean one thing!! Was it perhaps to do with a pretty lass? She enquired laughingly. Giles immediately blushed dramatically, leaving them in no doubt that Mabel had hit the nail right on the head. Giles finally gave into their familial taunting and he told them all about a young woman who had very much attracted his attention. He waxed lyrical about her beauty and humour, her intelligence and compassion. Eventually, he admitted that it was his employer who had stolen his heart but he did not know if she felt the same. The two women tried to caution him against making a buffoon of himself but equally they could see that he was determined in his intentions.

It was an incidental mention of her name that changed everything. Giles unwittingly referred to the young woman who permeated his thoughts by day and night, as Elise. Peggy's stomach lurched a little to hear the name and she became suddenly light headed and sank into the nearest chair. Mabel rushed to her with concern but Peggy feigned having moved too quickly and incurred a head spin. Nobody thought any more of it. Giles continued to chatter but Peggy's thoughts had shut off from his words while she tried to absorb this unbelievable twist of events. It was admittedly an unusual name but Peggy reasoned with herself that it would be highly unlikely that 'this' Elise could possibly be one and the same as the child, Henry and Elizabeth named Elise and called their own. Surely this would be too cruel to be true but then as Peggy tuned back into Giles's excited monologue, he was saying something about Elise's father being dead and she lived with her mother. Peggy at this point began to believe that this could be too much of a coincidence.

Elise was so excited to be going to find the Mill House, in the grounds of her childhood home. If it was good enough to repair and spruce up, she could be going to look at her future home. How wonderful it would be to remember all the happy times she spent with her father. Taking her mother's advice, she made herself a promise, that she would not entertain those memories of his death, which would make her sad. History was the past and she could not bring back her father so she must not taunt herself with 'what ifs'. She must only allow herself to bring on the good times and it was he who wanted her to enjoy this happy place, so she must honour that!

Giles was proud that she had asked him to go with her and they set off for Broadway, as early as possible in the morning. Elise hadn't been back to Broadway since they left more than a decade ago, for she had not wanted to revisit emotional memories but now she was positively enthusiastic to return. Incredulously, it was only now for the first time, she asked Giles where about he lived in the village. He described the road he would take, out of the village towards Snowshill. She laughed at the coincidence and said that that was the very road they needed to get to the Mill House. With animated chatter on the subject, it gradually transpired that they were both referring to living at Stapley Manor but the Mill House, as it was known to Elise, had become known to Giles as the Gate House, for they did not know its history.

The Mill House was just as she remembered it, except for it being very much more overgrown. The windows were barely visible now beneath the ivy growth and the trees were bigger and fuller in leaf than she remembered.

They rummaged around the rooms, finding intriguing bits of this and that as evidence of someone at some point, living there, albeit frugally. They spent time checking for its safety, trying to establish if it was worthy of making it sufficiently sound to live in. They believed that with some care and attention here and there, it could be.

Samson wanted to introduce her to his mother and while they were so close by, it seemed a good opportunity. Leaving the cart, they walked the length of the driveway to the front door and walked in. Aunt Mabel greeted them and with a broad smile made Elise welcome, then called for Peggy to come in from the kitchen, where she was feeding Albert his lunch.

Peggy came in flustered and removing her apron, fluffing up her hair as she walked, making no improvement whatsoever to her unkempt appearance. As soon as she came through the door to the salon and set eyes on the young woman, her legs weakened to the point she thought they might give way beneath her. It was like looking at a reflection of her former self. It quite took her breath away. Trying hard to disguise her reaction, she sweetly offered them both a drink. Her heart hammering, Peggy fought through the polite chitchat, trying to shake off her confused thoughts and not think too much on the possibility of such a coincidence.

Just then Albert came through from the kitchen looking for Peggy, his stained napkin tucked into his shirt and soup dripping down from his lips. Upon seeing Elise, he threw open wide his arms and welcomed Nancy May! They all looked at each other in embarrassment but Peggy could forgive his mistake, for the two women did indeed look very much alike. The more she considered it, the more she believed her worst nightmare was coming true.

Elise found it amusing to hear Samson's true name for the first time, for she had become so attuned to his nickname, that 'Giles' seemed not to fit. They heard the story of how he had come to be known to her as Samson and she thought how the revelations of the day about Samson, would bemuse her mother when she returned home!

Sitting around the table, with Peggy, Giles, Mabel, Fred and with Albert roaming the room, distracted, looking for something he'd lost, Elise broached the subject of this being her previous home. Not for a moment appreciating the can of worms she was about to open.

A stunned silence hung in the air for moments before the conversation continued. Elise suddenly put a few pieces of her mental jigsaw together from her sketchy understanding and realisation clouded over Elise's happiness and her stomach plummeted. She quickly calculated that if Giles had lived there since the date she and her mother left, then for whatever reason, these people in front of her, must have moved into her home just as she and her mother were forced to move to Primrose Lane. She had no real understanding of why she and her mother had moved from Stapley Manor immediately after her father had died but she did have vivid recollections of her mother sobbing and of the unhappiness, which had hung in the air. Again, she pondered upon the coincidence, that Giles had said he used to live there too!

Looking about the room, Elise had flashbacks about how she remembered it in its former opulence. Memories scurried across her mind as she simultaneously tried to participate in the polite conversation around her. She was trying to piece together in her mind the scattered bits and pieces of recollections but the parts of the puzzle, refused to make sense to her. She was going to have to ask her mother!

Then, suddenly, without any real thought, she referred to Peggy, asking, "At what number Primrose Lane, did you used to live?..."

Again, a hushed silence permeated the room. Peggy didn't seem to be able to make her mouth work to respond. Mabel stepped in to relieve her own embarrassment and not understanding Peggy's gross hesitation, "My sister lived at number twelve and my husband and I lived a few houses down at number eighteen."

Elise could not stop herself, "How strange! My mother and I went to live at number twelve when we left here ..." Giles looked at her curiously, realizing she was putting parts of the jigsaw together.

As if that was not enough, Elise questioned, "Did you know my mother? Elizabeth?"

Telling the truth, Peggy replied, "It's a small village! Perhaps I may have seen her years ago but I cannot say I know her." She desperately wanted the conversation to turn before Elise asked if she knew her father! "What brings you both to Stapley Manor?"

Elise spoke now with greater excitement. "It has just come to light, that my father left me the Mill House in his Will... Samson, sorry... Giles...tells me you call it the Gate House! I remember it was a very special place for him and it seems he was keen for me to keep and enjoy it. I do hope that you will not mind us being such close neighbours?"

Peggy's heart felt like it had stopped at hearing how much Henry loved the Mill House...just as she did, yet her nightmare was getting deeper. She had had many such nightmares over the years and now, she wanted to wake up and this would be all but a trick of her imagination.

"We never think about it", she lied. "I imagine it will be too derelict for you to do anything with it." She added hopefully to put her off thinking about living there. "Surely you could not make it habitable?!"

Unfortunately, the response, which this suggestion evoked, was much too positive for Peggy's liking. Both Elise and Giles effusively explained their plans for renovation and noted the term 'their' plans, not just Elise's. Peggy felt even more sickened to see the communication sparking between her son and Elise. It was a sense of togetherness she was not expecting. There was a definite close relationship blossoming, which Peggy sensed was more than just friendship. Dear God! This could not be happening!

Leaving Stapley Manor some time later and having another viewing of the Mill House, they got back in the cart and set off back to Harvington. Elise could not let go of the apparent coincidence of their younger years and could not help but feel that something did not sit right and so she aired her thoughts with Giles. How could it be that as her father died, she and her mother were caused to leave Stapley Manor, when the house had belonged to the family since it was built and her father clearly had enough money to remain there. That much had become clear from his will, leaving ample funds for Elise and her mother. She remembered her mother's tears as they sat that first night in the cottage at Primrose Lane and so she did not believe her mother ever wanted to leave Stapley Manor. On the other hand, how could it be that Giles's father, who it transpired had moved from job to job and not wealthy and lived in an impoverished cottage, could possibly afford to take on Stapley Manor. It simply didn't make sense. Giles recalled the angry disappointment in his father as they moved in and found there were no staff to serve on him. Giles had never understood either, how come they were so poor but as his father grew more dependent upon alcohol, it was left more and more to him to keep the house going.

They both sifted through their minds to piece together their understanding of what had happened but they had both been so young when they moved and much of what had happened had been kept from them. Children were seen and not heard. Memories were all so sketchy, yet a terrible lull of disbelief hung over them both as the horse clip clopped along, pulling their rattling cart. Giles held out his hand to grasp hers and a genuine sense of togetherness enveloped them both. Elise vowed to ask her mother. She was an adult herself now and deserved to know the truth. Whatever had happened, they both felt that the two families were somehow linked. It was quite the mystery. Both Elise and Giles agreed however, that whatever transpired, history was in the past and they could not change it. They confessed to each other that, all that mattered, was that they could be together.

CHAPTER 19

Elizabeth found herself sitting in the now familiar green leather chair, opposite to a greying solicitor, as he began to explain his most recent findings. There was never much in the way of polite preamble with Mr. Foster. He was always straight down to business without any cursory, introductory chat. She had got used to that over the years and today, she smiled inwardly, to note that he had not changed.

"You may remember Mrs. Carter, that last time we spoke, I had forewarned you of an unusual circumstance relating to your husband's last will and testament? I offer my apologies for the lengthy delay in being able to come to any conclusion in this matter but it has been a long and difficult process." Elizabeth's heart rate had increased and her chest was throbbing in anticipation of whatever drama Mr. Foster seemed to be considering.

"Mrs. Carter, I do not know how much you are aware of the duel as it unfolded." Elizabeth, shuffled in her seat as she uncomfortably recalled that dreadful night.

"It should be clarified, that had your husband's demise been under natural circumstances, his intentions, of course, had been for you and your daughter to continue to reside at Stapley Manor. You understand that that changed, under the agreement of the duel?" He looked to her for understanding. She nodded.

"I must once again ask you to recall the night of your husband's demise."

Pausing again and glancing up at his client he could not read her expression. "It would seem that your husband ... upon the instruction to fire, took his own life." Elizabeth, had of course, known this fact but still burst into tears, for it was not a subject she wished to revisit. Leaning forward and grasping a bottle, the solicitor poured a generous amount of amber liquid into a goblet. "Perhaps a glass of brandy, Mrs. Carter?" He slid forward the glass across the polished surface of the desk, encouraging her to take a sip. Doing so, she eventually replied, "Yes, I am aware of the circumstance, Mr. Foster but I do not see how this affects Henry's will."

Mr. Foster continued, "It was assumed, of course, that with the conclusion of the duel, Mr. Turner had every right to claim your family home: He was the sole survivor of both the duel and the agreement it represented. However, acting upon behalf of your husband, it was my duty to clarify something, which had troubled me. I have only before heard of one other example of such a situation as this and so I chose to consult my learned colleagues on such a point. There has ensued lengthy legal debate about the correctness of this outcome. It has therefore been concluded that we can claim, that there is in this instance, 'a loophole.'"

Elizabeth was none the wiser, "I am sorry Sir, but I am afraid I do not understand exactly what you are saying."

Mr. Foster tried to simplify his findings, "Well, fundamentally, we are considering the validation of witnesses present at the duel, who are prepared to swear that Mr. Carter took his own bullet first, therefore confirming that he took his own life. If this is proven to be the case, then the result of the duel will be considered null and void." Elizabeth still looked quizzically at Mr. Foster. "Mrs. Carter, this would mean that Mr. Turner has no right to claim Stapley Manor as his home. He would be residing there under false pretences." Elizabeth, dragged another gulp of brandy.

"It is however unfortunate, that we currently lack other, perhaps independent, witnesses to carry through this claim. Four men were present. The statements from Albert and his 'second', cannot be accepted, as clearly they are considered biased in opinion. Henry has gone. That only leaves Henry's 'second' and although his butler and life long friend is of reliable character and truthful, his word is not sufficient on its own."

The clock ticked loudly in the corner of the room whilst this information was considered.

"However, it has come to my notice, that there is a possibility of one more witness. If this person can be traced, we might be successful in reclaiming your home!"

Elizabeth picked up her glass and swigged back the remaining liquid in one swallow, then coughed. Her head was blank with disbelief.

Returning from the solicitor's that afternoon with mixed emotions, Elise was keen to hear her news.

"Oh Elise! I am quite exhausted! I am not at all sure what I can tell you..."

"Oh Mamma! You do looked fatigued! Let me make you a drink."

"Thank you my dearest child. What would I do without you? You do know, you are my everything, don't you?" she said almost tearfully.

"Oh Mamma, of course I do. And I love you so much too. It must have been so upsetting talking about dearest Papa and knowing he was not there to support you. It is the most awful thing that he died. I miss him terribly too Mamma ... but we shall be alright, you know. I will work so hard to make sure we have enough money to keep us comfortable."

"You will make your father so proud of you, just as you always did, my darling. You were the apple of his eye." Elizabeth took up her favourite chair by the window, with a heavy tearful sigh. "I miss him so terribly, Elise. He was my whole world ... until you came along, of course." She smiled at her daughter through glazed sadness. It broke Elise's heart.

Elizabeth reflected on her interview with Mr. Foster and his astonishing revelation about Mr. Turner's claim on the house. She began to recount as best as she could the dialogue, which had unfolded earlier that day.

Elise paled to hear the extraordinary possibility of reclaiming Stapley Manor but could not imagine the chances of this ridiculous turn of events actually coming to fruition.

"Mamma. Please do not hold your hopes on this ludicrous dream. It is unfair of Mr. Foster to tantalise you with such a notion. This can never happen! We have said goodbye to that house and we have moved on. We are happy here and we have sufficient funds to support ourselves. Papa is no longer there and it will never be the same without him. Let this go Mamma. Please!"

CHAPTER 20

Giles arrived home tired one evening after a full day's work at Harvington. His mother greeted him at the back door as she was coming in from feeding the chickens and without preamble, told him of her recent news.

"Oh Giles... I am so glad to have you home!" Giles immediately thought that his father had been causing issues and was not at first too concerned. He shrugged off his coat and asked casually what the problem was.

"We have had a visitation from the solicitor. Well not actually the solicitor... he sent a messenger. He came this morning and I was just doing the washing..."

"Mother... calm down. Tell me slowly. What was this about?"

"Sorry son. It's just that I'm all of a doings. It's made me so worried. He wants you to go to see him in his office in Evesham, as soon as possible."

"Well what's that about, then?"

"He wouldn't say but I wonder if it's about Nancy May?"... she added, "Do you think she's been found Giles?"

"I have no idea. Why would it be about Nancy May?"

"Well what else could it be about? I don't know! Dear God, I hope she's been found. Oh!! But what if she's been found..." She could not bring herself to finish her sentence. It would be too awful indeed to say that next word. "Please God she is not ...dead!" Peggy flopped into a kitchen chair and sobbed.

"Mother! Do not distress yourself so. You must not assume it is about Nancy May! It might be something completely unrelated. It is not worth getting yourself in such a doings. I will go tomorrow and find out what this is all about. I will come straight back and reassure you. Besides, don't you think I would know if Nancy May was dead? You know how sensitive we are about each other. I'm sure she is alright mother."

Putting his arm around his mother's shoulders, he suggested she now make herself a hot drink.

If only they had known it but at that very moment, Nancy May was preparing to say her final goodbyes to the band of gypsies and begin her journey back to Stapley Manor accompanied by Manfri. She was leaving with huge mixed feelings. These folk had become her family. Her friends. They had shared their lives with her and brought her into their circle of trust. Leaving Stow-on-the-Wold with Manfri, she reflected on the beautiful places she had seen throughout the seasons and their journey travelling through the idyllic Cotswold countryside from village to town, riverbank to copse. She had spent the most wonderful adventure with them but not wishing to overstay her welcome she finally accepted that it was time to take her leave and return to her mother and brother. For the time being and with heavy heart, she still had Manfri's company at least to enjoy for a few days longer. It was agreed that he would escort her home and stay at Stapley Manor for a brief few days, to rest the horses and allow Nancy May to show him around her home and the places which were meaningful to her. Unbeknown to each other, neither of them had any wish to hurry parting company with each other, so this means of prevarication seemed very acceptable to them both. Reluctantly, Manfri planned to thereafter reunite once more with the troupe in Evesham.

They elected to make one more night-time roadside stop along the way between Stow-on-the-Wold and Broadway. It was with enormous strength of willpower that Manfri once again slept outside to allegedly protect them against unwanted intruders. Yet his real reason was far from that! Next morning, they rode the vardo down the steep Fish Hill to admire together the panoramic views before descending through the village of Broadway, then upwards towards Snowshill. Manfri marvelled at the beauty of the village and the surrounding countryside. He could see why Nancy May loved the area so much and revelled in her stories of her childhood adventures as they 'clip-clopped" along.

She was certainly a fearless child, full of spirit, which he admired hugely. He had learnt that she was a pragmatic young woman with an infectious giggle and enchanting sense of humour. He loved how easily she could make him laugh. Yet she was also a person of deep emotion. She was very compassionate and thought of others before herself. She held few grudges but was sensitive of the opinions of others towards her. She spoke often of her beloved brother and of her mother but whenever the subject of her father came up, he noted that she changed the subject. He didn't push too hard on the subject but felt that there was something uncomfortable lurking in her relationship with him. He was curious to meet him!

It was not long before he did! The horse and wagon had made its way along the long driveway and was only yards away from the house, when suddenly out of the blue, a man came charging across the fields from a distance, waving a stick in the air, shouting obscenities at them. Nancy May was horrified as well as embarrassed. She called out to her father but he was so fixated on seeing only the gypsy caravan, that he did not seem to hear her. She asked Manfri to halt the horses and she leapt from the bench seat and ran towards her father, waving both hands in the air.

"Father. It is me... It's Nancy May! I have come home!" She shouted as loudly as she could but he still advanced towards them, yelling.

Such was the kafuffle, that Fred had rushed to the front door and swung it open to see what all the shouting was about.

Astonished, "Nancy May!" he exclaimed almost in disbelief, then turned inwards towards the hallway and yelled excitedly "It's Nancy May!! She's home!!"... He then ran towards the commotion and hugged Nancy May tightly, "My God! We have been so worried about you! Where have you been? Are you alright?"

From behind Fred came Peggy, running outside in disbelief, screaming with joy and relief. She ran down the steps weeping and flung her arms around her daughter, sobbing into the nape of her neck. As she released her at arms length to look into her eyes, then took a step back to be sure she was not dreaming, Albert approached from behind Nancy May and set about her with his stick. With several awful, unexpected strikes, she squealed with shock, "Oww!! Nooo!" Manfri had been watching the scene unfold from the elevated position of the vardo. As Albert approached them, his face angered and determined, his stick held strongly with purpose, Manfri anticipated his intent and jumped from his seat. He instinctively raced towards him but it was a moment too late to stop him making sharp contact with Nancy May's head. He finally reached him and snatched the stick from his hand and wrenched his arms behind his back in a strong restricting hold. Albert continued to yell and struggle. Peggy's hands flew to her face in abhorrence. Fred grabbed hold of Albert to relieve Manfri, who immediately pulled Nancy May into a warm embrace, with deep concern.

"Father... it's me Nancy May!" She turned to Albert with tears streaming her face.

"You filthy wench! I've told you before to get off my land. I don't want any thieving gypsy folk here! D'you hear me?"

Peggy shielded her daughter from Albert, whispered to Fred to get him inside. Still shouting abuse behind them, Peggy ushered her daughter indoors, with Manfri close behind. Mabel just caught the end of the pandemonium and greeted her niece with utter joy. Fred followed, struggling to keep Albert under control.

"I'll kill the pair of you!" Albert threatened, still writhing in Fred's grasp.

Fred tried to quell his anger, speaking quietly to Albert as he coaxed him along. He intended to get him up the stairs to his bedroom, where they had discovered he would usually calm down, often regressing to childhood. Unfortunately however, before he could get him away from the family, Albert blurted out something, which would trigger a whole new turn of events.

"Wouldn't be the first time I've killed a man!!" Peggy wished there was a hole in the floor to swallow her up. "See... you don't know, do you?! No! Well I'll tell you, I have! I've killed two men and I'll kill again if you don't get those stinking 'gypos' off my land!"

"Father!" Nancy May pleaded. "It's me – your daughter!" Peggy tried to pull her away from the distressing situation but Albert held court again.

"Don't you ever wonder how come you got to live in a place like this?? Hey??... Well I'll tell you! I won it fair and square in a duel."

"Father, please, not now." Why of all times would he do this in front of Manfri? She was mortified. Little did she realise, worse was to come!

"Don't you dare call me father! Or I swear I'll.." he wrestled with Fred and Manfri stepped forward to assist, as Fred's strength was weakening."

"Get your filthy hands off me or I'll ..." He stopped and looked Manfri in the eye. Between his teeth he spoke to Manfri alone, "You don't believe me do you?" Then he shouted, "Did you not hear me clearly enough? I've killed TWO men! That snivelling rat of a gamekeeper...he deserved it he did." Laughing hysterically now, "Even the stupid boys in blue couldn't work it out... shot 'im I did.. then the pig... so easy it was!" Got rid of him just like that, I did." He snapped his fingers to demonstrate the ease with which he could execute a man and thinking the whole thing incredibly funny, he laughed so hard he drooled down his shirt.

Fred stood back in shock and looked again at Albert. "It was you? YOU killed him! Dear God, no! You killed Jacob?"

Albert, swayed within Manfri's grasp and focussed on Fred. "Give the boy a toffee! You've got it!" he laughed sarcastically. "Yup, that was 'is name, 'Jacob'." He mimicked effeminately.

With one hefty swipe, Fred smacked his fist across Albert's jaw, snatching him from Manfri's hold and flattening him to the ground. Bending over him then kneeling, Fred was incandescent with rage, "You murderer! You bastard murderer!!" He grabbed his clothes around his neck in an effort to stop himself from battering him so hard he would kill him. He had never felt rage like it.

Neither Peggy nor Mabel had ever seen Fred anywhere close to enraged and were now transfixed with confusion, until slowly, it dawned on Mabel.

"Fred?" she began. Shaking with sickening understanding, "Fred... You... you and Jacob...were...?" She could not finish her sentence. Eyes wide with shock and trembling from head to toe, Peggy looked at her and by intuition also appreciated the wordless meaning of her thoughts.

Fred turned a glance shamefully towards Mabel, then dropped his tearful eyes. "I'm sorry", he whispered, "I'm so sorry. He was the love of my life. I didn't mean anything by it, Mabel. You have been so kind and sweet to me but I just didn't feel..." He broke down pitifully. He continued then and with quieter emotion, loosened his grip on Albert but holding his gaze with incredulity, he shrugged. "He was of no threat to you! Why would you do that... to such a kind and loving man? He was everything you could never be! He was just everything...to me..." Fred sat back on his heels and wept like a baby. Mabel too, flopped to the floor and wept. Nancy May picked up her Aunt Mabel from the floor and assisted her to the kitchen, where she made a hot pot of leaves and comforted her in her bleakness.

Manfri hauled up Albert from the floor and suggested he'd said enough. Albert look up at Manfri as would a child, "Can I go and play with my car now Daddy?" Manfri was taken aback but Peggy stepped in and with a nod of assurance to Manfri, she guided Albert away to his room.

Manfri stood silent, in disbelief of what he had just witnessed. What was for sure, was that he feared for Nancy May's safety. He didn't like it one bit, that he was planning on leaving her here.

Some time later, they were all sitting in the kitchen, reeling from the surreal episode earlier. Mabel was still in tears. Fred had disappeared, probably to compose himself in his embarrassment. Peggy was picking up where she had left off with Nancy May, hearing about her apologies for 'running away', as her mother put it.

Giles arrived home from the solicitor's office and was joyous to find Nancy May returned. Meeting Manfri, was at first a little strained, with memories of their first encounter with each other but as the hours went by and he saw the connection between him and his beloved sister, Giles concluded that he was a good man after all. Chatter was vibrant and celebratory and Giles was not at all shocked to hear about Nancy May's burns and subsequent need for care. He had known all along that his intuition was right. Peggy was grateful to Manfri's mother and wished him to thank her for her goodness.

Mealtime came around and a quick effort to put food on the table was all that Peggy could do. She took a tray up to Albert but found that he had put himself to bed, curled up with his toy car and his thumb in his mouth. Mabel subsequently announced that she was not hungry and quietly also took herself to her room.

As things quietened, Giles finally had the opportunity to tell them all, about the curious summons he had had to the solicitor's office. He explained how he was interviewed with regard to a duel their father had been involved in, just before they had moved to Stapley Manor. It had been believed that he had been hiding in the grass on the hillside and it was hoped that he could offer himself as witness all these years later as to clarify something about the event, which took place there that morning. Giles had assured the solicitor, that he was not the person they were looking for but as he left the solicitor's office, mulling over the conversation he had had with Mr. Foster, it triggered a memory of Nancy May coming home secretively one morning just before they moved and felt certain that she could likely be the person they were looking for. He hoped she was not in trouble.

Sitting around the table now, Giles asked Nancy May, if she could cast any light on the enquiry, secretly believing she could. Immediately, Nancy May admitted the truth about sneaking out to follow her father. Giles and Peggy were shocked beyond words to hear how she had kept secret all these years, such a gruesome memory. Manfri leant forward and took her hand, caressing her fingers with his thumb.

What she said next, completely shocked Peggy but not for the same reason as it shocked everyone else. Nancy May conceded, that the image she could not remove from her head, was that her father's opponent, brought this pistol to his own head and shot himself a split second before her father's bullet could strike. She spelt out the fact that Albert did not kill the first man, as believed. The man took his own life! Tears escaped Peggy's eyes

214

and Nancy May assumed that this was relief at knowing Albert did not kill him. Little did she know it was renewed grief, for a man she deeply loved.

The information did not excuse Albert from the second murder of course. Killing Jacob was unforgivable and they discussed what should they do now? Tell the police?

As a family, they agreed that in the first instance, Nancy May needed to visit the solicitor's office to present herself as the person present at the time of the duel. They did not know of what consequence her information might have on anything but it was the right thing to do.

At the close of day, Fred could not be found. They searched the house, then the grounds. The light was fading and it became a serious worry. As it became too dark to look further, they agreed he would probably be licking his wounds in an outbuilding somewhere and would be back for breakfast in the morning.

He was not! Giles, Manfri and Nancy May set out again at the break of day, in search of dear Fred. It was approaching midday, when Manfri made a macabre discovery of a body, floating face down in the river. Dead. He had the painful task of breaking the gruesome news to the distraught family.

The funeral was simple. No fuss. Small congregation. Mrs. Prowse agreed he be lain alongside her beloved Jacob. Mabel felt this was right and would befit Fred's wishes. Her loss cut like a deep wound, more so, as she mused about the secret life her husband had led. She pitied him.

Days later, Manfri was still staying at Stapley Manor. He did not wish to leave Nancy May, until he was certain she was safe from her father. Truth was, he did not wish to leave her. As soon as the funeral was over, Manfri escorted her on horseback to the solicitor's but remained outside to respect her privacy.

"Good morning! I am here to see Mr. Foster, regarding an incident in the summer of 1846. My name is Nancy May Turner."

The assistant looked at her with the strangest of glances, "That's over a decade ago!" she remarked incredulously.

"It is!" Nancy May replied, wondering why that would seem so strange at all. She was asked to sit and wait on an uncomfortable bench, which was no doubt a previous church pew.

A short while later, an officious male voice called out, "Miss Turner. Come!"

She walked into the dark, oak panelled, office, overcrowded with furniture and took a green leather seat in front of an aging gentleman, though she could barely see much of him, behind the piles of documents. The room smelled of stale tobacco and old parchment with a whiff of alcohol into the mix. So unpleasant that she wished this to be a brief encounter and she could escape to the fresh Cotswold air!

"Now! Miss Turner, I believe??"

"Yes Sir. I understand you have been looking for me?"

"Indeed we have! You have been hard to track down!"

"How can I help?"

"You were quite young when your family moved from Primrose Lane into Stapley Manor. Do you remember that time?"

"Yes Sir. I was about nine years old."

"Well, I would like you to cast your mind back to that time. In fact, I want you to think very carefully about the days BEFORE you moved. Do you have any particular recollections about those days?"

"Yes Sir, I do. Sir I am well aware that my father took part in a duel by the lake. His opponent died at the scene."

"...and how do you KNOW this, Miss Turner?

"Because I was there! I believed my father was up to no good and so I followed him. It was hard to keep up: It was still quite dark and I feared he would catch me out but eventually he reached the lake and met some other men there. Three I think. I needed to see better so I scrambled up the slope – the grass was dewy wet and I slipped a few times but found a place where I could crouch down to see what was going on."

Nancy May took a moment to reflect. She had gone through this scenario so often in her head. It would never leave her memory. "There seemed to be an agreement between the men, then they paced out ten steps each way. Pistols were brought out and a man called out a signal and ..."

Nancy May hated to go over this again. Speaking the words out loud was even harder than thinking them.

"Miss Turner. I must ask you to think very carefully about what happened next. This is very important. Tell me EXACTLY what you saw happen next."

A tear trickled down Nancy May's reddening cheek. "Someone called FIRE! My father raised his pistol like this..." she demonstrated his straight arm extended and mimicked pulling the trigger. "...and the other man put his pistol to his own head and shot..." Again she enacted the other man's movements, her chin wobbling with the distress of the memory.

"Take your time, Miss Turner. I have but one last question. Your response is crucial and I have to accept your first answer as true and correct. "In your opinion, which bullet do you believe killed you father's opponent? Do you think it was your father's, or the man who pulled the trigger upon himself. If you are not sure, tell me so."

There was no hesitation in Nancy May's response. She had gone over this so many times. "There is no doubt in my mind, Sir. The vision has been with me since I was a child. The man took his own life before my father's bullet hit. On the last second, he raised his gun to his own head, just as the command to fire was called, so that the bullets sounded in quick succession but the man's gun was already in position against his head. He fell to the ground with a thud."

"Miss Turner, you have been commendable in your strength and honesty and I am grateful to you for this. Please take a moment but when you are ready, you may leave."

"Of what consequence is my testament, Sir?"

"My enquiries are about finding just rewards, Miss Turner. You have played your part in helping me to establish what is fair. Always remember, no matter what the consequences to yourself or your family, you should be proud of the part you have played, in bringing justice, to a family who have been wronged."

Nancy May and Manfri returned to Stapley Manor in subdued mood. She still had no real understanding of the consequences of her statement and with the anticipation of Manfri returning to his troupe, left her with a sense of emptiness. Manfri also was realising his deep reluctance to leave Nancy May. He recognized his deep need to protect her from her father and in any case, he cannot imagine his day to day life without her. Telling himself that it will be but just over nine months until the travellers would return to Evesham when he could see her again, he hoped the time would go quickly. Perhaps after dinner, he would confirm his departure for the next day and ask her to promise to meet him at the fair next year.

As often was the case, Albert was in the garden, sitting on a stone bench in the sunshine mentally playing out a childhood game, laughing sporadically, calling out to an imaginary sibling, then staring, still and vacant for long periods of time. Despite Nancy May's abhorrence for her father, she still saw the pathos in his condition. She was not so much sad to see her father's deterioration, as she was sad that she had never really had a father to love or to love her. The past few days had caused her to truly reflect on her childhood and as a woman herself now, she deeply pitied her mother's life as his wife. God knows how he mistreated her and she wept for her miserable life. She wondered if she had ever had any happiness but hoped that somewhere along the path, she had found reward and love, for she was a caring, lovely woman and life had not treated her kindly. Nancy May reflected on Mr. Foster's words but regardless of how she tried to translate them, they still did not make sense: "No matter what the consequences to you or your family, you should be proud of the part you have played, in bringing justice, to a family who have been wronged."...

She decided that for the moment at least, she would keep her own counsel and not discuss this with her family. With her usual pragmatic maturity, she supposed all would be revealed soon enough.

Giles however, had bigger news. Really big news!!

He had invited Elise to share dinner with them at Stapley Manor to celebrate the homecoming of Nancy May and allow Elise to tell Nancy May herself, about coming to live at the 'Gate House' as he still referred to it. Peggy was beside herself with anxiety to hear his plan. How on earth was she going to keep up this pretence? It would be difficult enough to get through the evening meal but the thought of Elise moving in so close as her neighbour, would be too hard to bear. It was of course wonderful to see her beautiful estranged baby daughter as a grown woman and she could burst with the need to hold her and hug her tight but to hold such an immense secret and live this lie, was already becoming intolerable. More so now that Giles seemed to have intentions. That could not happen. She prayed for divine intervention, that the old house could not be made good enough to live in, or that for some reason, Giles could no longer work in Harvington, or in some way the two would be separated and this whole nightmare would go away.

However, for the moment, Peggy welcomed Elise as she would any other guest and every five minutes that passed, she was grateful for, as it was nearer the time when Elise would be going home and Peggy could relax, just a little. Mabel laughed at her sister's evident nervousness, believing it was because they were not in the habit of receiving guests, although it had also occurred to her, that it was perhaps because she could be entertaining her future daughter–in–law. She and Peggy were about to carry the tureens of food to the dining room, when Mabel made a comment to that effect and in reaction Peggy dropped the dish of potatoes she was holding. Fortunately it only fell as far as the kitchen table but it was enough to chip the dish. Peggy cursed, pretending it was too hot. Her excuse did not fool Mabel, who apologised for her comment, astonished to realise how touchy her sister truly was about the subject. With a rapid switch of dishes, nobody else knew any different, nor did anyone comment on Peggy's shaking hands and flushed face, as she served up the food at the table.

The meal went passably well and a generally convivial atmosphere made Elise feel welcomed. They had risked having Albert at the table, partly because Peggy felt it would be a suitable cover for her nerves and she could feign attention upon her confused husband, if needed. He sat quietly, stupefied at the change of routine. They were about to serve up a creamy pudding, when Giles prompted Elise to tell Nancy May her news about the Mill House. Peggy's stomach sank to see how excited she sounded at the prospect of moving in next door. Elise began by explaining the back story to what Nancy May would know as the Mill House and how she used to live in Stapley Manor. Things slowly began to dawn upon Nancy May as she pieced together all that was being said. It was as if unknown pieces of the jigsaw were coming to light and she looked around the table realising that she seemed to be the only one who was seeing through these details. At what point would it become obvious, that her father, who was sitting next to Elise, was the man who believed he had killed her father? And yet... she then reflected on the comment of the solicitor and wondered how that might fit into all of this.

Manfri noticed the worried furrow in Nancy May's brow deepen and although he had no idea what troubled her, he knew something was not right. He slipped his hand across to cover her white knuckles under the tablecloth and squeezed reassuringly. She glanced at him and tried to relax her facial muscles in response. How well he knew her!

At that moment, Giles scraped back his chair across the threadbare rug and stood away from the table, commanding attention. He pick up his glass of half finished ale and cleared his throat in preparation of his announcement. "I have something to tell you all, while we are gathered together." Raising his glass as though in royal salute to Elise and beaming from ear to ear, he continued with aplomb, "I wish that this was more than ale ... but I should like to ask you to all to raise a glass and welcome Elise to the family: She has agreed to marry me!"

Peggy's nausea overwhelmed her. "Something is burning in the kitchen!" She shot from the room and Mabel followed. Peggy brought back her entire dinner, which had not sat well from the start. "Whatever is the matter with you Peggy?"

Peggy collapsed to the floor, white as a ghost. "Are you ill?" It was all Peggy could do to shake her head. She broke down into a convulsive sob. Mabel crouched next to her and comforted her sister with a devoted hug. "You can tell me, Peg. What troubles you?"

"You will not forgive me, if I do! You will not understand."

"You're worrying me now! Peg, you have stood by me all these years and I will not fail you now. Trust me, I am here for you!"

"You say this Mabel but ... you will be ashamed of me!" Silence saturated the air around them, exaggerating the celebratory clanking of glasses and high-spirited merriment pervading the room next door. "Peg, Please! Tell me what is so painful to you that makes you thus!"

"It is Elise... Elise... she is my daughter!"

CHAPTER 21

Elizabeth is called for the last time to the solicitor's office. This time, now that Elise had reached sixteen, she asked her daughter to accompany her. They went into the panelled room with an open mind and protected heart, for they expected little from this latest and last investigation. After so many years since leaving Stapley Manor, they could never imagine being able to call it their own once more. They had prepared themselves to be advised that no further witness had come to light and the case was now closed.

Unusually, Mr. Foster seemed ebullient. Swinging wide open his office door in welcome and sweeping his extended arm in an overly exaggerated manner, he bid the two ladies enter.

Elizabeth introduced her daughter and as usual, Mr. Foster was straight down to business. As all three took their seats, he began.

"Mrs. Carter. Might I assume that I can speak freely? Do I assume that your daughter is now fully au fait with all that has gone before this meeting?"

Elise had many questions to ask her mother, following the curious coincidences, which had come to light surrounding Stapley Manor and the family who lived there. In addition, she was now to be married to Giles and believed that since she had now reached the age of sixteen and become what she now believed to be an adult, it was her mother's duty to tell her what she knew about her father's death and how it had come about that they had been caused to swap houses with Albert Turner and his wife and two children. Unable to keep her secret any longer, Elizabeth told Elise all that she knew, from the moment Albert rushed in that fateful night and Henry accepted the terms of the duel.

Elizabeth now gave Mr. Foster permission, to speak openly and without reservation. With this approval, he promptly continued. "I have some splendid news!" Elizabeth's heart was pumping hard and she sat forward on the edge of her chair. Elise reached across for her mother's hand and they squeezed each other's tightly.

"It has taken a great deal of time, legal wrangling and investigative research, for which I profusely apologise but finally, we have a result! We have eventually traced our necessary second witness to the event, which took place at the time of your husband's death." Unable to contain his excitement he almost shouted, "The outcome, is that it has been confirmed that your husband raised his given pistol to his own head and took the first bullet. By taking his own life, Mrs. Carter, the duel result is deemed 'null and void'. Thus, Mr. Turner (that is your husband's opponent), cannot stake a claim to Stapley Manor! Mrs. Carter, You remain the owner of this house and its grounds!"

Both Elizabeth and Elise hugged and wept until Mr. Foster offered them both a restorative warming drink, brought in by his secretary. There was no celebration in the confirmation that Henry did indeed take his own life but he was gone now, no matter by what method and they both knew that he would have wished that justice would have prevailed.

Once they had recovered from the truly unexpected revelation and simmered down their emotions, Mr.Foster resumed with a more sombre approach. "There is however, a difficult task ahead. That is, the removal of the incumbent occupiers. That is for me, together with the police if necessary, to exercise. So, what I am saying, is that it might be some little time before the house is likely to be vacated and your return possible.

Now that Elise knew Giles's family, this was going to be very awkward indeed. Elise put this to the solicitor. Re-positioning his spectacles in serious thought, he agreed, "Well, this is quite the conundrum, Miss Carter." Thinking about it for some moments longer, he offered a suggestion. "Perhaps, if I might be so bold as to make a suggestion... If there could be some open, convivial communication between your two families, this might be a way through this very difficult time. Perhaps you Mrs. Carter would agree to speak with Mrs. Turner? I have found in the past that this is often a good way through family disputes. Elizabeth was willing to try this. If it did not work, then she could always retreat and allow the law to step in but she hoped for Elise's sake, this first plan, might work. In any case, she would have to meet Mr. and Mrs. Turner soon enough, since Elise was about to marry their son! She could not pretend to be happy about Elise's future husband transpiring to be the son of their obnoxious former employee who caused so much hurt and grief all those years ago but she had become fond of Samson as she knew him and would not allow her opinion of his father colour her impression of him. He had proved himself to be a hard working, polite and caring young man and she saw nothing about him, which resembled his father. That being the case, it stood to reason, that the young man who was to become her son-in-law, must take after his mother, who must surely have set a fine example for her son to follow.

Mr. Foster had one last word of advice to offer Elizabeth and Elise. It was that under more usual circumstances, he might have suggested that they pursue through the courts for compensation for loss of use of the house for all of those years whilst Elise was growing up, as well as for the hardship and instability they had subsequently undergone unnecessarily. However, in this instance, he confirmed that the family are of insufficient funds and any kind of financial reimbursement would be unlikely. Elizabeth was quick to immediately reject any such sort of idea of a claim and the right to reclaim their home was more than she could ever have dreamt of achieving. With profuse thanks, Elizabeth and Elise left the solicitor and prepared themselves for whatever lay ahead.

CHAPTER 22

After provoking the ordeal with Fred, Albert never seemed to recover from Fred's physical assault and he rapidly deteriorated day by day. More regularly now, he was forgetting how to eat or getting confused with the time of day. He would mumble nonsensically or would get lost about the house. The family, were run ragged keeping an eye on him but ultimately, he took to his bed. He would not eat nor talk and there was a certain deadness about his eyes. Within days, he had lost significant weight from his already emaciated frame. His hands were all but skeletal and his face drawn and greyish pale. Peggy, Mabel and Giles all took turns in sitting by his bedside but Peggy's time was almost totally absorbed with his care: changing his bed regularly through necessity and laundering the poor quality sheets, cooking and trying to tempt him with food. Nancy May, would do anything else in the house to help out but she categorically refused to sit by her father's bedside. She would not be a hypocrite. It seemed ludicrous to think they were harbouring a murderer who had shown little remorse. At least they had no conscience that they had done the right thing, by calling in the police to arrest him. In their hearts they absolutely believed Albert's rant and confession of killing Jacob, which he had made in a rare lucid moment but it was unfortunate, that when the police arrived to interview Albert, he was completely incomprehensible and childlike. The boys in blue refused to take the claim seriously and left, reminding the family that the case was closed.

When Giles was not taking his turn to look after his father, he would continue travelling to Harvington to see Elise and work on her expanding farm, as he had committed to do. There was so much to be done at Stapley Manor however, that Manfri offered to stay with the family a while longer, ostensibly to help out around the place. There were fires to be kept going to keep the oncoming Autumnal chill off the rooms, animals to tend, vegetables to nurture in the garden ready for harvesting and physical help needed when Albert required changing. Of course, that was the least of it! Although Albert was no longer a physical threat to Nancy May, there was something more that was worrying her and Manfri was not yet ready to leave her side, whilst she was evidently so troubled. She had confided in him her concerns about Elise. There was something... just something... that she could not quite put her finger on. She saw Elise, as a beautiful, fun-loving, hard working, friendly girl. Yet her mother's reaction to her was, well, odd! Why was her mother so... uncomfortable around her? Why did nobody else notice this? Nancy May knew only time would tell but it bothered her that somehow the atmosphere would change whenever Elise came to the house, which made her mother agitated. Clearly, something was not right and Nancy May could not settle, until she knew exactly what it was. There were also the unknown repercussions, of her own statement. The more time passed, the less Nancy May understood Mr. Foster's parting comment and the inference that there might be some kind of impact on her own family.

It was perhaps two weeks after Nancy May had visited the solicitor that a formal letter arrived in the post, beautifully written in educated script, addressed to Mrs. Albert Turner. Such was the rarity of such an envelope arriving on their doorstep, that Mabel and Nancy May stood intrigued at her side, as Peggy held it in her rough, hard working hands, curious as to the sender. Coaxed on by her sister, she carefully opened the seal as though she did not wish to damage even the envelope and finally, pulled out an immaculately folded piece of paper and turned it right way up to read its content.

Peggy announced that it was from Elise's mother and with churning stomach, she began to read out aloud, for all to hear.

"Dear Mrs. Turner,

I believe that on this occasion, a calling card is not quite appropriate. Given the circumstances of our history and knowing that your husband is rather unwell, I thought perhaps I should write to you direct.

It would appear that our families are soon to be inextricably linked by the marriage of Elise and Giles and I believe it would be appropriate for you and I to meet, so that we might discuss wedding arrangements.

However, some other important information has recently come to my attention, which is rather more pressing and I would also very much like to discuss this with you, at your earliest convenience.

Might I propose Friday of this week? Would morning time be suitable for me to call upon you?

I look forward to your reply.

Yours faithfully," Peggy finished, "She has signed herself Elizabeth."

Peggy pulled out a chair and sank into it, with her head in her hands, allowing the tears to trickle between her fingers. The letter had unceremoniously fallen to the floor. Mabel and Nancy May exchanged worried glances and each made an almost indiscernible shrug of their shoulders, indicating to each other that they had no idea what troubled her. Nancy May hazarded a guess. Kneeling beside her mother, she gently reached out for her hand and held it in both of her own. Peggy sniffed hard in an effort to cease her crying but her chin continued to wobble uncontrollably and tears flowed constantly.

Gently and sympathetically, Nancy May spoke softly, "Mother, I wonder if I might know why you are so distressed." Peggy flashed her a look of absolute horror. "You have kept it from us all this time and it must have been so hard for you to keep such a secret ... but I know how we came to live here." Peggy, for that sweet moment felt relieved but listened to what her daughter thought she knew. Nancy May continued, "In fact, I know exactly what happened! That was why I was required to go to the solicitor's office. They needed to have an eye-witness's account of the duel, that took place between father and the man I now know, who used to live here."

Peggy and Mabel listened in astonishment, not about the fact that Henry took his own life, because they already knew that but that Nancy May, at the age of nine, had escaped from the house and followed her father. Worst of all, that she should have witnessed such a terrible event, then kept it close to her chest for all those years and had not even shared it with her brother. What a stoic young woman she was! Yet, all of this was still no comfort to Peggy for it was not what worried her most of all.

Nancy May, however, needed to tell her mother the worst of what she suspected. "Mother, I must tell you something which weighs heavily upon my mind. After I had told Mr. Foster what I had seen all those years ago, I had no idea of the possible consequence of my telling the truth but he suggested, that there might be repercussions for my family in order to bring justice, to a family which has been wronged. Is that family, Elise and her mother? Do you think this may be the reason for her wish to meet you?"

"I believe you are right my darling girl. What a clever girl you are! All those years ago, we swapped homes after Henry...

Mr. Carter died..." With cold realisation, Peggy considered the implication of this now but could not see how Nancy May's statement could change anything.

Nancy May had no regret in telling the truth to the solicitor. In fact, she felt astonishingly unburdened. Yet, she now held a sense of guilt that her statement may well have brought implications, in some way, for her family. She had been so glad for having Manfri stay over longer to help out but she knew that soon he would be returned to the camp and even the thought of that left her with a huge sense of loss. She surprised herself at how much she already missed the vardo and the cosy, intimate nights listening to Manfri's soporific breathing and the sense of security having him so close. She missed the troupe too, with their rituals, music and laughter and the close sense of community she had never before experienced. Their sense of wanderlust was enviable and she could easily imagine herself adapting to such a lifestyle. That sense of adventure and self-sufficiency had always appealed and having experienced a little of it, it now made here life here in Broadway, feel rather dull. It was a surprise to her that Manfri offered to stay a while longer until, as he put it, things settled down and he knew she was safe. Apart from her mother and brother, nobody had ever before seemed concerned for her like that... and she liked it. She liked him! The thought struck her hard. Her mind swirled over the many memories she had made with him over the period of a few weeks and she suddenly came to the conclusion, that what she was feeling, was love. Had she fallen in love with him? Perhaps she had but what she did know for sure was that she did not want him to leave and held her breath each morning until she knew he would stay another day. She dared not bring up the subject with him, for fear that his plan to leave might be imminent, so they coasted day to day without mention of the subject.

Friday came and Elizabeth arrived as arranged, by coach. It was an unassuming vehicle but at least she could afford that. Since Elizabeth's letter had arrived, Peggy had worried about this lady returning to Stapley Manor, knowing how grand it was in those days. Despite all of Peggy's efforts and hard work, the house had become dishevelled and impoverished, a hugely poorer version of what it once was. She and Mabel decided that since the parlour was the smallest of the reception rooms, they would dress it with as much of their best furniture as they owned, which was in itself poverty-stricken. Peggy was touched by everyone's understanding and support and so they all set to work.

Manfri took it upon himself to light a roaring, welcoming fire and carried through the two best armchairs to be placed either side of the fireplace. He then brought and placed one of their only circular wooden tables for the bay window. The best of their rugs was in Peggy's bedroom so he brought that downstairs and placed it in the centre of the room. It was beginning to take shape. On the mantelpiece Mabel placed Peggy's best ornaments and she had one cherished picture in her bedroom but she loaned it to Peggy for the wall above the parlour fireplace. Manfri was happy to help with that and once hung, they all agreed that it looked good there.

Nancy May found some linens in her mother's chest of drawers. She laundered all the lace cloths and with starching and pressing they were used to cover a multitude of battered furniture. The antimacassars were placed to cover the worn arms of the armchairs bringing them back to life and Mabel laid one of the more fragile cloths across the table in the window, which covered the entire table down to the floor. Upon its surface she placed a huge vase of foliage from the garden, interspersed with the remaining flowers from the autumn garden.

To fill the space, which remained in the far corner of the room, they decided to put a further table. It was rather wobbly and unsafe after Albert had fallen upon it in one of his drunken moments but with a little work, Manfri managed to stabilise it. Mabel then covered it in another white laundered cloth, on top of which Peggy placed a precious, gleaming, silver tray, which held a glass decanter and two highly polished glass goblets. Two wooden chairs were polished and set symmetrically aside the table. With that, the room seemed almost respectable and one could be forgiven for believing that each room would be furnished in the same, respectable way.

They all four stood back and admired their efforts. Manfri was complimentary and tried to discourage Peggy's dip back into under confidence, he cajoled and lightened her mood and she thought what a wonderful, kind young man he was. Between them they made a plan to keep some kind of dignity for Peggy, by arranging that Mabel would open the door to their guest and act as maid. Yet as the hour drew close and Peggy nervously awaited the arrival of Elizabeth in the parlour, she allowed her inferiority complex to take hold.

Sure enough, her guest's demeanour was just as Peggy had recalled. As she entered the room, ushered in by Mabel, Elizabeth presented herself with as much grace and elegance as Peggy had remembered from the fleeting moments they had previously met and although bereavement and increasing years had naturally taken their toll, she was still a beautiful, genteel, woman of certain years. Peggy felt inadequate, embarrassed and even perhaps shameful, before her.

Elizabeth stood, straight backed with silvering hair swept up into a bonnet, which she had declined to remove, as her stay would be brief. She accepted a seat offered by Peggy and they faced each other from either side of a blazing fire. Elizabeth seemed not to recognise Peggy at all but then, why should she?

Their brief encounter was years ago and there was no reason for her to make any connection with the scullery maid whom she had seen only fleetingly and without significance. Peggy offered refreshments, which were politely accepted for the sake of cordial etiquette, then with the expected pleasantries done, Elizabeth took control of the conversation in a business like way.

Placing her china cup with a barely audible sound into its floral saucer, Elizabeth took the plunge to begin her dreaded conversation. "Mrs. Turner, I must cut to the chase. We each share a difficult past but time has moved on. What I am here to say, is very difficult but whilst I am sorry to hear about your husband's weakening condition, I must be honest with you, that I am glad to have this opportunity to speak with you alone, for I would find it very difficult to be civil to Mr. Turner. You must surely understand my reasons and I apologise if this offends you, for I have no qualms with you." As she took a few seconds to prepare the words as carefully as she had rehearsed them, Peggy's thoughts honed in on this last phrase and very much doubted that Elizabeth would be saying any such thing, if she only knew the truth about her relationship with her husband all those years ago and she felt mighty guilty.

Fixing her eye contact as steadily as she could with her host, who seemed to have equal trouble holding her gaze in return, Elizabeth continued with apparent confidence. "This, I am sure, will come to you with as much shock and surprise as it has come to me. I have recently been informed that the duel in which our husbands came face to face, was not all it seemed. My husband died, as you well know and so the outcome was assumed that your husband was the victor and thus had claim to this house and grounds, in accordance with the duelling agreement. As you know, I honoured that decision and vacated Stapley Manor with dignity. My solicitor, Mr. Foster, however, suspected that all was not as it seemed and he has worked tirelessly to prove his belief." Again she took a shaky breath to restore her strength in delivering this blow to a woman who she believed was an innocent participant in this hideous situation.

"I am not sure if you are aware, Mrs. Turner, that in actual fact, as the duel unfolded, my husband took his own life and so did not die as a result of your husband's bullet but by his own." She swallowed hard against the grief, which still threatened to again surface as it often did, even after all these years. "Mr. Foster had worked tirelessly over the years to prove that because of this, the outcome of the duel should be discredited." With relief that it was said, she looked downwards to her cup and saucer, her eyes unseeing through a mist of moisture.

It took moments for Peggy to respond. "Mrs. Carter. You will never know how sorry I am that your husband died. Truly I am. More so, that my own husband played a part in this terrible outcome. I am indeed, ashamed. However, I am not entirely certain as to your conclusion."

"Mr. Foster had to secure two eyewitnesses to the event and after all these years, the second has just come to light. Although he was unable to divulge to me the identity of that person, their statement confirms that the agreement was null and void. Stapley Manor still belongs to me. This is still my home and I have to ask you to vacate it, with as much decorum as I did in the first place."

Stunned silence pervaded the room.

Elizabeth continued. "Of course, it would seem only fair that you now exchange homes with me, as we did once before and I can offer you my house and grounds in Harvington, which is considerably more acceptable than that of Primrose Lane. Of course, I shall not expect you to move out whilst your husband is ... so unwell ... but I anticipate that you may be able to do so ...in due course." She hesitated with diplomacy.

Peggy was floored at the reality of her words.

Finding her pluck, it was now her turn, to deal a blow to Elizabeth. With surprising calm, she gathered herself and began. "Mrs. Carter. I thank you for your frankness, which I can only admire. I can in fact, furnish you with some information in return." Sitting with her back upright and straight as if she were a lady of class, her hands loosely clasped upon her lap, suggesting she was confidently relaxed and belying her inner tension. "It was my daughter who has stepped forward to give honest witness to the event and it is her you must be grateful to, for allowing you to stake claim upon this beautiful house once more."

Elizabeth drew in a sharp breath of astonishment.

"Nancy May was but a child and had no understanding at that time, of what she witnessed, nor was she aware of its consequences all these years on. She chose to keep private what she saw, until very recently, when she was summoned to the solicitor. She was of course, ignorant of the implications of her account and now, she will be unaware of such ultimate consequences upon her own family. Yet, I can assure you, that such is her honesty, that she would never retract her statement and would undoubtedly do the same again."

Peggy then stood and walked to the bay window to look across the open fields beyond. As she did so, Elizabeth reflected on how the room used to be when she lived there and it was in that very place where Peggy now stood, that she first heard the cry of her baby daughter. Her drifting thoughts were brusquely interrupted.

"There is something more I should disclose, Mrs. Carter." She turned to face her guest, staring wide-eyed and boldly into her eyes. "Something which, I know, will be very painful for you to hear and which I have kept a close secret for close to two decades. This too, will have huge implications, for both you and Elise and indeed my own son, Giles."

Elizabeth slid forward to perch tremulously on the edge of her chair.

Without any further preamble, Peggy simply announced, "I am Elise's birth mother!"

Elizabeth's hands flew to her flushed cheeks in shocked disbelief. Quietly the words slipped from her lips as though they were spoken without Elizabeth's consent. "You! You... you are my husband's..."

"Yes! ... I loved him too" she arrested Elizabeth's words.

"I knew from the moment I set eyes on Elise. You must surely see the likeness in me too and you will see proof when you meet Nancy May. They are clearly sisters, – half sisters." She corrected herself. Peggy looked from Elizabeth to the view outside and back again to her stunned guest. "Do not judge me on my past, for I have no shame in having loved Henry and besides, there was never any intent for it to happen nor to cause you sorrow, although I know we did."

It was important she spoke from the heart and said all that she had wanted to say for years. "I have to thank you though, from the bottom of my heart, for bringing up my baby into such a beautiful girl. It broke my heart to leave her here on this very doorstep. You will never know how much it took me to do that ..."

"Does she know yet? Does your husband know?" Elizabeth needed to know.

"Albert does not know and he does no longer have the capacity to understand, so it is best he remains ignorant. I have hidden this from him for all these years, as I feared for my life as well as for Henry and Elise too. Albert has never been a forgiving man! It was years later I suppose through gossip that had miraculously lain dormant for years, that he learned I had been unfaithful. It was then, in a fit of pique, that he came to your house that night to call Henry out but thank God, nobody knew about the baby."

"As for Elise, it is now no longer my secret to tell her, so much as our secret! We are now BOTH responsible for telling her – and tell her we must. I should say, tell them, for this relationship, marriage, cannot be allowed to happen! This will be a bitter pill for them both. I had no more idea who Elise was until days ago, than you knew who Giles was. This is a cruel twist of fate, which brings us to this point and so we must deal with this together. Do you not agree, Elizabeth?"

Peggy deliberately used her guest's first name in a subconscious attempt to bring them together as equals. Elizabeth, it seemed, was struck dumb and pacing about the floor, from one end of the parlour to the other in distress. This was NOT how she imagined this visit to turn out. It was a nightmare from which she could not wake.

Peggy did her best to take control of the situation. "Elizabeth, we need to bring them both here, together and talk to them. This secret MUST be broken and I believe it is best and kindest to do this as soon as possible and with them both together." Elizabeth was still in utter shock and not able to respond.

Peggy thought carefully to make a plan. "Elizabeth, when Giles comes home tonight from Harvington, I shall ask him to bring Elise here tomorrow and I would invite you to be here also. Can you do that?" Elizabeth nodded. "It will be our task to sit them down and tell them together. Are you agreed?"

With a reluctant whisper, Elizabeth managed to respond. "Yes. I agree. Though it will break their hearts!"

Peggy sadly nodded her agreement. Elizabeth stood to leave, then suddenly stopped before she reached the door and turned back to Peggy. "However, there is one more thing I must know." Peggy looked at her questioningly. With utter calm, Elizabeth asked, "Why do you believe that Henry was so fond of the Mill House, enough to be sure that he left it to Elise in his Will?"

Peggy flushed red. She had no desire to hurt Elizabeth more. "He loved it as a child did he not?"

"It was more than that, was it not?" Elizabeth pushed.

"It was where I gave birth to Elise."

Elizabeth asked one last pertinent and deeply personal question. "And is it where Elise was conceived?"

"Yes." Was the simple reply. She tried hard not to avert her eyes and almost succeeded.

With that, Elizabeth left the room and the house and once within the privacy of her coach, she cried all the way home.

CHAPTER 23

Neither Peggy nor Elizabeth slept that night and the next day arrived with sickening dread for them both. Elizabeth felt duplicitous. Elise had assumed that she and Giles had been summoned to Stapley Manor to discuss wedding plans and Elizabeth did not have the heart to prepare her otherwise. Giles travelled with them in Elizabeth's carriage and enjoyed the treat of his life, being driven like a gentleman.

Peggy, in the meantime could not face breakfast, not even Mabel's finest porridge. Mabel did her best to comfort her sister and recognized that this would probably be the hardest thing she would ever do in her life but assured her too, that it was also the wisest thing to do. It was the ONLY thing to do!

It was unusual, that Nancy May should be up so early and even more uncommon that she should be so perky. She almost bounced into the kitchen and helped herself to the porridge, chattering on with sentences tumbling from her mouth in no particular order. Insensitive to her mother's melancholic demeanour, she scraped a wooden chair across the flagged floor and flopped into it and scooped up a spoonful of the hot creamy cereal almost before her backside touched the seat. Mabel was transfixed with her manner and was still wondering at her ill manners when, with her mouth full, her niece spurted out her exciting news.

"Mother! Something wonderful has happened! Manfri is to return to his family. He is leaving this morning." Peggy was surprised that this was coming as good news but after another scoop of porridge her daughter continued, "and, mother, isn't it wonderful...he has asked me to marry him and return to the camp with him?! I am going to become a gypsy wife!!" Oblivious to any reaction around her, she babbled on, her eyes intent on the bowl of breakfast in front of her. All Peggy could think of was, 'Why today? Why would she do this, today? Today of all days!' Mabel, realizing that this was completely oversaturating her sister's emotional limits, filled the gap of silence, chatting to her niece and trying to understand what her future nomadic life, would be like. The only saving grace in all of this, was that they had grown to like Manfri in the short time they had got to know him. He appeared to be an honourable, caring, hard working and respectful young man. More importantly, it was easy to see his genuine love for Nancy May. They could at least be sure that he would care for their beautiful wayward girl.

"Nancy dear..." Peggy finally found her voice. "You do realise don't you, that your father is almost at his end ... and if you leave now, you may never see him again?"

"Mother, I am no charlatan! I will not pretend that I feel attachment to my father, let alone love. I have spent all my life watching you suffering his beatings and cowering from his abuse and since a little girl, I have avoided his company and loathed his attention. I will not pretend that I care enough now to await his death with sorrow or stand by his grave grieving. He has never cared about anyone but himself and you should remind yourself, Mother, that he is a callous murderer! I wish to have nothing to do with him."

Peggy had never heard Nancy May give in to such a tirade and sat dumbstruck, staring at her daughter. "Mother I wish you to understand, that I can leave here now with a clear conscience to live my own life, in the knowledge that my father can harm you no more! He can no longer beat you, humiliate and distress you. I do not want you to live in this permanent state of anxiety and fear. My God! When I think of the life you have led, I could weep! You have not deserved that! You have been a wonderfully protective and loving mother to us both and although I shall be leaving, you will still have Giles ... and now Elise to keep you company." Mabel, appreciating the irony of her innocent comment, glanced up at Peggy, knowing that that would not be the case but Nancy May reached for her mother's hand across the table and squeezed it tightly within both of hers. "I will be sure to visit once a year when we travel back this way. This will be the best of all my adventures, mother." She smiled broadly and looked to Peggy to do the same. The moment was interrupted however, with a call from Manfri, announcing the arrival of Elizabeth's coach.

Keeping tight hold of Nancy May's hand for just a precious moment longer, she pleaded to her daughter. "Nancy dear, will you stay with me a little while longer, as there is something I want you to hear." Nancy May nodded in agreement, with no possible perception of what was to come. Peggy cast a watery smile between Nancy May and Mabel, then stood to receive her guests and her son.

Entering the parlour, the buoyancy between the younger members of the family would in other times have been joyous. Within moments of their arrival, introductions took place between Elizabeth and Elise with Nancy May and Manfri. Almost in the same breath, Nancy May had excitedly announced their engagement leading to high jubilation between the young ones and the girls comparing notes on their respective engagements.

Elizabeth stood on the periphery of the group, looking onto the mêlée of happiness before her and was instantly taken aback at the similarity between the two girls. Any doubt she may have had about the truth, of which Peggy spoke the day before, was immediately dismissed from her mind.

The exuberant excitement was explosive. The noise levels rose higher and higher with clatters of laughter and screeches of delight, the girls hugging each other and the men offering congratulatory handshakes. Peggy had never before seen her twins in such high spirits. How cruel life could be! She could take it no longer. She grasped at a chair and sat in it before her legs gave way.

"STOP. STOP!!" Came Peggy's harsh voice.

Instant silence. Nobody had ever heard Peggy raise her voice like that.

Mabel pulled up her chair close to her sister's and put a comforting hand gently upon her shoulder. "Stop!" she repeated, even though the room was already quiet. All eyes were upon her in shock. Elizabeth wiped a tear.

'Mother...?" Elise frowned to see her mother's evident upset.

Peggy, Elizabeth and Mabel sat waiting for their attention to settle. Peggy spoke with sombre voice. "Please. Sit down. All of you." Each person looked to another for a clue as to what was happening. They obeyed Peggy's instruction but it was not lost on Elise, that her mother elected to move across the room and take a seat next to Peggy. There was a sudden stillness of gloom, which settled about the room.

"Thank you. What I am about to tell you, will change all your lives forever. I wish to God, it was otherwise." Tears began to wash her face and she fought to continue. Nancy May started to interrupt her but Mabel quietened her with a gesture of her hand. "Things are not as they seem, here in this room. Life has played the most cruel of tricks upon this family." Everyone's imagination was running wild, with no expectation of where this was going.

"Giles, my dear son! You cannot marry Elise! It would be both illegal and immoral.

"What? What are you talking about mother? That is ridiculous!" He stood from his chair, "I cannot listen to this! Have you gone quite mad? ... Why would you say such a thing? – I thought you liked her!!" He raged red and grabbed Elise's hand to leave the room.

"Giles, for goodness sake! Sit down!" she raised her voice forcefully.

In a desperate effort to reassure Giles, she stressed her words, "Of course I like Elise. I love her very much! Now, hear me out."

Giles and Elise reluctantly retrieved their seats in certain confusion and Peggy continued in quiet tones, addressing the group as a whole. "Two years after the birth of my beautiful twins, I fell pregnant again with another child, but I was unable to keep the baby because my husband was not the father." There was an audible gasp from Nancy May. I loved this baby very much, just as I did the baby's father but he belonged to another woman."

"He was married?" Nancy May was astonished at her mother's confession.

"Yes, my darling but you cannot control who you fall in love with and I had been very unhappy for a long time." Peggy took a moment to gather her composure. "Anyway, I was left with no alternative but to give away my baby to a couple, whom I knew would protect her and love her as much as I did. So, hours after she was born, I said goodbye to my beautiful baby girl and with deep sadness – more than you will ever know, I left her upon these steps." She gestured towards the front door.

Elise looked confused and worryingly could not catch her mother's eyes for reassurance. Peggy looked to Elizabeth and gestured her hand towards her, "This lady became her mother and brought her up to be the beautiful young woman who sits in our midst now."

Confused, Elise became panicked and looked to her mother to negate these words. Instead, Elizabeth spoke the most hideous words a child could hear. "My darling Elise. I have loved you for all of your life and I will always consider you my daughter but the truth is that I am not your true mother. Giles's mother, is your birth mother."

Moments lapsed. Nancy May spoke with hushed staggered breath, "But that means..."

"Yes, Nancy May! That means Elise, you are Giles's half sister." Peggy confirmed. "... and you cannot marry!" Giles jumped up from his chair making it fall over in his wake. He left the room, slamming the door behind him and ran into the fields beyond the back garden. He ran and ran as though to get away from the cruel words just spoken.

As though that was not the only consideration, Elise was still working through all that had been said. "So, if you are not my real mother, who is my father?"

"Your father is as you know him, Elise", explained Peggy. I loved him very much but I could not keep his baby. Your parents badly wanted a child, so I knew you would be safe and well looked after. You have grown into a wonderful young woman my dear and your parents were – are – rightly proud of you."

Elizabeth assured Elise. "Always remember, your father adored you! Believe me, you were the apple of his eye." Elise slumped to the floor stunned for moments before the tears came and her body racked with grief.

Elise turned sharply on Peggy, "How long have you known it was me? ...You welcomed me into your home and you watched me with your son..." She was sobbing through her words almost incomprehensibly. "How could you not have said anything? ... You are mistaken... This cannot be true!!. Mother tell her it is not true for God's sake!!" She flopped forward to Elizabeth's feet, resting her head in her lap, "Oh mother", she wailed, "Tell me this cannot be true. I cannot bear to lose Giles. I love him so much! This is so unfair..." Elizabeth stroked her hair gently with shaking hands. "My darling, I believe it to be true. This changes nothing between us child. I will always be your mother for I have loved you all your life, just as your father did."

Nancy May looked on to this nightmare before her and felt numb, as she tried to absorb what had unfolded before her. She could not imagine how her mother could have held this secret for so long and kept it from her father, for she knew only too well what her father would have done to her, had he known. The beating would have been so ferocious, that he would probably have killed her. At this moment, she pitied Elise and her heart was breaking for her beloved brother but her mother looked so broken, so frail, that her heart went out to her. Only she knew, how cruelly she had been treated, by her father, for all those years and in that instant, Nancy May was glad, that her mother had clearly found someone else to love. She moved across the room to Peggy and sat beside her, cradling her trembling body. With that small gesture of love, Peggy collapsed against her daughter with relief, grateful for the comforting embrace and in one heartfelt guttural scream of tearful emotion which burst forth from her lungs like a lion's roar, purged all her pent up sorrow and grief. Nancy May held her tightly until the hysterical outburst eventually subsided. Reading Nancy May's mind, Mabel reached for the brandy on the side table and transferred Peggy into her arms to coax her into taking a sip. Giving Nancy May a nod of approval, her niece, left the room with Manfri, in search of Giles.

The rickety bridge that stretched across the stream about a mile or so from Stapley Manor, was always a place for the twins to retreat for solitude whenever Albert became too much.

Nancy May knew where to look for Giles and sure enough they found him propped against the post of the bridge, with angry tears. He wished he could be brave enough to kill himself but he knew he could never find that kind of courage. How... how could this be happening? When he awoke this morning, his life was full of joy and love and the future lay ahead of him like a sunrise.

He felt his sister's reassuring arms around him and her soothing voice speaking words he did not hear above the sound of his heartbeat drumming angrily in his ears. He had no idea how long he had sat there, but by the time they moved away, he was cold and shivering.

Elise begged her mother to help her make a hasty retreat from the abhorrent situation, which had unfolded before her. Elizabeth had no hesitation in calling for their driver and with little more than a nod of acknowledgement towards Peggy, she guided Elise from the room, still weeping hysterically into her crumpled cotton handkerchief.

Departing from the ghastly scene and away from the living nightmare, they left Peggy in the blackest of melancholic moods with Mabel unable to ease her despair.

Manfri and Nancy May escorted Giles back to the house and coaxed him to sit in the kitchen with a large warming brandy. By this time, Giles had made up his mind to leave home. He could not possibly stay there in Broadway and especially so now that Elise would be taking up residence at the Mill House. Seeing her every day would be torture. Nancy May worried for his plan. He was not a natural adventurer and was a home bird at heart. Without a decisive set plan, she believed it would not end well and she could not bear to be unsure of his safety.

Manfri had offered for him to come join Nancy May and return with him, back to the troupe. He could travel with them for a while, as a guest. If the life was not for him, then he could choose any place to stay and rebuild his life. At least that would take him away from here for the moment and give time for him to calm down and make a sensible decision at leisure. Giles accepted graciously. Nancy May loved Manfri all the more for his thoughtful and generous kindness.

CHAPTER 24

Elizabeth and Elise had now cocooned themselves at the cottage in Harvington, where Elise needed much time to rebalance her psyche and lick her damaged emotional wounds whilst Mr. Foster, was again instructed to deal with the paperwork, pertaining to the ownership of Stapley Manor. Stapley Manor, was all but silent. Peggy and Mabel seemed to rattle in the cavernous rooms. Albert had passed away holding his childhood toy car, after a painful and agitated last few hours and his funeral was attended only by the Reverend, Peggy and Mabel. Nobody missed him.

Eventually, Elizabeth and Peggy managed to put their respective sadness to one side and for the sake of Henry's memory and their children's peace of mind, they agreed to work alongside each other, to make better lives for them all. After all, history was history. This was time to look to the future.

Magnanimously, Elizabeth had after much thought and consideration, revised her offer to Peggy, which was humbly accepted. It involved selling her home in Harvington and with the proceeds, allow Elise to renovate the Mill House to her liking, just as Henry would have wanted.

In addition, Stapley Manor would be generously refurbished so as to accommodate not only a luxury wing for Elizabeth herself but also enable her proposed plan with Peggy's approval. They would together create a home for illegitimate children and arrange for their education. These children who were so often cast out from society and known as 'filius nullius' or nobody's child, would otherwise likely end up in dire poverty or the workhouse. Elizabeth knew that this could so easily have been Elise's destiny, had it not been for Peggy's courage. Had she not managed to keep her pregnancy a secret, Albert could have thrown her onto the streets with her three young children in tow and Elizabeth would never have known the joy of motherhood herself.

In respect of this, a generously proportioned home was to be built in the grounds, with its own staff and gardens and would belong in its entirety to Peggy and her sister. This was gifted legally and documented by deed for Peggy's lifelong security. Elizabeth knew in her soul that Henry would have wished this. Furthermore, the name of Stapley Manor would be changed, eradicating it of all recent negative history and it would be renamed, Henry House, in memory of such a good and generous man.

Elise settled in the Mill House and remained a spinster for some years but found joy in having her two mothers close by.

The season had returned when the gypsies revisited Evesham and Nancy May could not wait to make the extra journey as far as Broadway, to see her mother once more. They arrived at the manor house, aghast to see its much-improved changing face.

As Manfri proudly helped his wife from the vardo, her bangles jangled in their familiar way as she fell into his embrace. In that single moment when their eyes met, their deep connection was clearly evident to anyone who may have chanced to witness it.

Alerted by the sound of horses neighing, Peggy glanced up from the paperwork she was studying and looked through the study window. Recognising the vardo, her heart pounded at the unexpected sight and the now unimportant pages slipped from her grip. Her hands flew to her face in shocked disbelief as she cried joyously to see her daughter's rounded belly revealed, as her colourful shawl slipped a little and she flashed her mother a broad smile in greeting.

Rushing outside to fling her arms about her beautiful daughter, the moment's excitement was soon to be interrupted by the sound of another cart venturing along the stone track behind them. Overwhelmingly, Peggy had a further unexpected and wonderful surprise, to see a second wagon follow at slow pace along the driveway, with someone she squinted to recognise as Giles ... with a scruffy, aged dog ... and his new wife, Kezia.

About the Author

Gail Fulton has recently moved to the Cotswolds with her husband and Border Collie, Monty. Their two daughters and a future son-in-law have also relocated to the area and they look forward to many hours of dog walks, dining out and laughter.

Gail has now retired from teaching but has also always been passionate about interior design and loved setting up their new home. Floral art is also one of her favourite hobbies too but another, is people watching! Gail gained an M.A. in Psychology, focusing her interest on personality development and she is still intrigued in body language, so loves her visits to coffee shops and observing behaviour. She and her husband delight in gardening and have created a wonderfully colourful space for socialising and relaxation. Together they love to explore the Cotswold countryside and have, over the decades, travelled extensively around the world, finding inspiration for her writing. Gail has since childhood, loved to write. Her repertoire has largely covered childrens' stories to travel logs, although she mostly enjoys the escapism of fiction. Her particular joy, is penning descriptive passages. To have now published two novels, is both exciting and fulfilling.

BV - #0013 - 100522 - C0 - 216/140/15 - PB - 9781914424502 - Matt Lamination